ENTER THE ZONE, IF YOU DARE—

MAYBE TOMORROW—The lesson he had to teach was one no one should have to learn. . . .

THE FOOD COURT—He was about to discover just how true that old adage was—you are what you eat. . . .

GORDIE'S PETS—Sometimes the worst monsters are those created by your own imagination. . . .

LADY IN CREAM-COLORED CHIFFON—You never know what might happen when art imitates life a little too closely. . . .

These are just four of the fascinating twists in reality that you'll take when you—

RETURN TO THE TWILIGHT ZONE

More Original Anthologies
Brought to You by DAW:

JOURNEYS TO THE TWILIGHT ZONE *Edited by Carol Serling.* Sixteen unforgettable new tales—some eerie, some scary, some humorous—all with the unique *Twilight Zone* twist. Included is Rod Serling's classic, chill-provoking story, "Suggestion."

ALIEN PREGNANT BY ELVIS *Edited by Esther M. Friesner and Martin H. Greenberg.* Thirty-six, all-original, imagination-grabbing tales that could have come straight out of the supermarket tabloid headlines. From the bride of Bigfoot to the discovery of JFK's skull on the moon to a surefire way to tell whether your coworker is a space alien, here's all the "news" that's not fit to print.

FRANKENSTEIN: The Monster Wakes *Edited by Martin H. Greenberg.* From a journalist who stumbles upon a modern-day descendant of the famous doctor . . . to a mobster's physician whose innovative experiments might lead to a whole new kind of enforcer . . . to the monster's own determined search for a suitable bride . . . here are powerful new tales of creation gone awry.

THE YEAR'S BEST HORROR STORIES *Edited by Karl Edward Wagner.* The finest stories—by both established masters and bright new talents—published in the genre in the current year.

Return To
THE TWILIGHT ZONE

Edited By
CAROL SERLING

DAW BOOKS, INC.
DONALD A. WOLLHEIM, FOUNDER
375 Hudson Street, New York, NY 10014

ELIZABETH R. WOLLHEIM
SHEILA E. GILBERT
PUBLISHERS

Introduction © 1994 by Carol Serling.
Survival Song © 1994 by Ray Russell.
Night of the Living Bra © 1994 by K. D. Wentworth.
The Kaleidoscope © 1994 by Don D'Ammassa.
Big Roots © 1994 by Pamela Sargent.
The Midnight El © 1994 by Robert Weinberg.
Maybe Tomorrow © 1994 by Barry Hoffman.
The Food Court © 1994 by John Maclay.
The Garden © 1994 by Barbara Delaplace.
Gordie's Pets © 1994 by Hugh B. Cave.
Lady in Cream-Colored Chiffon © 1994 by Elizabeth Anderson and
Margaret Maron.
The Praying Lady © 1994 by Charles L. Fontenay.
The Cure © 1994 by Phillip C. Jennings.
Still Waters © 1994 by Barry B. Longyear.
Messenger © 1994 by Adam-Troy Castro.
The Duke of Demolition Goes to Hell © 1994 by John Gregory
Betancourt.
Salt © 1994 by P. D. Cacek.
Always, in the Dark © 1994 by Charles Grant.
Afternoon Ghost © 1994 by Jack Dann and George Zebrowski.
The Sole Survivor © 1971 by Rod Serling.

DAW Book Collectors No. 969.

First Printing, December 1994
1 2 3 4 5 6 7 8 9

CONTENTS

INTRODUCTION

by Carol Serling

Rod Serling's special vision of a world "between light and shadow, between science and superstition" contin ues to inspire master storytellers and motivate novices. The extraordinary reception the first book in this series, *Journeys to the Twilight Zone*, received convinced me that we should *Return to the Twilight Zone*.

As the editor, I have culled through a large body of work to find the stories most faithful to the Rod Serling vision. Those that I have chosen are all new works, never before published, with the exception of Rod's story, which seemed to fit in perfectly. I believe that you will be entertained by and entranced with the provocative tales included in this collection and that these odysseys will live on in your consciousness long after you have put the book down.

Ride Robert Weinberg's ghostly "Midnight El" and a subway ride will never be the same again, or if you're planning an ocean voyage, you might want to first check out Rod Serling's "Sole Survivor." Closer to home, John Maclay's "Food Court" might give you second thoughts before you place your next order at the mall, or the youngster next door, who collects pets, *could* be "Gordie" in Hugh Cave's story. Then there's the bug collector who shows a most unusual interest in genetic mating patterns in Charles Fontenay's "Praying Lady." And please listen to your kid when she tells you her teacher is weird. Barry Hoffman's "Maybe Tomorrow" has a message to offer here. Beware of your TV, too. K.D. Wentworth has a set in "Night of the Living Bra" that's right out of the *Twilight Zone*.

Many of the authors in this book are well known to those of us who inhabit the *Twilight Zone* . . . Ray Russell, Charles Grant, Pamela Sargent, Charles Fontenay, George Zebrowski, Jack Dann. . . . Some of the stories are from those who at this point are relatively unknown, but who may very well be the next generation of fantasy and horror writers. In any case, I believe you will find that this book will open up vistas never before seen or dreamed of . . . or to quote Shakespeare in *A Midsummer Night's Dream*:

"And as imagination bodies forth
The forms of things unknown, the poet's pen
Turns them to shapes, and gives to airy nothing
A local habitation and a name."

Welcome back to the ZONE!

SURVIVAL SONG

by Ray Russell

(1)

                                   . . . What's that?—
Was I asleep? I think so. Must have dozed.
Is it still there? Yes, there it is. Still there
In that small patch of light just to my left.
Not much. Enough, I hope, to keep me going
A little while at least. But don't move now.
Don't make a dash for it. Too dangerous.
Have to lie low and force myself to wait
Here in the dark until the patch of light
Has gone away. It's only safe at night.

(2)

How long have I been crouched here motionless?
How long since I've had anything to eat?
I can't remember. Not like better days.
That was a lovely time—in spite of Them.
A lovely time *because* of Them, perhaps.

We didn't know what hunger was. Warm, snug,
Our bellies full. Eating, sleeping, mating.
Yes, a good time. Now most of us are gone.
The corpses curl and blacken everywhere,
Scabbing the senses with a crust of smell
Like all the mountains of manure in Hell.

(3)

The food's still over there in the patch of light.
I'd like to take a chance and grab it now,
But no, it's risky. Last time I tried that,
I barely escaped alive. Just play it smart,
Think about something else. About the old days.
What fools we were. Afraid of Them. And now,
With reason, we're afraid of one another.
Already some of us, I've heard . . .

                              . . . *Who's there?*
Did something, someone, scamper in the shadow?
Is someone getting set to make a break
And grab the food? I have to stay awake.

(4)

The old days. How we ran away from Them!
We never did appreciate Them, really.
They even kept us warm when winter came.
And yet we wanted Them to go away,
Leave us alone.

                    Well, now we *are* alone.
Little by little, all of Them moved out,

Letting us have the city to ourselves,
And it was very good for quite a while.
We ate and ate and ate and ate. Got fat.
Eternal Plenty—we were sure of that.

(5)

The bad time didn't happen all at once.
At first, we hardly noticed that the food
Was running out. It seemed impossible.
We are an ancient race, older than Them,
But when They moved away, the food went, too.
For some time after, there was plenty left,
But then it began to dwindle. Life got hard.
There are just a few remaining scraps,
Like that scrap over there.

                        It's dark enough
For me to make my move and grab the stuff.

(6)

I've got it! But what is it? Pretty bad.
But not as bad as starving. Used to be,
We had oil, sugar . . . now I'm glad to get
This little scrap of paper. Gulp it quick!
Great Cucaracha God, Your praise I sing:
You planned us well. We can eat *anything* . . .
                       . . . *Look out!—*

NIGHT OF THE LIVING BRA

by K.D. Wentworth

"Amarantha!" Orville's voice hammered at her from the front room. "What the hell have you been doing to this TV-box? I swear, poor Lucille Ball looks like something straight out of the bathroom tonight!"

Peeking into the front room where light from the round screen flickered across her husband's face, Amarantha frowned. "Never touched that infernal thing, not even to dust!" That ought to settle it, she thought. The whole world knew that Amarantha-May Morgan considered dusting to be nigh on akin to church-going and other such Godly things.

"Well, at least come in here and look."

Wiping her hands on the dish towel, she walked into the darkened front room where on former summer nights they had entertained friends and relatives instead of Lucille Ball and Uncle Miltie.

"See?" he said fretfully. "You can't tell me that there's Lucille Ball."

Squinting her eyes, she studied the picture, then groped for the chair in front of her. Without a doubt, that was not Lucille Ball on the tiny screen. Although she couldn't believe that it was true, it actually appeared to be a toilet bowl that was . . . *singing*.

"And no matter how I fiddle with the dial, it won't come in no better." Orville crossed his arms over his chest.

Amarantha sank down into her own chair as the toilet finished its song, something about "blue," then waltzed off into the sunset with another toilet, one apparently of the—her face warmed—opposite sex. The scene shifted suddenly to a slender young girl dressing, right there on the screen in front of God and everyone, pulling on a pair of trousers that had—her face went from warm to oven-hot—trousers with a zipper in the front, just like a man's!

"That's not Lucille Ball, either!" Her husband's heavy features settled into a decided leer.

The scene changed again to an impossibly small car speeding down the road. All sweeping curves, it didn't seem any bigger than a shoe box. Then some kind of name flashed across the screen, long and altogether unpronounceable with far too many "U's" and "I's" in it.

Orville leaned closer until his nose almost touched the screen. "That there's a Jap name!"

"Japanese? Don't be silly." She shook her head, watching the little car stop short. Everyone knew that "made in Japan" was only another way to say "made to fall apart." No one would ever risk their life riding around in such a thing as a *Japanese* car.

The driver of the car emerged and Amarantha felt her jaw go slack in surprise at the sight of the long earring that dangled from his left ear, not to mention the hair that stuck straight up like a bed of nails on top, then trailed off behind in a stiff braid.

The car disappeared, replaced by strange moody music and a bunch of folks standing around a—

She hastily averted her eyes. "Turn that benighted thing off!"

Orville leaned closer to the screen, then released his breath in a long hissing sigh. "Well, would you look at that?"

"Orville Morgan, if you value your immortal soul, you will turn that infernal thing off!"

"She don't have . . . no clothes on!"

Screwing up her eyes, Amarantha glanced at the tiny screen again, where a woman sat smack in the middle of some sort of business meeting, dressed in nothing more than a bath towel while no one else seemed to even notice and a voice droned on about "freshness all day."

"It's the Devil," she said finally, fanning herself with one hand. "The Devil has done got into that TV-box of yours. You'd best take it out back and chop it into firewood before we all wind up in Hell!"

Orville's brow wrinkled as the woman sauntered out of the building still draped in the towel, then caught a crowded bus. "No, I don't think it's the Devil, Amarantha, but there is something almighty strange going on here!" Pulling out his pipe, he filled the bowl, then held a match to the shredded tobacco and puffed furiously. "It must be them Commies trying to make us crazy; you know, give us all one of them nervy-ous breakdown-things like your Aunt Katie is always having."

"Commies, right here in Terlton, Oklahoma?" She locked her hands together to keep them from shaking. "Well, that's nigh on as bad. What'll we do?"

Standing up from his chair, Orville threw his chest out, standing at attention, just like his picture from World War II. "I'm gonna call Sheriff Holmes. They ain't taking us without a fight."

The tall, elegant woman, her ears and fingers dripping with diamonds, looked the camera straight in the eye. "Just say no." Her voice was as serious as last year's taxes. "Say no to drugs!"

"Well, call me a toadstool and squash me flat!" Sheriff Holmes' jaw sagged earthward. "Them Commies do seem dead-set against aspirin and Alka-Seltzer and such, don't they?"

"I can see it now." Orville paced back and forth in front of the screen. "Once we're all laid low over here with headaches, they'll just swoop in and take over the whole dad-blamed country."

On the flickering screen, the picture switched to a shapely young woman in a clinging sweater dancing smack up against a tall, broad-shouldered man. Orville and the sheriff leaned closer. Then suddenly the young woman disappeared and all that was left was her—

Amarantha blushed as the two men glanced at each other. All that was left was the top portion of the woman's—*unmentionable*—clothing, and very well fitted-out it was too. She heard a voice say something

15

about ". . . could have danced all night in my living bra."

A living brassiere? She tried to get her breath—why, it sounded positively disgusting! "Orville, you turn that thing off! Commies or no Commies, I won't have that filth in my house!"

"Wait!" Sheriff Holmes stepped in front of the TV. "I'm sorry, Amarantha, but if you turn it off, we might not be able to get this signal again." Picking up his broad-brimmed hat, he turned it around in his fingers. "This here could be big, you know." He glanced meaningfully at Orville. "I mean—real big." Dropping the hat firmly back on his balding head, he lowered his voice dramatically. "What if we got ourselves something from another planet here?" He looked her dead-straight in the eye. "What if this machine is controlled by—aliens?"

On the small screen, a scantily clad young woman ran her hands over her curvaceous body and arched her back so far that Amarantha thought it would break as large white letters appeared and an unseen voice implored them to call "1-900-MYBROAD" for a "hot, nasty time."

A look of bewilderment stole into Orville's cement-gray eyes as he turned to Sheriff Holmes. "Mybroad-what?"

The screen flickered invitingly, but since Sheriff Holmes wouldn't let her turn the misbegotten thing off, Amarantha kept the sound dialed down. Orville, of course, had gone off as always at 4:00 A.M. to drive his Rainbow Bread delivery route.

"It don't matter if the bug-eyed monsters are coming to eat us up," he had said early that morning when she'd asked him not to go, "that bread's still going stale if I don't get to work. You just keep your pretty little mind on the washing and such, and leave the problem of that TV to them what's trained for it." Then the screen door had slammed behind him, leaving her alone with that infernal box to wait for Sheriff Holmes to return with some government men.

Restlessly wandering about the gleaming house, she looked for some small task still undone, but in the six hours since Orville had left, she had scrubbed and waxed the linoleum, cleaned the bathroom, rearranged the cabinets, baked an apple pie, and defrosted the ice-box. Everything seemed to sparkle, in fact, but still she felt restless and dissatisfied.

Perhaps, she told herself, she should visit her sister over by Mannford, but her hand stopped as she reached to untie her apron strings. Somehow, it just didn't seem right to go off and leave that TV-box blazing away like that, with no one here to keep an eye on it. The government men weren't supposed to be here until sometime tonight, six o'clock or so, the sheriff had said.

So what now? Peering into the front room, she realized that a visible layer of dust had settled onto the genuine imitation-oak coffee table. Her mouth tightened. What could she have been thinking of? If word ever got out that Amarantha-May Morgan kept a dirty house, why, she'd never be able to hold her head up in this town again.

Grabbing the dusting cloth, she set to work on the coffee table, moving the porcelain shepherd and shepherdess aside, then dusting each piece carefully before she replaced it. Without meaning to, she caught fragmented images out of the corner of her eye—women hurrying up huge marble steps with leather briefcases tucked under their arms, women in white coats with stethoscopes dangling around their necks, women driving strange streamlined cars, women wearing police uniforms. . . .

Before she knew it, she found herself on her knees, watching a tall man in a gray suit and a beautiful woman who were shouting at each other. What on earth were they arguing about, she wondered, as the two paced back and forth, gesturing angrily at each other. Finally, she succumbed to temptation and, deciding that she would just listen for a minute, turned the sound back up.

"—just take your millions and go to hell!" Dark eyes glittering dangerously, the woman swept a hand back over her long, French-braided hair. "I'll raise this child myself. You don't even have to see it."

The man blinked at her in surprise. "Erica, you don't mean that," he said, his deep voice thick with emotion.

"Oh, yes, I do." She raised her chin, looking, for all that she was head and shoulders shorter than him, tall as a mountain. "You just wait and see!" Turning her back on him, she marched out of the room, never once bobbling on her incredibly high spike heels.

Amarantha plumped down in Orville's easy chair, her heart racing like a sewing machine at full speed. Raise a child alone? Why—her mind whirled—that would mean poor Erica would have to get a *job*, would have to go out and work just like a man. What on earth would she do with a baby?

The scene faded, replaced by another of the advertisements that seemed to make up most of what aired on this channel. A bumping, grinding song began to play and she leaned closer, caught up in the rhythm and the lyrics. ". . . I can bring home the bacon—then cook it up in a pan . . . because I'm a wo-man!"

Without her realizing it, the rest of the day flowed by, filled with tempestuous love affairs, scads of children with two complete sets of parents, kitchen floors that shone ice-bright, cleaned as often by men as women, babies in "disposable" diapers, people of all colors living side by side, shopping in the same stores, their children attending the same schools, women working at every conceivable kind of job from business executive to truck driver.

Her mind reeled under the assault of strange ideas and so many questions ran through her mind, such as: what was this "quality time" that they kept talking about and how was it different from Daylight Savings Time? Where was this McDonald's-place and why did a "Big Mac" taste so good? How was a "microwave" different from a permanent wave, and could you do one at home yourself?

Totally forgotten, the dust rag lay on the floor by her feet.

Then she saw it again, the same mysterious image from the day before, the brassiere that floated along by itself, "living" as the unseen voice said again, somehow taking on a life of its own. She watched as it sailed into a courtroom full of men and women and proceeded to serve as counsel for the defense.

But, where before it had seemed shocking, now it seemed brave and free, going unfettered like that into male territory, doing things she had never dreamed were possible.

She was still staring at the round screen when Orville banged the screen door open at five. Glancing up at him, she was surprised to see how drab he looked, standing there all rumpled and dirty in his ill-fitting gray uniform with the tiny loaf of bread emblazoned on his chest.

"What's for supper?" Shoving his battered black lunch pail at her, he stared pointedly. "I don't smell nothing cooking."

"Supper?" she echoed, then her attention was drawn back to the TV where a handsome young man with large spectacles and thick white hair was just asking an audience of women, "Well, what do you say, ladies? How *do* you know if you and your sex partner are compatible?"

"Amarantha!"

Her head swiveled back to Orville. "Y—yes?"

"I said, what's for supper?"

"Oh." Her eyes returned to the young man, Phil, she believed his name was, as he held an older woman's hand and smiled encouragingly at her. "I suppose that we could go to MacDonald's."

When they returned from the Dairy Queen, Orville pointed at the long dark sedan waiting in their driveway next to the sheriff's battered black-and-white. "See, I told you we'd be late!"

"It's not like they'll melt, you know," she told him shortly.

Orville slammed the door on his side of their old DeSoto. "I swear, woman, I don't know what's got into you today, first no dinner and now this. You never used to sass me."

Ducking her head, Amarantha hurried up the driveway. A blue-uniformed man stood up from the porch swing and held his hand out to her. "Mrs. Morgan? I'm General Bradford from Project Bluebook."

Squinting through the dusk at his broad face, she took his hand. "Pleased to meet you, General."

"And this . . ." He nodded at another figure standing behind him. ". . . is Dr. Whitt, our transmission and reception specialist."

Orville came up from behind with Sheriff Holmes. "Sorry we're late."

"Can we go in now?" Clutching a suitcase to his chest, Dr. Whitt's long, pointy nose swung from one face to another. "We really haven't a moment to lose. This phenomena could end any second!"

Throwing Amarantha another sour look, Orville unlocked the door and stood aside. Quickly the two government men and Sheriff Holmes crowded into the living room and clustered around the TV set. Hurrying in behind them, she stood on tiptoe to peek over their shoulders and saw a towel-clad man arguing with a woman over a small white object. "*Strong* enough for a man," the unseen voice said firmly, "but *made* for a woman." The man's face fell as he reluctantly surrendered the bottle to the triumphant woman.

"Amazing!" Dropping to his knees, Dr. Whitt began to unpack his case.

"It's them Commies, ain't it, Doc?" Orville hovered as the other man spread dials and meters and strange little boxes on the floor around the television.

"Commies?" Whitt paused to blink at Orville through his thick lenses, then a furrow appeared between his eyes.

"That's what I think." Orville glanced at the TV where the strangest contraption that Amarantha had ever seen was whooshing past stars and planets. "You should hear the things they say." He edged closer to Whitt and lowered his voice. "I think they're trying to knock out our aspirin industry over here. They say it over and over—'Just say no to drugs.'" He glanced furtively at the TV. "My God, Doc, think of the drugstores that would go out of business—and the factories!"

Without warning, the scene shifted to a ruined city where strange tanks ranged down streets filled with scattered rubble, and soldiers dressed in tattered rags fired at uniforms indistinguishable from their own. An unseen voice rattled on about some place by the name of "Beirut" and the "body count" while smoke drifted across the street like fog.

Orville shook his head. "Came on about the same time yesterday, but for the life of me, I can't figure out what them folks is fighting about."

"It's definitely not a local signal!" The scientist rocked excitely back on his heels, glancing from one dial to the next in rapid succession. "It's overriding the local station, but I can't get a fix on its source." A smile bloomed over his face. "General Bradford, I think we have an encounter of the first kind here."

"Perhaps." Bradford locked his hands behind his back in a stiff military stance. "But we can't make our final decision based on anything but the strongest of proofs."

"I recommend immediate quarantine." Whitt glanced up at Amarantha and Orville. "We don't want this source accidentally interrupted. It's a miracle that it hasn't happened already, and if it does, we might never recover it."

General Bradford ran a finger along his strong jawline. "I see your point."

On the screen, the smashed buildings were replaced by the aerial view of a shiny car stranded high atop a huge tower of rock way out in the desert somewhere. Orville expelled his breath in one long sigh. "How in the blazes did they do that?"

Moving in front of the tv, the general blocked their view. "Get a cameraman over here on the double!" he snapped at the scientist. "Whatever this is all about, we don't want to miss a moment of it!"

Then he turned back to the Morgans. "I'm afraid that you two are going to have to evacuate."

"Evacuate?" Amarantha's mouth tightened.

"Just until we're certain what we're dealing with here." Bradford straightened his shoulders. "It's a matter of national security."

Amarantha turned to Orville. "I'm not leaving my home because of a stupid TV-box!"

The scientist stood up. "Mrs. Morgan," he said sympathetically, "we simply have no idea what could be causing this phenomena. It could be intelligent life from another world, or messages from another dimension, or . . ." He ran a hand back through his thinning hair. ". . . perhaps even glimpses of the future."

She looked from one smug, self-assured face to the other. "And what gives you the right to decide what we should do?" Her eyes were drawn back to the screen, and then she realized that it was there again, that brave brassiere, running through the park, filled with the body of a real woman this time, lean and fit, blonde hair blowing back in the breeze, keeping pace stride for stride with the other runners, both male and female.

"Now, dear, I'm sure that the general knows best." Orville put a hand on her shoulder, but she paid no attention. She would bet a month's washing that no one told that woman in the living brassiere what to do, or where to go, or even, it seemed, what to wear.

Before anyone could stop her, she reached around the general and jerked the TV cord out of the wall, then watched as the pictured condensed down into a spot of bright light in the middle of the round screen and winked out entirely.

The scientist's voice rose in a howl of dismay. "Turn

it back on!" Elbowing her out of the way, he grabbed the plug and thrust it back into the socket, but when the picture re-formed, Uncle Miltie stood in the center of a stage, his usual bewildered self.

"No!" Whitt buried his face in his hands. "We've lost it, all because of a stupid woman!" Clicking the dial around, he hastily examined the other local station.

It was the same fare, Amarantha noticed with satisfaction, the same boring nonsense that Orville glued his nose to every night. "I guess that settles that."

The scientist stood up, defeat written in every sagging line of his body. "Once the signal was interrupted, we lost it." His voice was low. "We should take the set back with us, and the antenna, too, just in case there are some abnormalities in the way they're put together."

"Take it and good riddance." She settled into her rocking chair. "I never wanted the fool thing in my house in the first place." Across the room, the government men sweated and struggled with the heavy set as they wrestled it out the door.

Orville sighed as the screen door slammed behind them. "Don't hardly seem fair for them to take it away now, just when it was fixing to play Lucille Ball again."

Two months later, Amarantha held the screen door open as several government men reluctantly returned the TV while another climbed to replace the antenna on the roof. "Does this mean there's nothing wrong with this outrageous contraption?"

"No, ma'am." The larger of the two mopped his bald head with a uniform sleeve. "Dr. Whitt tested it up and down and six ways from Friday, but it never got anything but local stations."

"Well, as far as I'm concerned, he could have kept it." She frowned as the two plugged it in, then retreated out the door. Then, as she heard their truck drive away, she reached out and touched the cabinet's dark wood. Since the government had taken it away, she and Orville had paid calls on their friends again and started receiving them here at home.

Now Orville would go back to Lucille Ball and she would be left with her dust rag for company, same as before.

Of course, it had been interesting when it played all those other things. Idly, her fingers wandered down to the dial. Maybe she ought to turn it on, just to be sure that it hadn't been damaged. Not that she wanted to watch it, of course, but it was a valuable machine. That fool, Orville, had paid far too much for it.

Clicking the knob on, she watched the screen, holding her breath without even realizing it. The tiny white dot in the middle suddenly expanded outward, filling up the screen with the biggest bathroom she'd ever seen, big as some folks' houses, and there were two people sitting there in some kind of steaming tub set right down into the floor.

A tiny prickle of hope ran up her spine. White letters appeared over the scene and began to scroll upward, partially obscuring the couple who had begun to stroke and kiss each other in a rather frenzied manner.

She sank into her chair. It was back, that strange, outrageous, sometimes frightening, but wonderful world where men and women listened to each other, at least part of the time, and did the same jobs, right down to taking out tonsils and cleaning ovens, that place where it seemed that anything was possible.

She pursed her lips. This time though, she would make sure that they kept it all to themselves. There was so much to learn in that TV-world, so much knowledge and bravery. She couldn't wait to see what would happen next.

On the screen, the letters stopped rolling, then the outline of a white rabbit's head appeared.

"This," said a cheerful male voice, "has been a production of the Playboy Channel."

THE KALEIDOSCOPE

by Don D'Ammassa

Ted Croner never realized how unhappy he was with his life until he found the kaleidoscope in a box in his basement. Beth had been after him to clean out the trash left by the previous owner for almost a year, and he'd actually taken a few cartons out to the curb from time to time. Unfortunately, Ted was a dreamer and had visions of finding some forgotten treasure hidden within the trash, a rare stamp from British Guiana, forgotten jewelry, private correspondence between Thomas Jefferson and Alexander Hamilton. He sorted through each box very carefully before abandoning its contents to the trashmen, and so far the only item he had valued enough to rescue was an elderly radio that might, if he invested a couple of hundred dollars to have it repaired, fetch almost that much from a collector.

But then he found the kaleidoscope.

He identified it immediately, although it was unlike any he had ever before seen. Fashioned of some lightweight metal, now heavily tarnished, it had an unusually long shaft and supported a prism barrel fully twelve inches in diameter. He cleaned matted dirt off the eyepiece and tried to look through it, but the light in the basement wasn't strong enough to project a clear image. Ted threw open the bulkhead door and climbed up into the backyard, then raised the kaleidoscope to eye level.

It was the most beautiful thing he had ever seen. The facets were tiny and complex, the images sharp, brightly colored, and surprisingly detailed. Although they were too small for him to make out the individual shapes clearly, they appeared less random than the usual colored stones or pieces of translucent plastic, almost seeming to have discernible, specific forms.

Ted reached around to the barrel and gave it a turn. Or tried to. It wouldn't move, even when he exerted considerable pressure, and he lowered it from his eye, regarding it with undisguised venom. The two metal surfaces were so close together that he couldn't examine the space between, but surely it was meant to turn so that the pattern inside could be altered. He set the shaft between clenched thighs and used both hands, hoping to break the seal of grease and time and free the mechanism. It surrendered, but only by the tiniest fraction of an inch, locking in place once more despite every effort he made to turn it further.

"Ted? Is that you out there?"

He turned, saw Beth staring down from the second floor window, and waved diffidently.

"As long as you're outside anyway, would you mind going next door for me? Karen said she'd loan me her roasting pan and I need it for tonight. And check the mailbox on your way back, will you?"

"All right," he answered sullenly, setting the kaleidoscope down on the wall of the brick patio. But despite the show of reluctance, he was secretly pleased. Ted's opinion of their next door neighbor had quickly moved from admiration to lust, and the fact that they both taught at Managansett High School, although in different departments, had added fuel to the fire. He had recently talked her into carpooling, and thought he'd done an excellent job of concealing his frequent, covert appraisals of her legs and breasts. It was hard to believe she had two kids, and that the older, Joe Junior, was almost a teenager.

Karen Pereira was in her kitchen, emptying groceries from a row of paper bags, when he knocked on the side door.

"Hi! Beth said something about a pan I'm supposed to borrow?"

"Oh, sure. Just a sec." Karen gestured for him to come inside and pulled a step stool out of the corner, used it to retrieve a stainless steel roasting pan from the top of a cupboard. She was wearing a very short skirt and Ted averted his eyes quickly, lest he be caught.

"Say, it looks like the Prescotts' cat sneaked in when you weren't looking." The tabby's left ear had long since been torn into an instantly recognizable shape and it was staring at him balefully from its perch on a nearby counter.

Karen descended and handed him the pan, but her

expression was puzzled. "What do you mean, the Prescotts' cat? Boots has belonged to us since she was a kitten. Andy and Samantha have that awful dog they bought for the twins."

Ted tried to cover his frown with a laugh; he was *sure* that the Prescotts owned a cat and the Pereiras a dog. "Sorry, I wasn't thinking."

He was still worrying about the exchange when he walked out to the street to check the mailbox, wondering if his memory was failing him or if he'd just been made the butt of some obscure joke. Andy Prescott's van was parked in front of the Pereira house, he noticed, and for some reason Joe Pereira had left his pickup truck across the street in the Prescotts' driveway. A moment later, Prescott himself came out through his front door, climbed into the truck, and backed it into the street, waving briefly before driving off.

Ted was surprised to see that Andy had shaved off his mustache.

The mail was depressing, a handful of circulars and an even larger handful of bills. He left it on the hall table and carried the roasting pan into the kitchen, setting it on the table.

"Here you go, dear. Where do you want it?"

Beth glanced up from where she was relining the lower cupboard shelves with contact paper. She had gathered her waist length, bright red hair up into a bun and pinned it in place, out of her way.

"Just put it anywhere. I hope you're making progress with that mess in the basement."

"I'm working on it." But instead of returning to the task, he retrieved the kaleidoscope and carried it into the small, windowless room he called his "office."

Ted used an unbent paper clip to scrape along the inside, clearing away several small clumps of unrecognizable matter that had been lodged between the inner surface of the barrel and the outer perimeter of the shaft. After finishing one complete circuit, he braced the shaft between his legs and tried once again to turn the mechanism, this time with slightly more success. It rotated perhaps an eighth of an inch before stopping. Ted glanced through the eyepiece, thought he could see changes in the revealed pattern, but only in some of the peripheral details.

Frustrated, he set it aside, decided to walk next door and see if Joe Pereira had an aerosol lubricant he could spray inside. Joe would be home, sitting in front of the television in all likelihood. It was baseball season and he was an avid Red Sox fan, nor was he willing to stir from the house while his right arm was still in a sling. He'd broken it a week earlier in a fall from the telephone pole where he'd been stringing cable and was still embarrassed by his clumsiness.

"Joe, you in there?" He rapped on the sliding glass door to the Pereiras' family room, trying to see through a crack between the drawn bamboo drapes.

"Hey, that you, Croner? C'mon in; my hands are full."

Ted obediently slid the glass door open and stepped into the air-conditioned interior. The television was off, but Joe Pereira was standing at the far end of the room, arranging six-packs of beer in a small refrigerator. That was surprising, since Joe had never been much of a drinker, despite Andy Prescott's many attempts to entice him into a night of barhopping.

"No game today?" Ted nodded toward the silent television.

Joe straightened up, looked momentarily puzzled. "Oh, is it baseball season already?"

"Has been for two months."

"Yeah, well, I've never been much for sports. You know how it is." But Ted didn't, and he was becoming very confused, particularly since he'd just watched his next door neighbor swing the refrigerator door shut with an arm which had suffered a compound fracture only a few days before.

"What can I do for you, neighbor?"

Ted blinked, having completely forgotten why he had come over in the first place. He improvised feverishly. "I just wanted to check with Karen and see if we can switch off in the car pool next week. I need the car during the day on Monday."

The other man's eyes narrowed. "Why would you and Karen be car pooling? She's all the way the other end of town from the high school."

Ted was definitely confused; he'd been very careful to suggest trading off the driving in front of Joe right from the start, and hadn't pressed seriously until he was sure the man wouldn't object. "Did Karen quit her job?" His heart sank; one of the high points of this year had been discovering that his and Karen's free periods coincided, and that she invariably spent the time in the faculty lounge.

"No way. She's hoping the Callanders will make her a full partner eventually."

The Callanders were brother and sister, owners of the most prestigious (actually, the only) accounting firm in Managansett. In fact, Andy Prescott had worked for them for several years, and was in line for a partnership himself.

And when had Joe Pereira found time to grow himself a mustache?

Ted was never quite sure how he managed to extricate himself from the conversation. He walked home in a fog of confusion, not even noticing when Samantha Prescott walked out to bring in the mail, carefully holding her broken arm pressed against her side.

Back inside his own house, Ted stumbled into the living room, slipped behind the bar, and poured himself a few fingers of brandy, downing it so abruptly that it burned the back of his throat and he began coughing uncontrollably. Alarmed, Beth came running in from the kitchen, pounded his back, and steered him over to the couch.

"What in the world?" She sat beside him, watching closely as he regained his composure, drew a deep breath, and sat back.

Beth's long red hair was suddenly blonde, and barely reached her shoulders.

Ted Croner lay awake for a long time that night, long after his wife's breathing had evened out and the traffic noises from outside had weakened and finally ceased almost entirely. He lay with his eyes open, staring up into the darkness, wondering if he'd lost his mind. Everything had been quite normal this morning, but now things were all mixed up. His wife and neighbors remembered a different past than his, had mysteriously exchanged pets and interests and who knew what else. And since that was clearly impossible, he must have gone crazy.

A passing car's headlights played through the branches of a tree just outside the bedroom window, throwing a crazy quiltwork pattern on the near wall. Like my sanity, he thought, shattered into myriad pieces and rearranged, the way colors and shapes were altered in a kaleidoscope.

The kaleidoscope.

He sat bolt upright, his forehead suddenly covered with perspiration. Could it be? No, that was crazy. But he'd already decided that he was crazy, hadn't he? And if that was the case, then why not indulge his insanity a bit further?

Quietly, not wanting to waken Beth, Ted slipped out of bed, tiptoed out of the room and down the stairs to the ground floor. He almost expected the kaleidoscope to be gone, but when he flicked on the overhead light, it was right where he had left it.

He picked it up tentatively this time, as though it might be dangerous. And if his insane idea was right, it probably was. This time he examined every inch of its surface, searching for some legend, some inscription, any mark which might help to identify it or its origin.

But other than a few scratches and gouges, there were no distinguishing features whatsoever.

After several minutes of concentrated effort designed to find significance in the current pattern, Ted decided to try moving the barrel again. As before, it resisted his efforts, but he continued to strain until his hand slipped and he scraped his palm badly along one edge. Frustrated, he stood up, weighed the kaleidoscope thoughtfully in one hand, then carried it downstairs to the basement.

Ted wrapped the shaft with an old towel before placing it between the jaws of his vise, then wrapped a second loosely around the barrel to protect his hands and improve his grip. Even with this increased leverage, he thought he had failed, but just before he abandoned the effort, there was a tiny sound, metal sliding on metal, and the barrel turned a quarter inch before once more refusing to budge. He released it from the vise, examined the new and now noticeably different pattern, then carried the kaleidoscope back upstairs.

The house was the same. He looked out the windows on either side and couldn't spot anything changed in either direction. Back in his bedroom, he briefly turned on the light; Beth slept peacefully, her shoulder length blonde hair twisted beneath her head.

"You *are* going crazy," he whispered to himself, turned off the light, and went to bed.

He felt much better in the morning, even though Beth's hair was still blonde and Joe Pereira's truck was once again parked in the Prescotts' driveway. It was

Sunday, and no one seemed to be up and about. Obviously he'd had a brief lapse of memory, disorienting and undoubtedly upsetting, but everything seemed to have settled down now and Ted felt quite certain he could reconcile his erring memories with reality.

It felt even more unreal later, while he was sitting on the front porch, reading the Sunday paper. Oddly enough, nothing he found there conflicted with his memories; the strange discontinuities seemed to have confined themselves to details of his immediate suroundings. He'd half expected to discover that Dukakis was President, the Soviet Union had remained intact, and Martians were invading.

When Joe Pereira came outdoors wearing a T-shirt and shorts, and began washing the pickup truck, that should have been a sign that things were returning to normal. Except that he came out of the wrong house to do it. And when the Prescott twins started to play on their swing set, they did so in the Pereiras' yard, or what should have been the Pereiras' yard. The newspaper fell from Ted's limp fingers.

Later, after he'd regained the ability to move and talk, he explored his newly rearranged environment by encouraging Beth to talk about the neighbors, a subject she was willing to discuss with minimal encouragement. From her freely offered store of rumors, facts, theories, and speculation, he learned several things that contradicted his memories.

The Prescotts and Pereiras had switched houses, obviously, and Andy was no longer an accountant but a real estate agent. When he cautiously asked Beth how her own work was going, Ted learned that rather than working for Catterall Realty, she was now an employee of Callander & Callander Accounting Services. The Prescotts still had the twins, Cindy and Julie, but now there was a third as well, another girl, Felicia. Felicia had been the Pereiras' daughter, but Joe Junior was now apparently an only child.

Karen Pereira was a teacher again, currently on a short medical leave because of the skydiving accident that had left her with a broken arm. Ted remembered Andy Prescott's fascination with skydiving, but apparently the closest he now came to participating in sports was his fanatical devotion to the Red Sox. Beth also made a passing reference to a miscarriage he was quite certain she had never had, at least not before, and wondered from which of his neighbors that particular attribute had come.

Nor was Ted himself immune from the changes. He found a scar on his arm that was an exact match to one he'd seen before, but it had belonged to Joe Pereira at the time. He'd gone to bed needing a haircut and wakened with a crewcut. And when Beth made lunch, linguini in a spicy sauce, he discovered that he had somehow managed to shed his allergy to tomatoes.

He might still be crazy, he realized, but Ted decided that a more satisfying, if less plausible, explanation was that the mysterious kaleidoscope was somehow changing reality, shifting bits and pieces of the lives of the three families back and forth. If he could somehow learn to control the process, pick the best parts of each for himself and Beth, he'd have it made.

And then he thought of something else. If the kaleidoscope could shift a child from one family to another, why not a wife? He no longer loved Beth, hadn't thought of her in those terms for years now. She was still attractive in an undistinguished sort of way, but she'd put on some weight over the years, and her idea of good sex was conservative, predictable, and as brief as possible.

Karen on the other hand. . . .

But how could he control it? Even if he could somehow loosen the barrel so that the mechanism turned freely, how could he choose a single attribute to change? Perhaps everything was reflected in the new patterns formed in the inner chamber, but if so, he hadn't the faintest idea how to interpret them.

After lunch, he walked into the study, closed the door, and spent nearly two hours staring through the narrow eyepiece, fancying he saw human forms, houses, pets, trees and vehicles and abstract forms all mixed together. But even if his eyes and imagination were not seeing what he wished to find rather than what was actually there, he still had no way of manipulating the discrete parts of his reality.

Except by trial and error.

Ted spent much of the afternoon on the back patio, watching the kids play in the adjacent yard and across the street, noticing that the dog and cat had switched back to their original houses, although they were still with the wrong families. Felicia Prescott was a precocious seven-year-old, and when she came outside to play with the twins, he discovered where Beth's red hair had gone. Andy Prescott had his mustache back, but now it was Karen who insisted on watching the Red Sox.

"Ever since she went to work in field maintenance for the phone company, she's been interested in sports," Joe confided when he wandered over to visit his neighbor late in the day. "I guess she picked it up from the guys she works with."

Ted ignored the kaleidoscope, trying to work out the implications in his mind. There had been so many rapid changes, he wasn't sure he remembered the original configuration of the neighborhood well enough to set things back, even if he could figure out how. Was it Andy or Joe who had originally sported that pencil-thin mustache, for example? And had Samantha Prescott always worn glasses?

He was also bothered by the fact that only he seemed to recognize that things were not as they had been before. Of course, he was the one operating the kaleidoscope, but the scar and his absent allergy demonstrated that he was just as vulnerable to the changes. But unless his wife and neighbors were extraordinarily good actors, none of them suspected anything was amiss. Ted also entertained the possibility that despite all the evidence, he was actually experiencing some weird variety of breakdown, that he was either imagining the changes or creatively reediting the past in order to convince himself that magic was at work.

Ultimately he decided to accept as his working hypothesis that the kaleidoscope was genuine, that the changes were real, and that further alterations were possible. If he *was* in fact crazy, it could do no harm, and if he was sane, he had a chance to substantially improve his situation, to say nothing of acquiring Karen Pereira as his wife. Karen Croner . . . he liked the sound of it.

The kaleidoscope proved to be as stubborn as ever when he finally picked it up. Frustrated, he carried it down to the basement, where he discovered that he now owned the fully equipped workshop that Joe Pereira had proudly shown off shortly after the Croners moved into the neighborhood. A quick search revealed an aerosol lubricant spray, which he used liberally around the circumference of the shaft. This time, when he tried to turn the barrel, it moved freely, a full half turn before he stopped.

The pattern had changed significantly, but he still couldn't interpret the shapes and colors. Setting the kaleidoscope down on the workbench, he walked upstairs to explore his new world.

Samantha Prescott met him at the top of the stairs. No, actually it was Samantha Croner who stood there, wearing her waist-length red hair loose across her back.

"There you are!" Her eyes flashed angrily. "Would you please talk to your daughters about their behavior? They've done nothing but fight since they got up this morning."

Stunned, Ted turned toward the living room, his feet moving automatically, found the twins sitting sullenly at opposite ends of the couch. Julie's right arm was in a sling. He glanced out the front window, noticed a pickup truck parked inside his carport, then jumped as a tabby cat ran across the floor practically under his feet.

"No, this isn't what I wanted," he whispered to himself, then turned and bolted back to the basement door, brushing past his new wife so quickly that her jaw dropped in amazement. Ted practically ran to the bottom of the stairs, snatched up the kaleidoscope, and gave it a full turn without even coming to a stop. A discarded rag shifted under one foot and Ted lost his balance, threw out both hands automatically to break the fall, and lost his grip on the kaleidoscope.

He hit the floor hard enough to take his breath away, slowly found the strength to roll over onto his back, and drew deep, ragged breaths until the pain subsided. A few seconds later he sat up, then stood, then began to search for the kaleidoscope. But not only was it no place to be found, he quickly realized he was no longer in his own basement. The workshop had been returned to the Pereira house, and he along with it.

A sudden premonition chilled him and he raced upstairs, not even nodding to his wife, Karen, before rushing out the front door.

As he had suspected, he lived in the Pereira house now, although the mailbox read Croner; at least he hadn't swapped identities. To his right, in his original yard, Beth . . . Pereira? . . . was working on hands and knees in the flower garden that Samantha Prescott had planted in the yard across the street early in the spring. Andy Prescott was outside, meticulously trimming weeds from the streetside edge of his property, using the weedwhacker Joe Pereira had bought at Sears the previous year.

Ted started down the front walk, just as Joe came out through his own front door, with a familiar object cradled in one arm. "Hey, Andy! Come see what I found!" As he stepped down from the porch, Joe was already attempting to turn the barrel of the kaleidoscope.

"Oh, my God!" Ted wasn't sure if he had said the words aloud. He started across the lawn, trying to figure out how to convince Pereira to surrender the kaleidoscope, and never even noticed the delivery van whose driver vainly slammed on the brakes when Andy Prescott blindly and foolishly stepped into the street without looking for traffic. There was a thud audible above the screech of tires on asphalt and Prescott flew twenty feet through the air before slamming down onto the pavement, where he made feeble efforts to move. At the very same instant, Joe Pereira used his well-muscled right arm to turn the kaleidoscope's barrel.

Ted stared up into the sky, feeling the pain of his broken body as an abstract thing, no longer a part of his personal reality. Faces came into view, Joe Pereira, Andy Prescott, a stranger wearing a uniform cap of some sort. In some remote, emotionless corner of his mind, Ted realized that he was dying and wished that there was some magic device he could use to change the world, to erase his foolish lack of attention, to preserve his life.

But there was no such thing, of course.

BIG ROOTS

by Pamela Sargent

After Father died, I stayed on at his camp. I had put off leaving for a lot of reasons. One was that I felt at peace there, in a way I hadn't for a long time, and another was the need to settle matters with my sister Evie. Maybe I still would have been there, struggling against a world intruding on my refuge, if my sister hadn't appeared to me in the guise of a False Face and the spirits had not spoken.

The camp was a cabin with two bedrooms, a kitchen and living room that were on the side facing the lake, and an attic with cots and sleeping bags. We called it a camp because that's what everyone in the Adirondacks called their summer places, whether they were shacks or mansions. Father had sold his house after Mother died, and lived at the camp during the last two years of his life, before my sister put him in the hospital.

My grandfather had built the camp and cleared the land around the cabin, but the pines were crowding in, and long knotted roots bulged from the ground in tangled masses along the path that led down to the lake.

One of the pines, during th
death, had grown larger, its tru
size of a sequoia's.

I didn't know why this tree
faster than the others, but its pr
I would sit under the pine and thi
ing out under the land, bu
ground. We had deep roots in these mountains, my
family and I, and I had felt them more lately. My
grandfather's people had come there early in the nine-
teenth century, but my grandmother's Mohawks, the
Eastern Gatekeepers of the Iroquois, had been there
even earlier. She had grown up on a reservation in Can-
ada, and my grandfather had met her in Montreal and
brought her back here after their marriage. This land
had been a Mohawk hunting ground, the forest they
had traveled to from their villages to hunt beaver and
deer, and where they had sometimes encountered forest spirits, long before white settlers had moved into
the mountains. My grandfather had brought his wife
back to her roots.

I had pulled up the canoe and was sitting on the
dock, thinking about Grandma's life while watching the
loon. The bird had taken up residence in our part of
the lake a couple of weeks earlier, and I wondered
when more loons would join it. The loon would float on
the water, moving its black-feathered head from side to
side like an Egyptian belly dancer, then dive. It would
stay underwater for three or four minutes, and I could
never predict where in the bay it would surface. I had
been like a loon underwater myself for the past year,

amp, diving below the turbulent surface
life. The bit of money I had saved was run-
. Pretty soon, I would have to emerge.

e wind picked up and the trees sighed. Sometimes
heard voices, as if people were chanting and singing elsewhere in the forest. Now I heard the sound of a car in the distance. It would be Evie; I was expecting my sister. Our great-aunt and a couple of cousins lived in the nearest town, but they hadn't called since the funeral, and I wanted nothing to do with them anyway; Aunt Clara had led the family faction that disapproved of my grandfather's marriage. My brothers, who lived in Seattle and Atlanta, had already said they wouldn't be visiting this summer, and I hadn't made any friends in town. So it had to be Evie, along with her husband Steve and her three kids by her first husband, my niece and nephews who couldn't sit in place without a VCR and a boom box for more than two minutes. It would be Evie, because anyone else would have called first to ask directions, since the only way to the camp was along a narrow dirt road through the woods. It would be Evie, because we had business to discuss. She was here to change my mind.

I got up and climbed toward the cabin. A winged shape soared overhead; I looked up as an eagle landed in the uppermost branches of the largest pine. Evie's blue Honda was rolling down the rutted dirt driveway that led to the cabin. She would unload a television, a VCR, and a ton of rented cassettes, to keep her kids quiet, and Steve would sit in the kitchen making jokes while Evie and I cooked supper. The noise from the TV would be deafening, because all the movies my niece and nephews watched had lots of special effects. I was sure the sounds would frighten the eagle away.

But when Evie got out of the car, I saw that she was alone. "Got the whole weekend," she said, "and I'm taking Monday off. Steve's watching the kids, so it'll be a real vacation for me." She went around to the trunk and opened it. "Brought some food in the cooler, so we won't have to cook tonight." Evie took after our father, and he had gotten his looks from his mother. My grandmother had looked like Evie when she was young—a tall woman, with coppery skin, thick black hair, and dark brown eyes. I had our mother's blue eyes, and my black hair had gone gray early, so now I colored it reddish-blonde. I didn't look anything like my grandmother, but I had her soul, which was more than you could say for Evie.

I helped her carry the cooler and her suitcase inside, relieved that the kids and Steve weren't with her, but still wary. Ten years lay between my younger sister and me, and we had never been that close. We had gone for years without even phoning each other while she was having kids and getting a divorce and I was drifting, afraid to come home. She wouldn't have come up here alone just to relax and visit with me.

The two bedrooms stood on either side of the bathroom, separated by a narrow corridor. I had been using the bedroom our grandmother had slept in during her summer visits, and took Evie's suitcase to the other. The quilt covered the bed that took up most of the small room, and a crucifix hung above the headboard.

I never slept in that room, mainly because I didn't like the idea of sleeping under a crucifix, especially one that made Christ look so peaceful hanging there, as if he were only snoozing. I also knew my grandmother had come to hate the sight of the cross, which only reminded her of the nuns who had tried to beat a white soul into her. I could have taken it down, but then Evie would have been whining, "Where's Dad's crucifix?" even though she hadn't been to Mass since her divorce. My father had wanted to die here, in the room he and my mother had shared, but Evie had insisted on the hospital, so an ambulance had come up the long dirt road and driven him the fifty miles to the city. Father had lasted less than a month there, barely enough time for my brothers to realize that he was actually dying and to get to his side to make whatever amends they could.

"Mother must have hated this place," Evie said as she opened the suitcase.

"I never heard her say so."

"Well, think of it, Jennie—sitting around here, away from all her friends, taking care of us and waiting for Dad to come up on the weekends."

Maybe she had hated it. I wouldn't know, because Mother had been the kind of person who kept her thoughts to herself. The camp had been my father's boyhood summer refuge. Even after all our summers there, Mother had moved around the rooms, occasionally peering into a corner or picking up an object from a table, as if she were a guest exploring unfamiliar surroundings. But maybe Evie was only projecting her own

48

feelings onto our mother. That would be like my sister, imagining that everyone felt exactly the way she did.

"But I guess you wouldn't understand that," Evie continued, "being practically a hermit yourself."

I would have to put up with three days of this, Evie asking when I was leaving, how I could possibly get through another winter, when I was going to find a job and get on with my life. She would get to the business about the land, too; I was sure of that now. It didn't matter. I was ready for her this time.

We went to the kitchen. "Hungry yet?" Evie asked.

"Not really."

"Let's have a drink, then. Better make mine a ginger ale, or diet soda if you have any."

"You sure? I've got some of your bourbon left."

"Steve and I are trying for a kid," she said, "so I'm laying off the booze."

"You must be kidding," I said. "You have three already. How can you afford it? What's going to happen to your job?"

"Steve wants a kid of his own. Can't blame a man for that, can you?"

"Go sit on the porch," I said. "I'll get the drinks." She wandered toward the porch. Evie had always been big, and she had gained more weight since her last visit; maybe she was already pregnant. I poured her a diet cola, along with gin over ice for myself. Once, I had liked Martinis, but had come to think of them as a drink for rich white Republicans, so now I didn't bother with the vermouth. "Your grandmother drank." Mother had harped on that, on how much trouble it had caused everyone. "Her Indian blood—that's what it was." That was Mother's explanation for any behavior she didn't want to blame either on environment or her own genes.

The screened-in porch faced the lake. Evie was sitting in one of the chairs, smoking a cigarette; apparently she hadn't given that up yet. I sat down near the standing ashtray and took out my own cigarettes. Tobacco was a sacred plant for the Iroquois; I had read that in a book. For my grandmother's Mohawk ancestors, it was a means by which their prayers could reach the spirits, and rise to their Creator. That was, I supposed, a pretty good reason not to quit. My indecision would travel out along the smoky tendrils, to be dispersed as it rose toward heaven; the spirits would answer my prayers. A stream of smoke from my cigarette drifted through the screen, then broke up into uneven strands.

Evie said, "I have to talk to you."

"I figured."

"Curt called me last night. I talked to Sam a couple of days ago, about the land. They think selling it off's a good idea. People want lakeside property, and this land's worth more now."

Of course my brothers would agree with her about selling. The land Father had left us was his only legacy. We owned everything around this small bay; the closest place, about a mile south, was another cabin overlooking the narrow channel that connected the bay to the rest of the lake. The shallowness of the channel kept large motorboats out of the bay; days could pass without my seeing more than a canoe moving along the shore. It was why the loons came there and blue herons nested in the nearby trees; I thought of the eagle I had seen earlier.

"Dad didn't leave us this land," I said, "so that we could sell it."

"He must have known we'd consider it. Why didn't he put it in the will if he didn't want us to sell?"

"Because he was too sick to think about it. Because there wasn't time. I know what he would have wanted."

"You know. You always know, Jennie. You always know all this stuff about everyone in the family that nobody else knows." Or which might not even be true, her voice suggested.

I knew things because the rest of them never bothered to listen to anybody. I said, "When I knew Dad was dying, I kept waiting for him to tell me to get on with my life. But he never did, and it wasn't until a little while ago that I figured out why. He wanted me to stay here, to protect this land."

"That's crazy. He was so doped up toward the end he probably couldn't think straight. He must have figured you'd have enough sense to get back on your feet by now. This land's worth nothing to us this way. If we sell it, we can—"

"It isn't ours," I said, "not really. It's like we're the caretakers, that it's a trust. I've been feeling that way the whole time I've been here. It isn't our land, it's our people's—Grandma's people."

"Are you on that again?" Evie stubbed out her cigarette. "How can that stuff matter to you? Look, I loved

Grandma, but she wasn't all that much use to anybody when she was alive. If Grandpa hadn't had to waste so much money on her, maybe there would have been something for us." She took out another cigarette and lit it. "You can afford to be sentimental about these things, but the rest of us have kids. I'd like to be able to do something for them."

That was the excuse that explained everything. "I have kids, so that gives me license to be an asshole. I have kids, so I'm entitled to do things I'd shy away from or have doubts about otherwise, because I have to think of them." At least that's how it sounded to me. Whatever happened to "I have kids, so maybe I should try to pass on some wisdom and principles?" But my sister didn't live in that world. Maybe no one did any more.

"And Curt's got a son almost ready for college," Evie went on. "He told me he wants Brian to get somewhere." That sounded like Curt. My brother would think he was doing the world a big favor if he gave it another lawyer or M.B.A.

"It isn't as if the state hasn't set aside plenty of un-developed land already." Evie gestured with her cigarette. "We're not rich, you know. We can't keep this our little private bay forever."

I tried to think of what to say, but the gin was getting to me. Evie wouldn't understand if I told her that I still caught glimpses of deer coming to the bay to drink, that we had to keep the land as it was so that the deer could still come here. I couldn't tell her that having more people around would probably frighten off the turtles that sunned themselves on the logs across from our dock. Evie would be thinking of future college bills and expensive technology for her kids and the new baby with Steve, not deer and turtles.

"It won't be the same," I said. "I saw an eagle in that big tree today. He won't stick around if builders start tearing things up. We could leave something behind, Evie, a bit of untouched land people might appreciate having someday."

"Listen." She leaned toward me. "We can still keep some of the land around this camp. You'd hardly notice the difference. We could sell the rest off in large parcels, so there wouldn't be too many places built." She sounded like a white woman, with her talk of selling the land and carving it up, but that was how Evie thought of herself. It's that Indian blood that caused most of the family troubles; better forget you have any.

"I'll just bet the developers will listen to you," I said. "They'll say, Sure, I'll just put one summer home here and make fifty grand instead of building five and pocketing a hell of a lot more."

"There are limits," Evie replied. "what with having to put in septic systems and all. If you ask me, this place could use some development." She squinted as she stared toward the lake. "For instance, that big tree there is completely out of hand. Somebody should have cut it down a long time ago. If you cleared out some of those trees, you'd have a much better view."

"That tree stays." I was on my feet. "It's Grandma's tree—she planted it herself when Grandpa built this place." I don't know how I knew that. During the year

I had been living at the camp, I had looked out at the tree without ever thinking about it. Why had Grandma planted a pine there, when pines already surrounded us on all sides? Yet somehow I knew she had planted it. Maybe she had told me once, and I had simply forgotten until that moment.

I went into the kitchen, took some ice out of the refrigerator, and poured myself more gin. The evening wind was picking up when I got back to the porch. The pines sang, the wind rising into a muted cheer and then falling into a sigh, but a deeper moan nearly drowned out the song. I heard a rumble that might have been distant thunder, but the sky was still salmon pink, the clouds fingers of navy blue.

"It was cruel," I said then, "what Grandpa did to Grandma."

"What do you mean?" Evie asked.

"Buying all this land and saying he did it for her."

"You call that cruel? It showed how much he adored her."

"No, it didn't," I said. "He was saying, Here, I bought this land, this little piece of the mountains that used to belong to your people, because I made a lot of money in lumber. And you can have a little of your land back because a white man got it for you."

"You're crazy, Jennie. Grandpa loved that woman. Do you think he would have stayed with her all those years if he hadn't?"

That was the way the rest of them saw it. Grandpa was the long-suffering saint and Grandma the alcoholic he hadn't been able to help. He had checked her into every expensive hospital he could find, but that had not kept her from going back to drinking when she got home. He had sold his business to stay with her, and at the end of his life, the money was gone. Grandma had outlived him even with the drinking; she tapered off toward the end, spacing out her drinks, but not enough to save either her liver or my father from her medical bills. No wonder the rest of them blamed her for their lives of tract houses, credit card bills, and tedious jobs.

Maybe I would have blamed her myself, but I had spent too much time as a child sitting with her when my brothers exiled me from their games. To Evie and my brothers, our grandmother was only an old drunk who sat in the corner and mumbled to herself; that was the Grandma they remembered. They didn't have the patience to listen to her, to see that her disjointed musings made sense once you put them together. The Grandpa I had heard about in her words wasn't the loving husband Evie saw, but the man who had forced her to live among people who despised her, who had refused to let her go.

"The wild Indians'll get you." That had been Curt's favorite taunt at our camp when he was tormenting our younger brother Sam. "When you're asleep, the wild Indians'll climb in your window and scalp you." Indians had nothing to do with them. They had never noticed how Grandma closed her eyes when she heard Curt's words, how her hand had tightened around her glass.

"I don't even know my clan," I said.

Evie exhaled a stream of smoke. "What?"

"I don't even know my clan. Grandma used to say

that. She'd say it in this low voice, so nobody else would hear, but I did." She had said it as if knowing the name of her clan would have freed her from her prison.

"Probably said it when she was drunk." Evie leaned back in her chair. "It doesn't matter, Jennie. It's got nothing to do with us." She was quiet for a while. "Being alone up here all this time—no wonder you sound so funny. Look, if we sell, you'd have enough to make a new start. You can think of where to live, have time to find a job. Hell, maybe we can get enough so you don't have to work at all."

As the gin slowed me down, I wanted to shout that I was going to find work—waitressing, office work, or whatever—in the nearest town, that I could lay in enough wood for the winter and buy enough meat for myself cheaply from a hunter once deer season started. I knew what I had to do; it was time to lay it all out and show Evie she had to go along. I was about to raise my voice when the cabin suddenly shook, and the floor dropped from under my chair.

The disturbance lasted only a moment. Before I could speak, the floor was once more firmly under my feet, the evening still except for the gentle sound of the wind.

"Whoa," Evie muttered. "Did you feel that?"

"Just a quake," I said. The mountains had them once in a while, mild ones that barely made three points or so on the Richter scale, but I had never felt one quite like that. Usually, everything would get very quiet, and then there would be a sharp sound like a sonic boom, and after that a small bounce before things settled down. This time, the quake had come from deep underground, as though the earth was giving way.

"Jesus," Evie said, "I thought the whole place was going to fall down. I'll have that bourbon after all."

I got her the drink, and then another one when we sat down in the kitchen to eat the sandwiches she had brought, and by then Evie was wandering down memory lane, droning on about our adventures at the camp when we were younger. She seemed to get most nostalgic about the times the boys had ganged up on me, or about how Curt and Sam would always push me off the dock, even when I was dressed, even when the water was freezing cold. I didn't mind. At least she had forgotten about real estate for the moment.

She went to bed early, tired from her drive, and I sat on the porch with another gin, trying to think of how to persuade her and my brothers not to sell our land. Brilliant ideas about how to convince them flashed through my mind, only to be forgotten a second or so later. My face was stiff, my body numb. I was really drunk by then, and felt as if I were wrapped in cotton and looking at everything from inside a long tunnel. The big pine tree near the path seemed larger, and then I saw a face in the bark, a carved mask like the ones my ancestors had made.

That had to be an illusion, a trick of the moonlight shining through the boughs. The face changed as I stared at it, reshaping itself into that of a wolf. Seeing a face in the tree didn't frighten me, though, because I had noticed other strange things lately—marks and symbols on trees that looked as though they had been made by knives, the throbbing sounds of drums in the night until hooting owls or the snarl of a bobcat drowned them out. I had grown to accept these passing sights and sounds, which seemed to belong to the forest and mountains.

I must have fallen asleep after that, and woke up on the studio couch in the living room, my head pounding. I lifted my head, then realized I would never make it to my bedroom without collapsing or vomiting—maybe both. My head fell back, and then I was outside, under the big pine.

Two men in feathered caps and deerskin robes stood near the tree. One lifted his hand, and then I looked up to see the eagle flutter its wings in the branches overhead.

"Do you know what tree this is?" one man asked.

"My grandmother's," I replied.

"It is more than that. Your grandmother planted the cone from which it grew, but that cone fell from an ancient pine, the one under which I had my vision of peace, the vision that united the Five Nations of the Iroquois. I am the Peacemaker, child, and this tree—"

But before he could say anything more, I was back on the couch, covering my eyes with one hand against the light. "Jennie," my sister said.

"Jesus Christ." My jaw ached, and even moving my mouth hurt. "Turn off the light."

"You're drunk," she said.

"So what?"

"Is this what you do when you're alone, just drink yourself silly?"

"No. This is what I do when you guys won't leave me alone."

She pulled me up from the couch and helped me toward my bedroom. "You ought to know better, Jennie, what with— "

"I had a dream. I have to tell you— "

"You probably had a nightmare, in your condition." She let me fall to the bed, then took off my shoes.

"It wasn't a nightmare." Something else my grandmother had said was coming back to me. Dreams were important; in the old days, an Iroquois who had a vivid dream would go to every longhouse in his settlement, recounting his dream until he found someone who could explain it to him. I didn't think Evie would be able to explain my dream to me, but it clearly had something to do with our land and the tree outside, so I felt it was something I had to tell her. Maybe the dream would persuade her to give up her plans.

"I was outside," I continued, "and these two men—I'm positive they were Mohawks, or Iroquois anyway, were standing— "

"Give it a rest," Evie burst out. "I'm going back to sleep. Talk to me when you're sober." She stomped out of the room.

I don't know why I thought telling her about the dream would bring her around. The fact was, I didn't have to come up with brilliant schemes for keeping the land. All I had to do was tell Evie I wasn't going to sign any papers, and she and my brothers wouldn't be able to do a thing. I hadn't wanted to state the matter quite so bluntly, but she had pushed me to it, so there was nothing else to be done.

But I didn't know if I would have the fortitude to hold out against my brothers and sisters forever. I could disappear, but the rest of them—Curt especially—wouldn't give up until they found me, and they might use my disappearance against me. If they got desperate enough they might even get me declared incompetent, and they would have enough grounds, what with my wanderings, erratic work history, and bouts of manic-depression. I had gotten my mental shit together before coming home, but it could still look bad, so I'd have to make sure they couldn't find me. If that meant leaving the forest that had finally calmed the storms that often raged inside me, I would still have the comfort of knowing the land was safe.

I slept for a while and woke up with a bad case of the dries. Somehow, I managed to stumble into the bathroom for a glass of water, and then the telephone in the kitchen started ringing. I found my way to it, shading my eyes against the morning light as I leaned against the wall and picked up the receiver.

"Hello," I mumbled.

"Hey, Jennie! This is Curt. Gosh, it's great hearing your voice again—been a long time."

I sank into the chair below the phone. "Yeah."

"Evie said she was going up there this weekend. Wish I could be there with you guys."

I always got nervous when my brother sounded

cheerful, especially at that hour of the day. "She's trying to talk me into letting the rest of you sell," I said.

"Well, I know, but don't think we're going to get rid of the camp or anything. I was talking to Sam last night, and we were thinking that maybe you should get the deed to the camp, along with your share of whatever we get for the land. We owe you something for taking care of Dad before he went to the hospital, for coming home when he got sick." So Curt was offering me a bribe. "I know the place means a lot to you, so maybe you should have it. Of course, I hope you'll let your old brother come to visit once in a while."

I was silent.

"You'd have enough money to get another place for yourself, get a new start, but the camp would be there for the summers. You could—"

"I won't sell."

"What?"

"I'm not going to let this land be sold. I won't sign any papers. I won't go along with you."

"Jennie? Jennie?"

I rubbed at my aching temples, refusing to answer him.

"I want to talk to Evie," he said at last.

My sister was standing in the doorway. I got up, handed her the phone, and went to my bedroom. Evie was talking in a low voice, but sounds echoed in the kitchen, so occasionally I caught a few words. "Crazy" was one. The words that disturbed me most, though, were "power of attorney." So they were considering that option already.

A rumbling sound came from under the cabin. Another small quake, I thought; they were certainly coming more often lately. I heard Evie hang up, and then the banging of pots in the kitchen. I dozed off, and woke to find Evie carrying a tray into the room.

"You need breakfast," she said as she set the tray down. "There's coffee, eggs, and toast. You'd better rest today—you look like you might be coming down with something. I'll stay here until you're feeling better, and then I'll head into town to pick up more groceries."

She handed me the coffee; I sipped at it. "You should know better than to drink so much," she went on, "what with your manic-depression and all." She was already laying the groundwork, but not out of malice. Like my brothers, she was probably half-convinced that I really was demented, and that it would all be for the best in the end. Evie could persuade herself that I would be better off in treatment, with others handling my affairs. She would play nurse this morning until I felt better, and then go off to town, where she would probably call Curt from a public phone so that they could decide what to do next. They would tell themselves they were saving my life, that they were helping me.

"You look like death warmed over," Evie said as she lit a cigarette. I set down my cup. She seemed to be holding a glowing coal to her lips as coils of smoke drifted toward the ceiling. Her dark eyes glittered, and her face was as still as a mask.

Masks, I thought, and recalled something else I had read. I had been reading a lot while living at the camp, going into town to buy old books at garage sales and to take others out of the library. That was how severed I was from our traditions; I had to pick up a lot of my people's lore from books. Now I remembered reading about the False Faces.

The shamans called the False Faces would come to the longhouses to heal the ill, bearing hot coals in their hands. They would put on their masks and sprinkle ashes over the ailing person, and if by some miracle they saved him, he had to become one of them. I drew in Evie's smoke; an ash from the end of her cigarette fell on my hand.

She was a False Face, I suddenly realized, but one who served evil spirits. She would nurse me and heal me and bring me back from the dead. Then I would have to join her and my brothers and the society of those who bought and sold and tore at the land instead of living lightly on it, giving back what they took from it. I would have to live in their world.

"Get away from me!" I was on my feet, struggling against her as she tried to restrain me. Evie was three inches taller, and a good thirty pounds heavier, but I broke her grip and pushed her against the wall. She fell, and then I was running through the living room toward the porch. It was dark out there for that time of day. I lifted my head and gazed through the screen.

The big pine had grown during the night. Its trunk was much wider, almost cutting off the dock from view. Nothing could grow that fast, and yet the great tree's roots now twisted over much of the cleared land around the cabin. I looked up through the lattice of green branches at a patch of sky. The pine had grown past the trees around it; I could no longer see the top.

"Oh, my God," I said under my breath.

"You crazy bitch." I turned to see Evie stomping toward me. "I tried to be reasonable about this. You really are nuts, and—"

"Get out!" I shouted. "Get the hell out of here." I went at her, but she jumped back before I could hit her.

"You'll be sorry for this, Jennie."

"Get out!" I swung at her, then ran after her as she retreated across the kitchen. My knee caught the table, and I was suddenly on the floor. By the time I got up, Evie was gone.

I stumbled toward the door. Evie was making for her car across a maze of roots. A bulge in the ground appeared near the cabin, as if a giant mole was burrowing nearby. "Evie!" I shouted, but she was inside the Honda and barreling up to the road before I could get to her. Brown tentacles snaked after the car, scattering dirt and grass. I don't know if Evie saw the roots. Maybe by then she was too concerned with getting away from her crazy sister to notice anything.

The ground heaved under my feet; roots spread out around me as I walked back to the cabin, swelling in size until they reached nearly to my knees. The pine now blocked most of the path leading down to the lake, and the smaller trees around it nestled in the furrows between its roots.

The cabin shook, but I felt calm as I sat down at the kitchen table. It came to me that I had been waiting for something like this, and that the pine and its burgeoning roots might solve my problem. Nobody would want to buy land near a spot where trees behaved this way.

I went to my bedroom, picked up the remains of my breakfast, then made more coffee. The floor trembled, but I made no move to leave. A glance out the kitchen window revealed that the roots had surrounded my car and that more had tunneled up to the road; I would never be able to drive over them. I might be able to get to the camp overlooking the channel on foot. Maybe the people there, the closest neighbors to me, had seen the giant pine springing toward the sky. Perhaps its roots were already moving in that direction.

Father had posted a list of numbers near the telephone. I found the number of my neighbors, then dialed it quickly.

"Simmons here," a voice said in my ear.

"Mr. Simmons, I'm your neighbor, Jennifer Relson, from the other end of the bay. I think I'd better warn you that a tree around here seems to be out of control."

"What?"

"It's growing really fast. I can't even see how tall it is any more, and the roots are going all over the place. What I'm trying to say is they might come your way."

"What?"

"The tree's roots," I said. "They're growing all around this camp now, high as walls!"

"Look, lady, I was just on my way out. I don't know what you're smoking, but—"

I hung up. Maybe he would believe me when he saw

the roots moving toward him, if they got that far. How far could they spread? I went outside to find out. The tree's trunk had grown as wide as the cabin; the pines around it swayed as smaller roots twisted across the ground, then burrowed into it. I climbed over roots, into the ways between them, and over more roots again until I could see the lake.

The yodeling cry of loons greeted me; five more had joined the one I had been watching. The pine didn't seem to be growing any more, but long bands of brown bark were winding among the trees on the other side of the bay. I sat down, resting my back against a root. Dark veins snaked through the forest until the hills across the lake seemed enmeshed in a network of tunnels.

Strangely, none of the maples and pines seemed harmed by the roots, which bulged up and around the trees without crushing them. The loons bobbed on the smooth, mirrorlike surface of the water, the turtles basked on their logs, and deer had come down to the opposite shore to drink. The birds and animals were undisturbed by the roots branching out around them; the loons filled the air once more with their wild laughter.

I turned away from the lake and clambered back over the roots. Above, the cabin nestled among curved brown walls, an outpost of order in the midst of disorder. The phone was ringing when I went inside. I waited for a bit, then picked up the receiver.

"Listen, Jennie," my sister said. "I'm trying to understand, I really am. I'm willing to come back if you'll promise to be sensible." There was the sound of country-and-western music in the background, which meant Evie was probably calling from the Brass Rail, the only bar in town. "If you don't," she continued, "I'm going to call Curt and Sam, and discuss this, and we'll decide what to do about you."

"But you can't do anything," I said. "You won't get past the roots. They're all over the place now."

"You're out of your mind."

"Didn't you see them on your way out?"

"I thought it was only your manic-depression, but you're really out to lunch. That does it, Jennie. I'm calling Curt as soon as—"

"Go ahead and call. You'll just be wasting your money. There's nothing you can do." She didn't answer. "Evie? Evie?"

The line was dead. I wandered through the cabin, trying to sort out my thoughts. The electricity still worked, and water came out of the bathroom faucets. If I didn't look through the windows at the bark barriers entwined around the place, I could almost believe everything was still normal. Somehow, the burrowing roots weren't affecting the cabin, but that probably wouldn't be the case for long. Eventually I would run out of food, and the roots would keep me from driving into town for more. There was no reason to stay anyway. How could my sister and brothers sell this land now?

I packed some food and a canteen of water, then struggled over the roots down to the dock. The roots winding among the forested hills had settled down, but now a brown wall cut off Mr. Simmons' camp from view. He had said he was on his way out when I called; he would certainly be surprised when he tried to drive back. There was no point in going to his place anyway. I would try for town. I didn't think about what I would do if the roots had spread that far.

I dropped the backpack into the canoe, then climbed in and paddled out, looking back when I was halfway across the bay. The pine towered overhead, as tall as a skyscraper, dwarfing everything around it, its needles as long as arrows. The surface of the lake was dappled by the green shadows of giant boughs. There had been some peace for me under the tree my grandmother had planted; maybe its limbs would grow vast enough to shelter the world. I paddled out from the shadows toward the far shore.

I beached the canoe at a spot where the land sloped gently up from the water, then shouldered my backpack. The tangle of roots on the hillside above had cut me off from a path that led to the nearest road. I scrambled over one thick root, into a ditch and up another root, then sat down to consider my options.

Even if I managed to find the road, making it to town might be pointless. If the roots had spread that far, I would only find chaos, and be forced to try for refuge somewhere else. I lifted my head and gazed across the lake at the camp. The cabin was hidden, the great tree a branching green canopy shielding the forests below. Roots were looped among the reeds near the shore; I thought of them tunneling under the water.

The mountains beyond the bay, made blue by the distance, were now covered by thin brown webs.

So the roots had already spread that far. In the middle of this unexplainable event, sitting on top of a root that gently pulsated under me, I was surprised to find that I could still think rationally. Reason told me that my only choice now was to find the road, follow it to town, and figure out what to do after I found out what was going on there. If I kept climbing this hill, I would eventually reach the road, however many roots barred the way.

The tree was still stretching toward the sky, as if time was accelerating. I imagined the great pine springing into space, its boughs embracing the moon as its roots clutched at the earth. A wedge of ducks, quacking loudly, dropped toward the lake; the water blossomed around them as they landed. Maybe that was keeping me sane, the fact that the birds and animals I had seen were acting normally, that the roots had not harmed or frightened them. Perhaps the animals were somehow blind to them. I narrowed my eyes and stilled my thoughts, and the roots became translucent, as if I were gazing at one image superimposed on another. But the root under me still throbbed, as though sap and nutrients were coursing through it, and I felt the ground shake as another root slithered past my feet. The great pine and its roots might save this bay from intruders. I wanted them to be real.

As I stared at the lake, an eagle flew out from under the great pine, soared over the bay, then dropped toward me and landed in a branch overhead. It watched me for a while, waiting.

"Well?" I said. The bird fluttered its wings, then lifted from its perch.

The eagle wanted me to follow. I didn't think of why a wild bird of prey would want me to follow it anywhere, but sensed that it did. The eagle led me. Whenever I was lost and uncertain of which way to go, it would return and circle above me before flying on.

I climbed over roots and down into wide ditches, then thrashed my way through underbrush. Roots were looped around berry bushes and arched over creeks. The staccato tapping of woodpeckers filled the forest, and once I glimpsed a rabbit before it hopped over a root and disappeared. I kept going, following my feathered guide through the tangled tendrils of wood until my backpack seemed as heavy as a boulder and my arms felt like useless baggage; my legs were cramping from climbing over so many roots. It was beginning to dawn on me that I should have come to the road by now, that the eagle was only leading me even farther into the forest.

I leaned against a tree, cursing myself for my stupidity. Had I been thinking clearly, I would have stayed in my canoe, headed through the channel and then hugged the shore until I reached town that way. Now I was too lost even to find my way back to the canoe. I might have given up then if the eagle hadn't flown back and landed on a branch just above me.

"I suppose you want me to go on," I said. "Not that I have much choice." The bird tilted its head. What was the point, after all, of going back to a world where I had always felt displaced, where something inside me had constantly threatened to burgeon as wildly as these roots? My previous life had been as uncontrolled as this growth, a manic lashing out followed by a burrowing into depression. Like the pine my grandmother had planted, I had been waiting to gather my strength. I don't know whether my grandmother had meant this to happen, or if she had been ignorant of the pine's power, but I would take my chances among the roots burrowing into the earth, among the trees the great pine was protecting.

"Grandma," I whispered, "you planted some kind of tree."

The deep green light of the forest grew darker. The eagle disappeared. I struggled on until I reached a small clearing. Ahead lay the largest root I had yet seen, a rounded ridge of bark as high as a good-sized hill.

I was too tired to go on. I stretched out, propping myself against the backpack. The air was still; the birds were silent. My ancestors had believed there were spirits in these mountains, but I was more fearful of animals that might be lurking nearby. Then a darker thought came to me, the kind of grim reflection I often had just before falling asleep, a thought that becomes a sinkhole swallowing every fragment of hope.

Maybe I was as crazy as Evie believed. Maybe the sudden growth of the pine tree and its huge, spreading roots were a delusion. I wanted to save this land so badly that I could imagine the supernatural had intervened to save it. I had called up this vision, and the small part of me that was still sane was able to perceive that the surrounding land and wildlife were unaffected by my imaginings. Maybe I would wake to find everything as it had been, and be unable to find my way out of the woods. Fear locked my muscles and dried up my mouth. I might wander these mountains until I joined the roaming spirits of Indians who had never been laid to rest.

"Perhaps you will," a voice said. "Maybe this is all an illusion after all." The voice was inside me, but I opened my eyes to see a woman standing near the root. She wore a long cloak decorated with beads and a band with eagle feathers over her brow, but the darkness hid her face. "Perhaps what you see is only a vision that will vanish, and you will return to the world you remember. But you cannot find your way back to your canoe without help, and even if you made it to the town, what then?"

"My sister's there," I replied, "and she thinks I'm a few cards short of a deck as it is. She'd have all the reasons she needs to put me away. Can't really blame her, you know—she has other priorities."

"Do you want to go back?"

The answer shot out from me before I could hold it back. "No."

The woman vanished. The ground lurched; I looked up to see trees swaying wildly. I jumped up and grabbed for a tree limb as the earth yawned under my feet. Roots were sinking all around me, groaning as they burrowed into the ground. I guessed what it meant. The tree had reached out with its roots and would now send them deep into the world to entwine them around the earth's heart. Then I lost my grip and was suddenly rolling down the hill until something hard rushed up to meet me.

I must have lain there throughout the night, because when I opened my eyes, the forest was green with light again. I was afraid to move, expecting to feel bruises and aches, fearing that I might have broken bones. But when I finally sat up, my body obeyed me easily, bringing me to my feet as effortlessly as it had when I was younger.

Most of the roots had vanished, but I felt them pulsating beneath me. The giant root still lay across the hill, and now I noticed that the trunks of the trees around me were marked by lines and patterns that pointed upward. My backpack lay near me; I slipped it on. I had as much chance of reaching safety by following the carved markings as I did doing anything else.

I hurried up the hill, then climbed the root, clinging to ridges in the bark, resting my feet in its cracks. The backpack tugged at my shoulders and pressed against me with its weight. I kept going until the ground was far below me and it was too late to turn back. I climbed, afraid to look up or down, until I reached the top.

There were no giant roots in the valley below me, only maples and pines of normal size. They stood around a field planted with corn and squash, and in the distance, I saw the wide leaves of tobacco plants. Smoke rose from the roofs of the longhouses beyond the field; people waited in the doorways, men and women in deerskin robes adorned with beads.

I don't know where this land is. It may be the past, or a far future, but I don't know enough astronomy to look up at the night sky and find out. It could be a world that might have been. Whatever it is, something has guided me here, to the place where I will make my home and live out my life.

I stumbled down the other side of the root and went to find my clan.

THE MIDNIGHT EL

by Robert Weinberg

Cold and alone, Sidney Taine waited for the Midnight El. Collar pulled up close around his neck, he shivered as the frigid Chicago wind attacked his exposed skin. Not even the usual drunks haunted the outdoor subway platforms on nights like these. With temperatures hovering only a few degrees above zero, the stiff breeze off Lake Michigan plunged the wind chill factor to twenty below. Fall asleep outside in the darkness and you never woke up.

Taine hated the cold. Though he had lived in Chicago for more than a year, he had yet to adjust to the winter weather. Originally from San Francisco, he delighted his hometown friends when he groused that he never realized what the phrase "chilled to the bone" meant until he moved to the Windy City.

Six feet four inches tall, weighing a bit more than two hundred and thirty pounds, Taine resembled a professional football player. Yet he moved with the grace of a stalking tiger and, for his size, was incredibly light on his feet. A sly grin and dark, piercing eyes gave him a sardonic, slightly mysterious air. An image he strived hard to cultivate.

Like his father and grandfather before him, Taine worked as a private investigator. Though he had opened his office in Chicago only fourteen months ago, he was already well known throughout the city. Dubbed by one of the major urban newspapers as "The New-Age Detective," Taine used both conventional techniques and occult means to solve his cases. While his unusual methods caused a few raised eyebrows, no one mocked his success rate. Specializing in missing-person investigations, Taine rarely failed to locate his quarry. He had his doubts, though, about tonight's assignment.

Before leaving his office this evening, Taine had mixed, then drunk, an elixir with astonishing properties. According to the famous grimoire, *The Key of Solomon*, the potion enabled the user to see the spirits of the dead. Its effects only lasted till dawn. Which was more than enough time for Taine. If he failed tonight, there would be no second chance.

The detective glanced down at his watch for the hundredth time. The glowing hands indicated five minutes to twelve. According to local legends, it was nearly the hour for the Midnight El to start its run.

No one knew how or when the stories began. A dozen specialists in urban folklore supplied the detective with an equal number of fabled origins. One and all, they were of the opinion that the tales dated back to the first decades of the century, when the subway first debuted in Chicago.

A few old-timers, mostly retired railway conductors

and engineers, claimed the Midnight El continued an even older tradition—the Phantom Train, sometimes called the Death's Head Locomotive. Despite the disagreements, several elements remained constant in all the accounts. The Midnight El hit the tracks exactly at the stroke of twelve. Its passengers consisted of those who had died that day in Chicago. The train traversed the entire city, starting at the station closest to the most deaths of the day, and working its way along from there.

Knowing that fact, Taine waited on a far south side platform. Earlier in the day, twelve people had died in a flash fire only blocks from this location. There was little question that this would be the subway's first stop.

Slowly, the seconds ticked past. A harsh west wind wailed off the lake, like some dread banshee warning Taine of his peril. With it came the doleful chiming of a distant church bell striking the hour. Midnight—the end of one day, start of another.

The huge train came hurtling along the track rumbling like distant thunder. Emerging ghostlike out of thin air, dark and forbidding, blacker than the night, it lumbered into the station. Lights flashed red and yellow as it slowed to a stop. Taine caught a hurried vision inside a half-dozen cars as they rumbled past. Pale, vacant, *dead* faces stared out into the night. Riders from another city, or another day, he wasn't sure which, and he had no desire to know. Young and old, black and white, men and women, all hungering for a glimpse of life.

Hissing loudly, double doors swung open on each car. A huge, shadowy figure clad in a conductor's uniform emerged from midway along the train. In his right hand he held a massive silver pocket watch, hooked by a glittering chain to his vest. Impatiently, he stood there, waiting for new arrivals.

The conductor's gaze swept the station, rested on Taine for a moment, then continued by. The ghost train and all its passengers were invisible to mortal eyes. There was no way for him to know that the man on the platform could actually see him. Nor suspect what Taine planned to do.

Once he had been a ferryman. The ancient Greeks knew him as Charon. To the Egyptians, he had been Anubis, the Opener of the Way. A hundred other cultures named him a hundred different ways. But always his task remained the same—transporting the newly dead to their final destination.

They came with the wind. Not there, then suddenly there. Each one stopped to face the conductor for an instant before being allowed to pass. The breath froze in Taine's throat as he watched them file by. Those who had died that day.

His hands clenched into fists when he sighted three pajama-clad black children. The detective recognized the trio immediately. Today's newspapers had been filled with all the grisly details of that sudden tenement fire that had resulted in their deaths. None of them had been over six years old.

Wordlessly, the last of the three turned. Lonely, mournful eyes stared deep into Taine's for an instant.

The detective remained motionless. If he reacted now, it might warn the conductor. An instant passed, and then the child and all the other passengers were gone. Disappeared into the Midnight El.

The conductor stepped back into the doorway. Raising one hand, he signaled to some unseen engineer to continue. Seeing his chance, Taine acted.

Moving incredibly fast for a man his size, the detective darted at, then around, the astonished doorman. Before the shadowy figure could react, Taine was past him and into the subway. Ignoring the restless dead on all sides, the detective headed for the front of the car.

"Come back here," demanded the conductor, swinging aboard. Behind him, the doors thudded shut. An instant later, the car jerked forward as the engine came to life. Outside scenery blurred as the train gained speed. The floor shook with a gentle, rocking motion. The Midnight El was off to its next stop.

Taine relaxed, letting his pursuer catch up to him. Surprise had enabled him to board the ghostly train. Getting off might not prove so easy.

"You do not belong on the Midnight El, Mr. Taine," said the conductor. He spoke calmly, without any trace of accent. Listening closely, Taine caught the barest hint of amusement in the phantom's voice. "At least, not yet. Your time is not for years and years."

"You know my name, and the instant of my death?" asked Taine, not the least bit intimidated by the imposing bulk of the other. Surrounded by shadows, the ticket taker towered over Taine by a head. His face, though human, appeared cut from weathered marble. Only his black, black eyes burned with life.

"Of course," answered the conductor. His body swayed gracefully with every motion of the subway car. "Past, present, future mean nothing to me. One look at a man is all I need to review his entire life history, from the moment of his birth to the last breath he takes. It's part of my job, supervising the Midnight El."

"For what employer?" asked Taine, casually.

"Someday you'll learn the answer," replied the conductor, with a chuckle. "But it won't matter much then."

The phantom reached into his vest pocket and pulled out the silver pocket watch. "Thirteen minutes to the next stop. This train, unlike most, always runs on time. You shall exit there, Mr. Taine."

"And if I choose not to," said Taine.

The conductor frowned. "You must. I cannot harm you. Such action is strictly forbidden under the terms of my contract. However, I appeal to your sense of compassion. A living presence on this train upsets the other passengers. Think of the pain you are inflicting on them."

Darkness gathered around the railroad man. He no longer looked so human. His black coal eyes burned into Taine's with inhuman intensity. "Leave them to their rest, Mr. Taine. You do not belong here."

"Nor does one other," replied the detective.

The conductor sighed, his rock-hard features softening in sorrow. "I should have guessed. You came searching for Maria Hernandez. Why?"

"Her husband hired me. He read about my services in the newspapers. I'm the final resort for those who refuse to give us hope.

"Victor told me what little he knew. My knowledge of the occult filled in the blanks. Combined together, the facts led me here."

"All trails end at the Midnight El," declared the conductor solemnly. "Though I'm surprised that you realized that."

"After examining the information, it was the only possible solution," said Taine. "Maria disappeared three nights ago. She vanished without a trace from an isolated underground subway platform exactly at midnight. No one else recognized the significance of the time.

"The police admitted they were completely baffled. The ticket seller remembered Maria taking the escalator down to the station a few minutes before twelve. A transit patrolman spoke to her afterward. He remembered looking up at the clock and noting the lateness of the hour. But when he looked around, the woman was no longer there. Somehow, she disappeared in the blink of an eye. Searching the tunnels for her body turned up nothing."

Taine paused. "Victor Hernandez considered me his last and only chance. I promised him I would do my best. I never mentioned the Midnight El."

"My thanks to you for that," said the conductor, nodding his understanding. "Suicides cause me the greatest pain. Especially those who sacrifice themselves to join the one they love."

"She meant a great deal to him," said Taine. "They were only married a few months. It seemed quite unfair."

"The world is unfair, Mr. Taine," said the conductor, shrugging his massive shoulders. "Or so I have been told by many of my passengers. Again and again, for centuries beyond imagining."

"She wasn't dead," said Taine. "If I don't belong here, then neither does she."

The conductor grimaced, his black eyes narrowing. He looked down at his great silver watch and shook his head. "There's not enough time to explain," he said. "Our schedule is too tight for long talks. Please understand my position."

"The Greeks considered Charon the most honorable of the gods," said Taine, sensing his host's inner conflict. "Of course, that was thousands of years ago."

"Spare me the dramatics," said the conductor. A bitter smile crossed his lips. He nodded to himself, as if making an important decision. Slowly, ever so slowly, he twisted the stem on the top of his watch.

All motion ceased. The subway car no longer shook with motion. Outside, the blurred features of the city solidified into grotesque, odd shapes, faintly resembling the Chicago skyline.

Taine grunted in surprise. "You can stop time?"

"For a little while," said the conductor. "Don't forget, the Midnight El visits every station in the city and suburbs within the space of a single night. On a hot summer night in a violent city like this, we often need extra minutes for all the passengers. Thus my watch. Twisting a little more produces a timeless state."

"The scenery?" asked Taine, not wanting to waste his questions, but compelled to ask by the alienness of the landscape.

"All things exist in time as well as space," said the conductor. "Take away that fourth dimension and the other three seem twisted."

The phantom turned and beckoned with his other hand. "Maria Hernandez. Attend me."

A short, slender woman in her early twenties pushed her way forward through the ranks of the dead. Long brown hair, knotted in a single thick braid, dropped down her back almost to her waist. Wide, questioning eyes looked at the detective. Unlike all the others on the train, a spark of color still touched Maria's cheeks. And her chest rose and fell with her every breath.

"Tell Mr. Taine how you missed the subway two weeks ago," said the conductor. He glanced over at Taine, almost as if checking to make sure the detective was paying attention.

"There was a shortage in one of the drawers at closing time," began Maria Hernandez, her voice calm, controlled. "My superior asked me to do a crosscheck. It was merely a mathematical error, but it took nearly twenty minutes to find. By then, I was ten minutes late for my train."

She hesitated, as if remembering something particularly painful. "I was in a hurry to get home. It was our six-month anniversary. When I left that morning for the bank, my husband, Victor, promised me a big surprise when I returned. I loved surprises."

"Yes, I know," said the conductor, his voice gentle. "He bought you tickets to the theater. But that is incidental to the story. Please continue."

"Usually, I have to wait a few minutes for my train," said Maria. "Not that night. It arrived exactly on schedule. When I reached the el platform, the conductor was signaling to close the doors. The next subway wasn't for thirty minutes. So, I ran."

Again, she paused. "I would have made it, too, if it wasn't for my right heel." She looked down at her shoes. "It caught in a crack in the cement. Wedged there so tight I couldn't pull my foot loose. By the time I wrenched free, the train had already left."

"Two weeks ago," said Taine, comprehension dawning. "The day of the big subway crash in the Loop."

"Correct," said the conductor. "Four minutes after Mrs. Hernandez missed her train, it crashed headlong into another, stalled on the tracks ahead. Fourteen people died when several of the cars sandwiched together. *Fifteen* should have perished."

"Fate," said Taine.

"She was destined to die," replied the conductor, as if explaining the obvious. "It was woven in the threads. A mistake was made somewhere. Her heel should have missed that crack. There was probably a knot in the twine. I assure you her name was on my passenger list. Maria was scheduled to ride the Midnight El."

"So, when she didn't, you decided to correct that mistake on your own," said Taine, his temper rising.

Mrs. Hernandez stood silent, as if frozen in place. Her story told, the conductor ignored her. "I thought a living person on board disturbed the dead?"

"With effort, the rules can be bent," said the conductor. He sighed. "It grows so boring here, Taine. You cannot imagine how terribly boring. I desired company, someone to talk to. Someone alive, someone with feelings, emotions. The dead no longer care about anything. They are so dull.

"The Three Sisters had to unravel a whole section of the cloth. They needed to weave a new destiny for Mrs. Hernandez to cover up their mistake. Meanwhile, Maria should have been dead but was still alive. Her spirit belonged to neither plane of existence. It took no great effort to bring her on the train as a passenger. And here she will remain, for all eternity, neither living nor dead but in a state between the two. Immortal, undying, unchanging—exactly like me. Forever."

Taine's fist clenched in anger. "Who gave you the power to decide her fate. That's not your job. You're only the ferryman, nothing more. She doesn't belong here. I won't allow you to do this."

"Your opinion means nothing to me, Mr. Taine," said the conductor, his features hardening. His left hand rested on the stem of the pocket watch. "There is nothing you can do to stop me."

"Like hell," said the detective, and leaped forward.

A big, powerfully built man, he moved with astonishing speed. Once tonight he had caught the conductor by surprise. This time, he did not.

The phantom's left hand shot out and caught Taine

by the throat. Without effort, he raised the detective into the air, so that the man's feet dangled inches off the floor.

"I am not fooled so easily a second time," he declared.

Taine flailed wildly with both hands at the conductor. Not one of his punches connected. Desperately, the detective lashed out one foot, hitting the other in the chest. The phantom didn't even flinch. He hardly seemed to notice Taine's struggles.

"In my youth," said the conductor, "I wrestled with Atlas and Hercules. Your efforts pale before theirs, Mr. Taine."

The conductor's attention focused entirely on the detective. Neither man nor spirit noticed Mrs. Hernandez cautiously reaching for the silver pocket watch the trainman held negligently in his other hand. Not until she suddenly grabbed it away.

"What!" bellowed the conductor, dropping Taine and whirling about. "You . . . you . . ."

"Just because I obeyed your commands," said Mrs. Hernandez, "didn't mean that I no longer possessed a will of my own. I was waiting for the right opportunity." She gestured with her head at the crowds of the dead all around them. "I'm not like them. I'm alive."

She held the pocket watch tightly, one hand on the stem. "If you try to take this away, I'll break it. Don't make me do that."

Taine, his throat and neck burning with pain, staggered to Mrs. Hernandez's side. "Let us go. Otherwise, we'll remain here forever, frozen in time."

"Nonsense," said the conductor. "I told you the rules can only be bent so far. Sooner or later, the strain would become too great and snap this train back to the real world."

"But if Maria breaks your watch," said Taine, "what then? You admitted needing its powers. Think of the problems maintaining your schedule without it."

"True enough," admitted the conductor. He paused for a moment, as if in thought. "Listen, I am willing to offer this compromise. Maria cannot leave this train without my permission. The Fates will not spin her a new destiny as long as she remains on the El. Return the watch to me and I'll give her a chance to return to her husband. And resume her life on Earth."

"A chance?" said the detective, suspiciously. "What exactly do you mean by that?"

"A gamble, a bet, *a wager*, Mr. Taine," said the conductor. "Relieve my boredom. Ask me a question, any question. If I cannot answer, you and Mrs. Hernandez go free. If I guess correctly, then both of you remain here for all eternity—not dead but no longer among the living—on the Midnight El. It will take a great deal of effort, but I can manage. Take it or leave it. I refuse to bend any further."

"Both of us?" said Taine. "You raised the stakes. And what about disturbing the dead? A little while ago you were anxious for me to leave."

"As I stated before, the rules can be bent. After all, I am the ferryman. And," continued Charon, the faintest trace of a smile on his lips, "what better way to sharpen your wits, Mr. Taine, than to put your own future at peril?"

"But," said the detective, "according to your earlier remarks, there's nothing in the world you don't know."

"There is only one omniscient presence," said the conductor. "Man or spirit, we are mere reflections of his glory. Still," he added, almost in afterthought, "the universe holds few mysteries for me."

Shadows gathered around the phantom. He extended one huge hand. "Make your decision. Now. Before I change my mind." His eyes burned like two flaming coals. "No tricks, either. An answer must exist for your question."

"Give him the watch," Taine said to Maria Hernandez.

"Then you agree?" asked the conductor.

"I agree," replied the detective, calmly.

Chuckling, the conductor twisted the stem of his great silver watch. Immediately, the scenery shifted and the subway car started shaking. They were back in the real world.

"We arrive at the next station in a few minutes," Charon announced smugly. "You have until then to frame your question, Mr. Taine."

Maria Hernandez gasped, raising her hands to her face. "But . . . but . . . that's cheating."

"Not true," said the conductor. "I promised no specific length of time for our challenge." He glanced down at his watch. "Your time is ticking by quickly. Better think fast."

Taine took a deep breath. Not all questions depended on facts for their answer. He prayed that the ferryman would not renege on their bargain once he realized his mistake. "You trapped yourself," said the detective. "I'm ready now."

"You are?" said the conductor, frowning. He sounded surprised.

"Of course," said Taine. "Are you prepared to accept defeat?"

"Impossible," replied the conductor, bewildered. "I know the answer to every question."

"Then tell me," said Taine, "the answer to the question raised when I first boarded the train. When is the exact moment of my death."

"You will perish . . ." began the conductor, then stopped. He stood silent, mouth open in astonishment. Slowly, the fire left his eyes. The phantom shook his head in dismay. "Caught by my own words."

Not exactly sure what the conductor meant, Maria Hernandez directed her attention to Taine. "I don't understand. Caught? How?"

"The conductor bragged earlier that he knew the date of my death," said Taine. "If he answers correctly, then he wins our bet."

"And," continued Maria, comprehension dawning, "by the terms of the agreement, you must remain on the Midnight El forever."

"Thus making his prediction false," finished Taine, "since I cannot die when he predicts. On the other hand, if he says that I will never die, then he does not know the date of my death. Which means he cannot answer the question. So, whatever he says, I am the winner. The bet is ours."

With a sigh, the conductor pocketed his watch. "You would have made good company, Mr. Taine." Metal screeched on metal as the Midnight El pulled into the next station. "This is your stop. Farewell."

They were outside. Alone. On a deserted subway station. With a cold wind blowing, but neither of them noticed.

Tears filled Maria Hernandez's eyes. "Are we free? Really free?"

Taine nodded, his thoughts drifting. Already, he searched for an explanation for Maria's disappearance that would satisfy both the police and her husband.

"As free as any man or woman can be," he answered somberly. "In the end, we all have a date to keep with the Midnight El."

MAYBE TOMORROW

by Barry Hoffman

Seventeen-year-old Lori Springer couldn't explain her feelings for her contemporary lit teacher. It was much more than a teenage infatuation, yet it wasn't love—of this she was certain. It was a need . . . a hunger. At times she thought he knew it . . . and wanted her as much as she desired him. Silly girl, she thought. He hardly knows you exist. Silly girl, my ass, her mind responded, to him *only* you exist. He talked to the class, but spoke only to her. She saw his eyes scour the class, linger on her, strip her bare—body and soul—then sweep over the others as if they were mannequins.

"He's so adorable," she confided to Carrie Lofton, on their way home that afternoon.

"He's old enough to be your father."

"You're just jealous. Have you ever looked at his eyes? I mean *really* looked into his eyes? They're so full of wisdom, yearning and compassion. He's seen things I've only read in books."

"Yeah, *Playboy*. You see wisdom—maybe, yearning—yes, but compassion? How about lust? Pure animal lust." She shook her head at her friend's foolishness.

"You look at him and see romance. He looks at you and sees a motel room."

"At least he notices me. No one else does. I'm not pretty; I'm not sexy; and, I'm sure no brain."

"Aren't we feeling sorry for ourself today?" Carrie said, teasingly.

They were at Lori's house, but she balked at going in.

"I'm not kidding, Carrie. I'm a nobody—at school, even in my own home. I dread going in with Jeremy on the loose. Don't you ever wonder why I never invite you over?"

"I didn't want to pry. Since you've brought it up, what's his problem, anyway?"

"Jeremy's autistic. Not the idiot savant of *Rain Man*, but an evil little boy totally wrapped up in himself."

"You don't mean that."

"Carrie, everything revolves around him. The older he gets the more attention he commands . . . and demands. Sometimes I wonder if he's really autistic or just faking the whole thing to get what he wants. He's nine years old and has us imprisoned in his own little world. I can't have company over—it upsets him and he flies into a rage. We can't go on vacation for fear he'll attack other guests. I can't even eat dinner with my parents without getting pelted with mashed potatoes, peas, or spaghetti. I think I could run away and my parents wouldn't notice for weeks."

"So you think Mr. Marsh will give you the attention you crave?"

"He thinks I'm special."

"He's told you so?"

"He doesn't have to. He doesn't look through me or past me like everyone else. He sees me—sometimes *only* me."

"Get off it, Lori. He's probably married with kids of his own. You're just another pretty body he can fantasize over. You know, look, but don't touch."

"You're wrong. You'll see. I am special to him. Not just a name . . . a face . . . a body. His plans include me. Me, me and only me."

With tears streaming down her face, she ran from her best friend.

In the days that followed, the bond strengthened. Lori couldn't tell Carrie. She wouldn't understand. No one would. Mr. Marsh spoke to the class about Poe, O'Henry, and Hemingway while, at the same time, talking to her of more important matters. Like fingers probing her body, his eyes penetrated her mind.

"Life has dealt you a rotten hand," he spoke silently to her while lecturing the class on the evils of censorship as embodied in Ray Bradbury's *Fahrenheit 451*. "And it's going to get worse."

"What do you mean?" she thought, and his voice singed her mind with a future so bleak her head felt like a volcano ready to erupt.

"Your brother will seek even more attention as he gets older. You'll turn to drugs for solace. Then, you'll get pregnant to gain the attention denied to you now."

"How do you know?"

"How can I speak to you while talking gibberish to these nonentities? I am the future—your future. I paint you a picture of pain and sorrow, but I can be your salvation."

"You can change the future?"

"Only you can alter your fate—but not until you know the depths of your despair. Do you want to know it all?"

"No . . . yes. I don't know. Please help me."

"The father will marry you," he continued. "Not from love, but from guilt. He'll turn on you when your child's born. The baby's colicky—constantly crying, keeping you both awake until your nerves are raw. Your husband beats you in frustration, sleeps with others, and finally leaves you . . . without a penny to your name."

"Is there no happiness for me?"

Silence.

"I don't deserve such a future. I've done nothing wrong."

"There is a way out."

"How? Please tell me."

"End it now."

"What do you mean?"

"You know what I mean. You've thought about it before."

"Suicide? No. Never! It's a cop out. And I'll rot in hell."

"Rubbish. You've been taught to believe that garbage. End it now and you'll be reborn. Reborn to parents who'll treat you as the center of their universe."

"I can't."

"You must."

"I won't."

"Then you'll die a slow death . . . every day of your life."

Day after day he hammered away at her. And day after day life at home became a whirlpool threatening to suck her under.

A girl at the special school Jeremy attended hit him in the head with a block. He ignored the attack . . . bided his time. Two days later, when she went to take a pee, he followed her and held her head in the toilet. Another child's screams brought help just in time. The school admitted defeat, though, and expelled the boy. Lori's parents kept him at home for the next two weeks, looking in vain for another school. It was unbearable for Lori's mother.

"I don't know if I can take it much longer," her mother said in exasperation. "All day long I follow him around as he prowls the house like a caged tiger. I turn my back for just an instant and he's butchering the couch with a fork. So after meals I count the knives; I count the forks; hell, I even count the spoons—though God only knows what havoc he could wreak with one."

"I know it's tough, honey. I spend half the day at work contacting schools. It's just a matter of time. We'll find a place for him."

"Just a matter of time? I've no more energy. I've got no life. Face it, we've got to institutionalize him. For his sake. And, yes, dammit, for ours, too."

"I won't have my son locked up, sedated, and left to vegetate. I won't hear of it, do you understand?"

"Paul, please . . ."

"Not another word."

Lori, locked in her room, soaked it all in. Another nail in her coffin, she thought. She looked in her mirror and wondered if a man could *ever* love her. She was utterly plain, though not hideously ugly. She thanked God for that. Thin, scrawny rather than svelte, just a smidgen over five feet, and even at seventeen her breasts were little more than nubs. Her blonde hair was like limp wheat fighting a losing battle in the face of a drought, sitting devoid of life atop her head. She'd had it permed; she'd had it styled, but within days it hung like a ragged mop. She'd unsuccessfully fought the ravages of acne with every new product that came on the market. It had begun to abate of late, but her sallow complexion which at the moment wouldn't tolerate makeup depressed her further.

She turned from the mirror and ventured into Jeremy's room. There he was, just sitting on his bed, peaceful as could be. He twisted a Rubik's Cube in his hands, forming patterns without any meaning.

"I'm wise to you, you little shit," she said. "You know just what you're doing. Autistic my ass."

He looked up at her and smiled, drool sliding down his chin.

In school the next day Mr. Marsh needled her while discussing the horror of Shirley Jackson's, "The Lottery," with the other students.

"Your parents find a school for Jeremy?"

"You know they haven't."

"Will they put him away?"

"You know my father won't allow it."

"He's not autistic . . . not anymore."

"What do you mean?"

"He revels in the attention he gets. Like an infant, all his needs are met, yet he has no responsibilities. Life revolves around *his* wants, *his* desires, *his* schedule. All of a sudden his mind awakens from its slumber, but he's not ready ... not willing to face a hostile world. It's all an act, now, and you know it. He'll be waited on hand and foot for as long as he wants. Where does that leave you?"

She was silent. She knew though. Knew, like he'd told her, she'd seek her own way of getting attention ... and fail.

Day after day he prodded, cajoled, and waved that carrot of a better life before her until her resistance crumbled.

"I won't go to hell?"

"No."

"I'll be reborn?"

"To parents who'll appreciate how fortunate they are to have you."

"Will you be with me?"

"I'm your future. Where you go I follow."

"What do I have to do?"

He told her.

He was as surprised as she when she slithered into class the next day. A single tear sliding down her face betrayed her churning emotions.

"I'm sorry," she told him. His eyes bored into her soul, while he patiently explained to the class how Stephen King had brought the horror novel out of the back rooms of bookstores. Yet his attention was solely on her.

"I tried. I really did. I closed the door of the garage, like you said, and kept the engine running. I started to doze off. No pain—just as you promised." She couldn't go on.

"What stopped you?" His voice was tinged with impatience . . . and fury.

He's pissed at me, Lori thought. Like I let *him* down. She felt bad, but a bit angry herself. It was *her* life she was taking. She'd do it . . . in her own sweet time.

He read her mind and she could feel his silent rebuke.

"I heard a song by Bruce Springsteen. I was just vaguely aware of it. Kind of like the music in elevators. The deejay said he had *two* albums due out at the end of the week. I was really looking forward to it. Just a few more days. Then . . . then I'll be ready."

"I understand," he said, softening, "and I won't push." But she didn't quite believe him. She saw his lip quiver, almost imperceptibly. He was exasperated . . . disappointed, Lori thought. "When do you plan to try again?" He tried to sound matter-of-fact, but she felt his annoyance like salt on a wound.

"Over the weekend. My parents are taking Jeremy for an interview at a school for autistic kids."

"The weekend, then." Curt, no nonsense. He ignored her the rest of the period.

All week he reminded her of the grim future she faced to strengthen her resolve. By Friday she was sure she'd been forgiven. She wouldn't let him down again.

Saturday she prepared herself. New parents—the center of their world. No more Jeremy. No more second class status. She kept repeating the words to herself. She was glad, though, she'd waited to hear Springsteen's new albums. She'd played them to death the night before and still hadn't gotten enough.

As she made for the car, the phone rang. "Shit!" she said, aloud. "The gods are conspiring against me." She could ignore it. She would ignore it. She *couldn't* ignore it. She just had to know who it was. It would only take a minute or two. No big deal.

"Lori? It's Mrs. Carlson. I just wanted to remind you about babysitting Justin on Monday."

"Monday?" Damn, she'd forgotten all about it.

"We've gotten benefit concert tickets. I told you last month. No problem, is there?"

"Uh, no, I'll be there. Seven o'clock, right?"

"Right. See you Monday, then."

Lori hung up, almost feeling Mr. Marsh's hands throttling her. He'll be pissed, she thought. Royally pissed. Well, she'd deal with him Monday. No use letting it upset her the entire weekend. She went upstairs and listened to Bruce Springsteen again. She almost felt glad Mrs. Carlson had called. No, she *was* glad. The music was so good.

Outwardly, Mr. Marsh took her presence at school, Monday, in stride. He introduced splatterpunk to the class, addressing her all the while.

"Nice to have your smiling face in class, Lori." His voice dripped with sarcasm.

"Please, let me explain. It wasn't my fault. I'd promised to babysit tonight, ages ago, and I couldn't disappoint Mrs. Carlson. I'd feel so guilty. . . ."

"Guilty!" His voice thundered in her head. "You felt guilty!"

"It's just one more day. Don't be so uptight. Look, as soon as I get home tonight, I'll just close the garage door and it's over."

He glowered at her the next day, when she appeared once again. *What now?* she knew he was thinking before he even asked. Sheepishly, she told him she'd started a book.

"So?"

"I just *had* to find out how it ended," she said, weakly.

"Why didn't you just turn to the last page?"

"Don't be silly." It was all she could do not to laugh out loud. "Getting there is half the fun." She didn't think he appreciated her logic.

Next, she had to tutor Robin Winston. It had slipped her mind. Every other Thursday. Robin had been doing so well, lately. She couldn't abandon the child, not just yet.

Then it was another book. She'd tried to resist the temptation. She really had. Just glanced at the cover. Before she knew it, she was on page seven and there was no turning back.

And then there was Murphy Brown, about to have her baby. Each promo seemed more hilarious than the one before. Did he really think she could do without seeing it? She only hoped it wasn't a cliffhanger; one that wouldn't be resolved until next season.

"Excuses, Lori. All I get are excuses," he told her day after day. "Sometimes I wonder if you really want that new life I've promised."

Nag, nag, nag, she thought, forgetting he could read her every thought.

"Don't give me that 'nag, nag, nag' crap. I've invested a lot of time in you. I'm sick to death of seeing you stroll in each day."

There was no tenderness in his eyes now. No understanding. No concern. She saw before her a predator. Worse, a leech; a parasite. Mean, greedy, and self-centered. The quivering of his lip was now a visible tic.

"Tonight. You'll do it tonight." It was a command. "Don't trifle with me anymore."

Lori was confused. Sure, he had reason to be upset. But, ending her life was not as cut and dried as it had seemed a few weeks before. Yes, life could be a bitch at times and his promises were enticing. Yet there was much she'd miss if she gave in to him. Things she'd always taken for granted. Her books; her music; those like Mrs. Carlson and Robin who depended on her . . . needed *her!*

"Have it your way, Lori," he said, again reading her thoughts. "You've made your bed, now sleep in it." His voice was filled with loathing, disgust . . . and defeat. He was used to getting his way, she thought. A spoiled brat, she thought. So much like . . . Jeremy.

"There are others who'll welcome my help," he continued. "Don't come crawling back for a second chance.

There are *no* second chances. No reprieves. No more tomorrows."

The voice in her mind was gone, replaced by Mr. Marsh calmly discussing the emergence of Clive Barker as the heir apparent to Stephen King. Gone now, gone forever. Oddly, she felt a great weight lifted from her shoulders.

There are others who'll welcome my help.
> *. . . welcome my help*
> *. . . welcome . . .*

She couldn't get the words out of her mind in the days that followed. It didn't take long to spot his next target; Marcie Robinson.

Mr. Marsh was explaining how horror flicks like *Halloween*, *Nightmare on Elm Street* and *Friday the Thirteenth* diluted their sensitivity to the written word. Lori saw a flicker of a smile pass over Marcie's plump face, though her eyes were glazed as if in a trance. She knew the feeling. Knew he'd chosen her . . . and with good reason.

Marcie's mother had run down a three-year-old a week before and been too drunk to even notice. A cop had pulled her over three blocks past the scene of the accident, gun drawn. Sickened by what she'd done, she'd promptly puked over the poor guy.

Word had spread like AIDS in a bath house, and Marcie had been taunted unmercifully. She'd found empty beer cans in her locker, been made the butt of cruel jokes, and had gotten into a number of fights.

Lori was sure their teacher was offering her the same

opportunity she'd rejected. And at the moment, Marcie was much more vulnerable.

After class she joined Marcie at lunch. A chubby girl, who wore clothes two sizes too large to hide the layers of fat, Marcie eyed her suspiciously, waiting for the inevitable putdown.

"I'm sorry about your mother," Lori began, not quite knowing how to draw the other girl out. "I bet Mr. Marsh has been sympathetic."

Marcie shrank even farther into herself. Yes, Lori thought, he'd gotten his hooks into her.

"I don't know what you're talking about." Scarcely above a whisper.

"Yes, you do. He talks to you . . . in your mind, while lecturing the rest of the class. To you and only you."

Marcie gaped at her in astonishment and confusion but said nothing.

"He's been telling you how much worse your life will become, hasn't he?"

"How do you know?"

"Because he ran his line by me; had me ready to kill myself. . . ."

"I don't believe you!" she interrupted. He's been here for me and only me. He says I'm special. I'm chosen. . . ."

"And if you kill yourself, you'll be reborn again to parents who'll treat you as the center of their lives."

"Yes, a mother who won't spend her whole day drinking. A father whose life isn't his work." She paused, letting the painful truth sink in. "That bastard. He said I was the *only* one. He was my guardian angel. . . ."

"Feeding on your weakness. . . ."

" . . . easy prey with everybody treating me like a leper because of my mom."

Lori could see his hold over Marcie shatter like a piece of fine china hitting the floor. It made her feel warm inside. She'd literally saved someone's life. Not much different from a fireman rushing into an inferno to save a helpless child. And that gave her own life added meaning.

" . . . a phony," Marcie was saying. "How I wish I could get back at him."

"You can," Lori said. She told her how.

For the next three weeks Lori saw Mr. Marsh pout, ever so slightly, when Marcie entered the room. The tic at his mouth extended to his eyes like he'd had a stroke and one side of his face had taken on a life of its own. Marcie had promised to take her life time and time again, but something always came up forcing her to postpone the deadly deed for another few days.

Finally, he'd had enough.

" 'Maybe tomorrow,' I told him," Marcie explained at the Carlsons', where Lori was babysitting that night.

" 'That's all I ever hear from you,' he told me. 'Maybe tomorrow. If I didn't know better, I'd think you were stringing me along.' "

"I told him things had gotten better."

" 'Things will get a lot worse,' he promised."

"My mother needs me. I need time. Maybe in a few weeks."

Then he'd fed her the line about others who'd welcome his help and had gone silent.

Soon he was casting his line again; his bait tempting to teenagers whose whole life revolved around their cloistered world. It was easy to hook the girl whose boyfriend dumped her because she wouldn't go all the way; another pressured to get good grades to earn a college scholarship; a third who'd just moved to town and resented having to make new friends among strangers.

Lori and Marcie spotted each and every one as they fell under their teacher's spell, and fanned their anger when they learned he'd misled them. They told each to string him along. They saw doubt creep into his face as he struck out time and time again. Like the stud who couldn't get it up anymore, Marcie had observed.

Like a ballplayer in a prolonged slump; an author with writer's block; a boxer too worn out to answer the bell—the creature that beckoned them to their graves aged before them.

His once lean face was now bloated, sores sprouting—like weeds—leaking pus, which he dabbed with a yellowed handkerchief. His eyes lost their luster and his thick black hair its sheen. He spoke barely above a whisper in class, every few sentences punctuated by a coughing fit that reverberated in the silent classroom.

One day he didn't show up. Called in sick. It stretched into a week, then a month.

Strengthened by their ordeal, the five girls he'd tempted visited him at a seedy rooming house.

He looked like death warmed over. He was bedridden and frail; so weak he couldn't sit up without their help. Yet his eyes lit up when they entered.

"You've reconsidered my offer," he wheezed, his lips so swollen the words came out slurred. Like a baby teething, saliva dripped down his chin. A boil exploded on his forehead, viscous liquid flowing down his fevered cheeks. "I knew I could count on you. You can do it now, before me. Pills, yes, I've got pills on the shelf. . . ." He looked at them beseechingly.

"Maybe tomorrow," they answered in unison, before turning away and leaving.

THE FOOD COURT

by John Maclay

Herman Garber was fat. Not overweight, not corpulent, but fat. And not just fat, but obese. Obese, at a dark-haired thirty-five, as anyone could be and still walk, or waddle, to and from his car, to and from his cashier's job at the mall. He had rolls of fat everywhere, from his neck to his chest to his belly to his ass. Even his arms and legs were like torsos in themselves. Moon-faced, wheezing, sweating, Herman was the stereotype of fat. Herman Garber *was* fat.

And, despite new studies which showed that some people were overweight by nature, Herman knew his own situation was ridiculous. He'd outgrown even the big and tall men's shops, his car had special springs, his bed was reinforced with concrete blocks. Chairs regularly buckled under his bulk, and last month he'd tilted another toilet from its moorings. And as for sex, it had been a long time since his manhood had broken the plane of his obesity.

He'd been a fat kid, a fat teenager, a fat adult. Where others had stopped at two hot dogs, he'd had four; a second piece of cake, he'd had the cake; a beer, he dealt in six-packs. Food was ever at his hands, bulging out his pockets, sticking in his chins. The McDonald's at the Recession-struck mall swore by Herman.

But late one night, after he'd closed the shop where he worked and oozed out into the aisle, Herman Garber had a vision. A waking of the proverbial thin person far inside his hugeness. A voice which said that something not only should, but could be done.

So, for the first time in his fat life, he made a resolution. To stop eating, stop rationalizing, view food as an enemy instead of a reason for being, a friend. Have salads and water, exercise as much as his absurd body would allow. At least get down to a weight that would make him a human being again.

Yes, Herman thought as he struggled down the corridor, past the sporting goods store. *Just Do It. And, in a year or so, I'll be a new man.*

But before he reached the double doors to the parking lot, headed home to his small apartment, he had an obstacle to pass. A place, late a pleasure dome with its glass roof, fountain, and palms, but now a scene from hell. A place that could bring him ruin.

In short, the Food Court.

The Food Court, with its deli, its steak and fries, its Chinese buffet, its Italian. Its bakery, its ice cream parlor, its candy store. Its fake-marble tables where he'd gleefully spent a thousand breakfasts, lunches, dinners, and in between.

The Court was closed and locked now, but a friendly security guard let him in. Besides, the proprietors of the various stands had often said he could help himself, he'd been so good to them. So he waddled around in the half-light, pants hugging his hips, shirt revealing the white of his belly. Knowing what he was about to do.

One last time, Herman thought, eyes bulging. *One last time,* a tear actually forming, *and then no more.* He went along behind the counters, filling a plate, then a tray, with samples of every leftover he could find. Then he settled himself on a chair, two chairs, and began.

But before he could raise even a forkful to his thick lips, he became aware of something. Shapes, no, figures on the periphery of the glass-roofed space, converging on him. Now another awakening occurred, of the sort occasioned by surprise, even terror.

At first Herman thought the apparitions were janitorial personnel. But no, they didn't wear the familiar uniforms of the mall. Then, perhaps, some late shoppers who'd been locked in. They weren't dressed in normal, casual clothes, however.

Instead, as they drew closer, he saw that they were in costume. Elaborate costumes, he discerned further, that mirrored the nationalities of the booths from which he'd selected the feast before him. Chinese, Italian, German for the bakery, even Old English for the fish and chips place he hadn't overlooked. French for the crepes outlet, Mexican for the tacos. A half-dozen in number, they settled around a table across from his own.

And spoke, or seemed to.

"We are the Food Court," they said, in surreal, nightmarish unison. "And we have come to judge."

This can't be, Herman Garber thought, then voiced it. "You're mistaken about the name. The Food Court is a place, not a legal thing."

But they came right back at him. "For you, it's a court of law, and you're on trial. To find you innocent or guilty of what you've done to yourself. Those meals, too many and too large, stretching infinitely back to your childhood. Resulting in the gross, triple-sized person you've now become."

Herman's rolls of flesh quivered with fear, and he even pushed his much-anticipated plate of late-night morsels aside. His very bulk made him unable to move, to flee the Food Judges he faced. One by one, then, they made their case.

"Chinese," the figure in a red and gold robe began. "How many times have you eaten Chinese? Not just a platter, but whole quarts of chow mein, shrimp in lobster sauce, pepper steak, moo goo gai pan?"

And to Herman's horror, the figure quickly *changed,* into a chunky mass of MSG-impregnated stuff, coated with bamboo-shoot scales.

"Italian," the next judge pressed, without missing a beat. "Really, now. A whole pan of lasagna, a dozen meatballs at a sitting, pasta without end?"

And, as his overtaxed heart raced, his accuser became a monster from the Mediterranean, with spaghetti tentacles reaching out at him.

The others were sickeningly consistent. In short order, Herman was faced by a humanoid who suddenly swelled up into a German chocolate cake, one that became a mound of fat-dripping fried potatoes, one that turned into a fold of pastry dripping raspberries in syrup. Not to mention a taco man, perhaps the most hideous after the spaghetti creature, with cheese, meat, and tomato chunks oozing out on all sides.

"Enough," the accused protested before it went any farther. "I'm guilty. I did eat you all."

Slowly, then, his judges changed back to their anthropomorphic forms. "So," Old English asked at length, "what do you have to say in your defense?"

Herman Garber thought for a long time. "I did it for love," he finally said. "For love of your aroma, your flavor, your myriad consistencies on the tongue. I ate not only to live, but as a way of life, of love."

He paused. "And maybe I did it as a substitute for something else. Action, other love, sex, who knows?" He looked down at his incredible bulk, his straining clothes. "But I'm willing to make amends."

The judges, he thought, while seeming to approve his speech, also laughed among themselves. At last, in an accent thick as cake, German replied.

"Good," it said. "And I, for one, am going to take a good big bite!"

That was when Herman lost control. No question of tilting another toilet from its moorings; he instantly befouled the chair, or two chairs, on which he sat. Sweat beaded on his moon-face, ran down his chins. When he saw what was about to happen, what were inexorably coming at him.

Mouths, huge mouths, belonging to the Food Court. Gaping, reaching, then tearing at his globuled flesh like so many piranhas. One at each of his torsolike legs and arms, another at his ballooned belly, another at the gargantuan spread of his ass. Smacking, consuming.

As they got each one of those thousands of ill-considered meals *back*.

There was no pain, only a deeper and deeper feeling of loss, of emptiness as his body was bloodlessly lessened. There was even a clinical detachment, and a sense of wonder, of humor, when his attackers paused intermittently to exchange comments, appraisals.

"I think that this thigh would be equivalent to my share," French might say.

"Agreed," Mexican might reply. "If you'll let me have half the belly."

So it proceeded, in the surreal twilight of the after-hours mall, through the long night. Until, one by one, the representative judges had eaten their fair share of him, and withdrawn. Leaving Herman Garber to look down at his slack clothing and realize that at last he was:

Thin.

But there was one more thing to be attended to. Quietly, then more urgently, Herman felt a churning in his stomach, then an undeniable upward thrust. And soon he was spewing the remaining contents of his body onto the fake-marble table in front of him, until he was empty indeed.

I wouldn't have done it exactly that way, he thought, looking up through the glass roof of the Food Court, literally that again, at the stars above. *But it beats a year of dieting,* he decided as he got to his feet and walked, improbably lightly, to the men's room, where he cleaned himself up as best he could. Then out to the corridor, past the security guard, who didn't even recognize him in his clownlike baggy pants.

The world is before me, he thought further, as he went out into the cool dawn. Got into his car, felt the springs not give at all, had to move the seat up six notches. *I can go running, I can have a woman, anything.*

After breakfast, that is, Herman thought as he drove home.

THE GARDEN

by Barbara Delaplace

Morning, and the first blush of dawn was yielding to the stronger glow of daylight. A chorus of birdsong (and othercreature song) filled the air, accompaniment to the tiny bustlings of animals and insects in the early light.

But faint sounds of stealth could be heard under the tuneful hubbub: the soft click of a touch-lock yielding, the quiet creak of a gate swinging open. An impossibly tall, slender creature slipped through the entrance, quickly closing the gate behind him. For a long moment he stood rigid and still, waiting. Finally reassured that his entrance had disturbed no one, he stepped away from the gate.

He stood within a walled compound, its size artfully concealed by careful groupings of shrubs and trees, its vistas broken by winding paths and meandering streams. He hoped that his smooth purple skin and slitted red eyes would not attract the stares they did in the world outside the gate, for his exotic appearance was matched by the profusion of exotic forms of plant life surrounding him. Varieties of flowers that had grown under native suns light-years apart were here placed side-by-side in splendid combination. Flame-colored azaleas were surrounded by the cool hues of colony-growing bush coral. Nightchime trees, trunks festooned with purple-flowered clematis vines, folded away slitted, light-sensitive leaves as the daylight grew stronger, their whispering music silenced until evening. Tri-hybrid roses shared beds with the iridescent blossoms of peacock tails.

But this was more than a floral paradise, for where there are plants there also are animals, living by and with and upon them, adding motion and sound and still more color. Tarellian lizards skulked among the flowers, clucking and chuckling to each other. They were answered by the rollicking notes of goldfinches, animate little flakes of sunlight busily hunting seeds for breakfast. Hummingbirds buzzed from blossom to blossom, competing with wind chasers and butterflies for their nectar.

Yet in this profusion of life, there were no people. The alien gave a silent prayer of thanks—he would be undisturbed. That was important. A short distance away, he saw the shimmer of a stream winding its way through the garden. Yes, that would be very suitable. He glided toward it.

His unshod feet scarcely dented the mossy ground, and any sounds of his passage were masked by the gurgle of the water. Even the shy blue-eyed lurkers were not disturbed as he passed their woven grass nests. He had nearly reached his goal; his narrow hand slid into a long pouch hanging from the beaded belt around his middle. Once through the shady arches of a massive cathedral shrub—

But he could go no farther, for suddenly blocking his path was a fearsome green-furred animal. Long fangs curved down from its upper jaw, and its muscular body was supported by powerful legs, armed with heavy dew-claws both fore and aft above each paw. Upon seeing him, it lifted its head and gave a deep trumpeting call, then moved closer. The alien's body began to tremble as he tried to back away, but a sudden collision with a tree trunk stopped him. He edged to one side, and the beast sidled over to block that route. It trumpeted again, then watched him intently with huge golden eyes. The alien's trembling increased.

"Hold him, Cerebrus!"

The words came from a tall, middle-aged woman, dressed in an unadorned dark green coverall. A belt around her waist dangled with cutting and digging tools; sturdy gloves protruded from a hip pocket. Her hand rested briefly on the creature's head, and she turned to the alien. "May I ask what you are doing here?"

"You are the possessor of this facility? That is to say, you are the . . . the proprietor?"

The alien's mouth moved, but no sound seemed to come from it. Rather, a voice emerged from a silver disk on a long chain about his narrow neck. The green-furred beast started slightly, its enormous eyes moving from the alien's face to the disk. Orange stripes became visible on its furry hide as it took a step closer. The alien's body began to shake again.

"Your companion, is it . . . will it hurt?"

"Do you mean, will he attack you?"

His eyes on the beast, the alien replied, "Yes."

"He does as I tell him."

The alien's trembling eased slightly but did not stop. "That is not . . . reassurance? . . . yes, reassurance."

"It wasn't intended to be. You haven't told me what you're doing here."

"I am . . . was—I was absorbed? . . . no, that is not right . . . this language! So many choices of words! It is not easy."

"A simple question like 'Why are you here?' only needs a simple answer."

"I was . . . drawn . . . to this place. It is so full of life, of energy. There is so little life in this city."

The woman smiled wryly as she replied, "I'd suggest a city of ten million inhabitants can hardly be called 'dead.' "

"I did not mean it was a city of death." The alien seemed to be speaking to himself. "I must be exact. Precision is required."

"What precisely did you mean?"

The alien tried again, eyeing Cerebrus nervously. "This place is filled with . . . peacefulness. Can you not see how much more . . . tranquil, yes, this place is than that too-busy world outside the walls?"

"Ah, now I understand you. Yes, the garden is indeed serene."

" 'Garden'? That is the correct name for this facility?"

"Yes, I am the gardener—I care for the garden."

"You do very good. The beings living here thrive at your touch."

"Thank you. But that doesn't explain why you broke in. The garden is not open to the public today."

"That is the reason I am here now. I cannot do what I must while there are others watching." His hand quickly slipped into his pouch as he spoke.

At the swift movement of the alien's hand, Cerebrus suddenly gave a piercing hiss and moved quickly between the gardener and the alien. The orange stripes became more vivid, and a heavy crest of skin, also glowing orange, flared from the creature's neck.

The alien stepped back hastily. "Tell your companion not to injure me. I mean no harm. I wish only to sit in quiet . . . contemplation of this . . . garden for a space of time. To restore the . . . balance of my inner self. And I wish to make a record of this beautiful place to remind me of the peacefulness, when I am away from it." His hand emerged from the pouch with a small lensed device. "Do you see? It is only a holo camera."

The gardener relaxed. Her hand stroked Cerebrus' neck, soothing the animal. "You may meditate here. You are welcome to make holo images of the garden, but please don't touch the plants—some of them are extremely fragile." Cerebrus' crest gradually flattened under her hand as she spoke, and the orange attack colors faded. The alien noted the calm green fur of the beast, and thanked her as fervently as the translating mechanism would allow.

"Would it be permissible for me to assume meditation stance by this small body of water?"

"Certainly."

"And could you," he asked timidly, "perhaps direct your companion elsewhere while I do so?"

"As you wish. Away you go, Cerebrus! Off duty!" The creature vanished into the shrubbery with a silence astonishing for so massive an animal. "I must see about transplanting some *Nicotiana*. If you call me when you're finished, I'll point out some of the more popular spots for making holos."

The alien thanked her, and watched as she walked away. Once he was sure he was alone again, he sat down on the grassy stream bank, folding his long limbs into the awkward-looking yet oddly graceful Seventh Serene Mist posture. His eyes became unfocused as his breathing slowed, and he lost himself in tranquil contemplation. . . .

The gardener was on her knees by a flowerbed, her deft hands transferring young plants from flats to their new home surrounding a magnificent rhododendron, when she heard the trumpeting call. "Another one?" she muttered as she rose to her feet and brushed the dirt from her hands. Still, the garden was supposed to be available to the public. Even when "the public" included oddballs like the alien down by the stream there, she mused. With the ease of long familiarity, she moved quickly through the garden toward the source of the sound.

When she reached the stream, she was greeted by the alien, who gravely thanked her for answering his call so swiftly. Surprised, she turned to him. "I thought it was Cerebrus calling me."

"I . . . presumed? . . . yes, presumed that cry was the usual way of . . . invoking a friend on this planet. If it was inappropriate, I ask forgiveness."

"Oh, no, don't apologize. It startled me, that's all." She paused. "Would you now like me to show you where you can take the best holos?"

"I would greatly enjoy."

"Come this way."

The gardener followed the stream bank to a small cedarwood bridge, then turned and walked across it. The sharp odor of the wood pierced the air. The alien followed her, but at the center of the span he stopped for a moment, peering down. In the water below were groups of pearly white flowers swaying in a ceaseless ballet, a dance that ignored the swirls and eddies of the current.

"Those blossoms there in the water," he said. "They are most fascinating."

"The swimming lilies? Yes, they are. I won an award from the Intergalactic Horticulturalists. No one else has been able to get them to grow, let alone dance, away from their native habitat before. It took me over a year to get all the conditions just right. They needed a sulfur supplement, of all things."

"You possess very great skill in teaching living creatures to grow well. These ones thrive also."

"Thank you. Of course, I can't manage a garden this size by myself any longer. I have a staff to assist me."

The alien studied the lilies' graceful movements as the gardener waited patiently. Finally, he turned to follow her again. But now it was she who was still, listening intently for something over the murmur of the stream. The chuckling and trilling of a flock of Tarellian lizards gradually emerged from the landscape of sound.

"Over there! Can you hear them? The lizards? I love to listen to them calling to each other."

The alien looked in the direction she indicated, and saw first the telltale movement of leaves, then the lizards themselves, as vividly luminous as stained glass, scampering from branch to branch. "They have so many beautiful colors."

"A delight to many senses at once, a poet would say. I've tried to choose living things that delighted more than one sense wherever I can. This way. . . ." She sauntered down a trail that passed beneath the branched vaulting of a group of Acturan tree ferns. "For example, these wind singers." She touched blossoms dangling from a vine wreathed about a branch, blossoms that matched the drab purple of the alien's skin. Their intoxicating scent floated through the air.

"They possess no attractive color."

"They have wonderful fragrance, and they make beautiful harmonics when the breezes catch them."

" 'Fragrance'?" Yet another unfamiliar word in this difficult language. "I apologize for my limited understanding. Could you tell me please what that is?"

"It's a sweet smell or a perfume."

"I have no . . . referent for that."

The gardener's expression changed from cool professional to something warmer. "You have no sense of smell?"

"No. My hearing device repeats your exact words. It does not translate them."

"I'm sorry you can't smell the wind singers or the other scented flowers. Fragrance was a major factor in my design of this garden—there're so many to choose from."

"I regret also. You see the world through different senses than my people."

"Among humans, smell is a very ancient sense. Even though we've lost the ability to perceive the world acutely with it, odors can call up vivid memories for us, memories we think we've forgotten."

"How unusual."

"It can be a very subtle thing. Sometimes people aren't even aware of it. They suddenly recall a childhood memory, without realizing it was the odor of a particular food, perhaps, that reminded them."

"Such a way of touching off emotions must give a gardener a complex tool to work with, when . . . patterning . . . a garden."

"It gives me a whole palette of intricate shadings to work with, to add to the wonder and enjoyment of a guest here." *A palette of shadings this guest would never enjoy,* she thought regretfully. Never to enjoy the jasmine or the ambrosia or the roses she'd so carefully nurtured. To be unable to breathe the clear scent of Cythan lemon grass, or be soothed by healer's balm, or delight in the spicy perfume of carnations. Smell was so important—

Suddenly she noticed the odor that was being wafted by the breeze, the turpentine odor of cottonleaf pods ready to burst. Thickets of cottonleaf were scattered all over this part of the garden, but not all of them were ready to spread their seeds. Now which? . . . she turned into the breeze, toward the source of the odor. "Excuse me!" Her hand reached out, pulling the alien safely to one side, out of range. The cottonleaf pods exploded in a mass of sticky, prickly seeds. "I'm sorry to yank you around like that. Those seeds are a complete nuisance to get off once they stick. I hope you didn't get any on you?"

"No, I am unscathed. My gratitude to you. How did you determine they were about to be set free?"

"From the scent of the pods. Just before they burst, they smell of turpentine—well, that won't mean anything to you, but it's a very distinctive odor, easy to notice. Once you've spent a couple of hours trying to get cottonleaf seeds out of your hair, you never forget again."

"It would seem a sense of smell is more than just a source of pleasure. It also can prevent unpleasant accidental experiences. How fortunate your species must be in the regard of the Creator of All Things to have been gifted in this way."

Her expression was skeptical. "Well, it depends on how you look at it, you know. There are nasty smells as well as delightful ones. And you can't shut off your nose to avoid them."

"Your . . . nose? That being the sense organ for odors?"

She smiled ruefully. "Yes. Forgive me, I should explain more clearly."

"Your explanations are most clear, I assure you," he said. But unlike much of his halting speech, this phrase came with the ease of long practice, and she suspected he was merely being courteous. "I desire greatly to experience smells, now that you have shown me." The tone of the alien's translated voice was in some way somber. "It is as though I lack a color in my vision."

"A philosopher once said that what you've never had, you can't miss. I don't agree with him. I know how you feel—you can miss intensely something you've never experienced, feel left out when you hear others talking about it." Her words came out hard-edged. "And they treat you as something to be pitied, and act as if you lack other things. Oh, well, it doesn't matter." Her hands swept down her thighs as if brushing dirt from her coveralls, brushing the subject away. "Well, even if you can't smell things, we can share other senses." The gardener's words trailed away as the wind picked up. The air was filled with the gentle echoing harmonies of the wind singers, each blossom sounding its own unique note, blending into a unified fabric of sound. "You see? Don't they sound beautiful in the wind?"

"Again I regret. I hear different . . . frequencies? . . . yes . . . than you. My hearing device is . . . adjusted for . . . vocal frequencies only."

"I share your regret. I planted the garden with beautiful sounds, as well as scents. I'm so sorry you can't experience it the way I intended it." She paused. "Please come this way. I'll show you a plant you don't need those senses for."

The alien followed her obediently down a side path

through the tree ferns. Shortly they emerged into a small clearing with an enormous shrub dominating the planting. The gardener pulled a dangling stem down and held it out for the alien. "This is silkenleaf. Touch it."

He was hesitant, remembering her earlier warning about the fragility of some plants. "I do not wish to cause damage. . . ."

"Oh, this one is very sturdy—it's meant to be touched. That's how its seeds are spread—they're very fine and powdery, and they brush away even if you just graze the leaves."

His slender fingers delicately brushed the silvery leaves, and he noted the glittering particles that floated free, surging in the subtle air currents caused by his movements. "This . . . sensation is . . . exquisite. Like *frana* webs."

"Frana?"

"A rare and delicate fabric woven by my people. It feels very much like these leaves. May I touch them further?"

She smiled. "Of course."

He stepped forward, into the mass of dangling limbs. His arms swept out and gathered the limber branches closer, so that he was cloaked in living silver from head to toe, leaf and seed, shimmering and twinkling in the sunlight. A sound of obvious delight came from him.

The gardener laughed with him, and their tones joined the soft rustle of the leaves as they brushed the alien's skin. He bathed in the sensations for a few moments longer, then stepped away from the plant. "That was most wonderful. I thank you for displaying the silkenleaf to me," and he bent on one knee before her.

She replied, "I enjoyed sharing it with you."

As he straightened to his full height, the alien noticed that his skin was now resplendent in silkenleaf dust. "I will have to perform cleansing—I am covered with the seed powder."

The gardener's face lit with delight. "I'll tell you a secret—I've had to 'perform cleansing,' too. Sometimes, if I've been working late and it's been a tiring day, I come here and wrap myself in the leaves the way you did. It's somehow soothing, I find."

"Yes. The living creature is content here. It spreads that content with its seeds."

"I'm glad to hear you say that. I'm not one of those people who talks to plants. I just hope I'm caring for it properly."

"Ah—but your garden glows with tranquil energy. Did I not say the energy drew me here? That bush just behind you—it is . . . vivid . . . with life."

"That's one of my new hybrid multigolds. We just transplanted it. It's dormant and won't be in bloom for several weeks yet."

"It . . . flourishes. Can you not see how full of life it is?"

"Not the way you can."

"But such color! I have never seen such a deep shade of ___." No sound came from the translator, though the alien's mouth moved.

"I'm sorry, could you say that again? I didn't hear the last word."

"___." Again no sound emerged from the device. "My species also sees in different . . . a wider . . . range of the spectrum, than yours. There must not be a referent in your language. I regret for you. The garden glows with so many colors."

"You see my world with different eyes," she said. Now the gardener's face was alive with curiosity. "Would you please describe the garden as you see it? I'd be fascinated to experience it through your eyes."

"I would have great pleasure in such description. No one of your species has ever asked me a thing like this. What would you like me to see for you?"

"Why, everything, of course."

The alien's voice was amused again. "That would take abundant time."

"All right. I've shown you some of the things I found most beautiful. Let it be your turn—describe the things that seem most beautiful to you."

"Ah, a fair exchange." He paused. "Did you know how wonderful the plants beneath our feet appear?"

"The grass? But it's just—so mundane. It's pleasant to walk on in bare feet, of course. . . ." Her voice trailed away.

"It . . . shimmers with energy. And where the breeze exhales upon it, or where sunshine falls upon it, there it changes color. A carpet upon which we walk, yes, but one with an ever-changing and subtle pattern."

"I never thought of it that way before. I'll have to tell Toma to cut the grass with more respect from now on." She smiled. "What else do you see?"

"If we return by the way we came here," the alien

said, leading the way back down the path, "I did notice another tree. . . ."

And so the guide becomes the guided, the gardener thought to herself, but without the habitual surge of irritation the thought usually gave her. Her familiar, beloved garden became a new and more wonderful place. The alien drew a picture in words of the world she had planted and nurtured—the gleaming of the dancing lilies in their endless swirling in the stream, the colorful flickerings of energy that were birds, the stately glow of the huge oaks.

And because he was eager to share his view of the world, and was not patronizing because she could not see the way he could, she lost the last of her reserve and just as eagerly questioned him. What did the bush coral look like? How did the inner vistas appear to him? Did he discern the patterns she'd intended for human sight in the mass plantings across the pond? He willingly explained all he saw, and his speech came with less hesitancy, flowed more easily the more he spoke.

Finally, they came to the gate. "Thank you so much. You can't imagine how I've enjoyed talking with you," she said.

"I have enjoyed it very much as well. I can return to my duties at the embassy with a refreshed spirit. I give you thanks."

She nodded as she reached to open the touch-lock on the gate. "Please, feel free to come again."

He bowed gravely to her, then slipped through the gate. She closed and locked it behind him. It was time for her to leave as well. She returned to the rhododendron and gathered up the now-empty seed flats and her gloves, piling them into the wheelbarrow. As she trundle the wheelbarrow back to the shed, her thoughts returned to her guest. *What a marvelous way to see the world!* And yet, she reflected, she would not want to be handicapped the way he was. Never to be able to perceive the garden the way she'd designed it to be seen, a landscape painted for several senses together.

The wheelbarrow stored away, she whistled for Cerebrus as she walked to the service gate. He was waiting there for her when she reached it, and gave her a low hum of greeting.

"You know my routine, don't you, old friend?" she said as she took his harness down from its hook, his enormous golden eyes following her motions. He stood quietly, shifting for her so she could easily close the fasteners on the straps.

Then, gripping the rigid harness handle, the handle that transmitted his every move to her, she opened the gate. "Forward, Cerebrus!"

And he guided her out into the noise and bustle of the city.

GORDIE'S PETS

by Hugh B. Cave

This new kid moved into our neighborhood in the middle of the school year. Gordie, his name was. Gordie Hasler. They put him in the seventh grade.

He was small for thirteen years old. Real small, with batwing ears and bulgy green eyes like a frog's. But smart. He was smart.

Like the day Miss Carmody set up a show-and-tell and he brought a black cat to school. He brought it in one of those carrier things, and put the carrier down beside his desk. Then, when his turn came, he didn't take the carrier up to the front of the room like you'd expect. He just reached down and opened its little door, and walked up without it and turned around to face the class.

The cat hadn't moved. It was still in the carrier.

"What I'm going to show you is how you can talk to animals and have them understand you," Gordie said, standing up there with his hands on his hips and a solemn look on that homely face of his. "My cat's name is Spooky," he said. "Watch."

Amy Michelli giggled, and two or three others joined

in, but he just stood there with a patient look on his face and waited for them to stop.

Then— "Spooky," he said, "come here, please."

Well, we've always had cats at my house, so I know they don't come when you call them. So maybe you won't believe this, but it happened. That black cat came out of its cage and walked right up there to where Gordie Hasler was standing, and sat down and looked at him.

"Spooky," the kid said, "do you know where you are?"

The cat answered him, and not with just with a "meow" either. You'll have to take my word for it, because there's no way anyone could write down how it sounded. But when Ev Neilson and the rest of us in the Tree-Street Club discussed it after school that day, we all agreed that Gordie and his cat held a conversation.

The Tree-Street Club? That's right, I haven't told you about that yet, have I? It was just a bunch of us guys— seven, to be exact—who lived in Arborhaven, where all the streets are named for trees. You know, like Birch Street, Elm Street, Maple Street, and so on. One of the things that galled us about this new kid was that he and his family had moved into the McKillops' house on Birch Street. Before Orrin McKillop moved away, he was our club president.

But about the cat, uh-huh, Gordie Hasler gave us a real demonstration that morning of how, like he said, a boy could talk to animals.

"Now listen, Spooky," he said. "I want you to go back

to your carrier there by my desk, but don't go into it yet. Just jump up and sit on it, you hear?"

The room got so still I could hear my own heart beating, I swear. And the black cat turned around and trotted back to its cage and jumped up on it, just like Gordie ordered it to. And it sat there looking at him, waiting for his next command. Or request. Or whatever the right word is.

Well, for ten minutes Gordie told that cat to do things and the cat did them. It walked around the room for him. It sat up and talked to him—not with words, of course, but with a whole bunch of sounds that could have been words in some kind of cat language. Then he sent it back to its cage and told it to take a nap until he could take it home.

And it did that. I *know* it did because I was sitting right there on the other side of it, and I *saw* that cat curl up and close its eyes and put a paw over its face.

Then to wind up his show-and-tell Gordie Hasler said, "Now I don't want anyone thinking this is some special kind of trained cat, because it isn't. I got it from an animal shelter in Coupeville, Washington, where I lived before my family moved here, and it's just an ordinary cat. So what I'm saying is you can talk to *any* kind of an animal or bird if you want to. To horses and dogs and deer—we had lots of deer there in Coupeville—and even to squirrels and chipmunks and quail and crows. You only have to *believe* you can."

"What about dangerous animals like lions and tigers?" Mario Fusto asked. Mario was a member of our Tree-Street Club.

"Well, that's something I never tried because there wasn't any zoo near enough for me to go to. There's one in Seattle, I think, but I was never in that city long enough to visit it."

"What about snakes?" said Vern Gibb, another club member. "Can you talk to snakes?"

"You bet. I have a boa constrictor at home that'll do most anything I ask it to. It can't talk back, of course, but it understands me."

Well, Miss Carmody let him go on for another ten minutes before she told him his time was up. You could tell she didn't want to stop him but had to. And when school let out that day, the Tree-Street Club got together, like I said before, to discuss what we ought to do about him. Because he lived in our neighborhood and would probably want to join the club.

"To be shown up by a normal kid from out of state wouldn't be so bad, maybe," Vern Gibb said. Vern was a tall, skinny redhead. "People have been saying our schools here are lousy anyway. But he's such a funny-lookin' little nerd. If we don't put him in his place, he'll make us look like dummies."

"Besides," Jay Pekram said, "he's moved into the very house our president used to live in. Like he was supposed to take Orrin's place, for God's sake."

Everybody had something bad to say about the kid. But finally Brad O'Dell said, "Wait, though. Aren't you guys forgetting his *sister*?"

That was the one good thing about Gordie Hasler—he had this sister. Her name was Amanda and she was a year younger than him, in the sixth grade, and man was she cute. She was just about the cutest chick in the whole school. Ev Neilson already had his eye on her.

"What we better do is pretend we like him and invite him to join our club," Ev said. Ev was a take-charge kind of guy who always went after what he wanted, with no fooling around. He was fourteen, the oldest in the club, and big and heavy. None of us really liked him a whole lot, but any club or gang needs a leader and he was a good one.

"What good will taking him into the club do?" Mario argued. "You think he'll ease up in school so we won't look so dumb?"

"Not right away," Ev said. "But after we teach him not to fool around with us, he will."

"How will we teach him that?" I asked.

"We'll take him on a snarf hunt, Lamont," he said. That's my name, Lamont Booker. "And after we do that, he won't never think he's smarter'n we are again."

Okay, we said, all of us laughing so hard that some kids coming down the school steps turned to look at us. And the next day, with it all planned out what we would do when the right time came, we invited Gordie Hasler to join the Tree-Streeters and hang out with us. And—would you believe this?—only a week later his sister had a birthday and we all got invited to his house for a party.

It was the first time any of us had set foot in that house since the McKillops lived in it, and we were in for a real surprise. Along with everything else that was queer about this Gordie Hasler, he had a whole houseful of dumb things that he talked to. He had three more cats in addition to the black one he'd brought to school, and the big snake he'd told us about, and hamsters and guinea pigs and rabbits and even two pet lizards. And he talked to all of them and claimed they understood him and talked back. Even the snake opened its mouth when he spoke to it. And the lizards had little balloons in their throats that they blew up. Man, I tell you it was weird.

But there was nothing weird about Gordie's sister Amanda. No, man. She was real cute, like I've said, and real friendly. More than once I saw Ev Neilson looking at her like she was an ice-cream cone and he was starving.

Well . . . when I look back on it now, I can see it wasn't Amanda's fault, what happened. She was just being nice to everybody because it was her birthday, and she didn't have any idea what kind of guy Ev Neilson was, so she didn't have her guard up.

And anyway it didn't happen right off, so when it did, she'd probably even forgotten she was ever nice to him.

How we found out about it, Mario and me were in my driveway one Friday night shooting baskets with the garage light on, and Ev showed up wearing a grin that just about cut his face in half. This was three weeks after Amanda's birthday party, and her brother Gordie had been a member of the Tree-Streeters for quite a while.

Ev's grin was one of those that says loud and clear, "Ask me what happened," so of course we asked him.

And he punched us on our arms and said, "Hey. I made out with Amanda."

We just stood there with our mouths open, both of us. Mario closed his first and said, "You *what?*"

"Not half an hour ago," Ev said. "I bumped into her in Quik Snak and was walking home with her. And right there in the empty lot on the corner of Birch and Dogwood, I did it,"

The lot he was talking about was a big one full of trees and underbrush, but kids had used it as a short-cut for so long there was a path running through it. You could do anything on that path and nobody on either street would see you do it.

"W-what'd you d—do with her?" Mario said, so excited he stuttered.

Ev told us what he'd done.

"But didn't she yell for help?" I asked him.

"Couldn't," he said. "I kept my hand over her mouth."

"All the time you were doing it?"

"All the time. Hey, come on, she wouldn't have yelled anyhow. She liked it."

"But, jeez," Mario said, "what if she tells her parents?"

Ev shook his head. "Actually, she was so mad she threatened to do that, but she won't. 'You do,' I warned her, 'and what the Tree-Streeters will do to your brother Gordie won't be nice. It won't be nice at all.'"

"But, hey," I said, "I thought you *liked* Amanda. Now she won't ever look at you again."

"Cripes," he said, "I didn't want her for a *girlfriend.*

You crazy or somethin'? Who'd want a girlfriend with a smartass, creepy-lookin' brother like Gordie? All I ever wanted was to do what I did to her. C'mon," he said, "let's shoot some baskets."

Well.

Amanda must have believed him. About what the Tree-Streeters would do to her brother, I mean. Because when we had our next club meeting, Gordie never said a word about it.

We met in Randy Seller's house on a Saturday when his parents were out for the evening. We drank some of Mr. Seller's beer, which Gordie wouldn't drink any of because it made him sick, he said. We played some Ping-Pong, which he was pretty good at, beating everybody except Randy, and nobody beats Randy because the table is right there in his own house and he plays with his dad all the time. But not a word was said about Gordie's sister or what Ev had done to her. Her name wasn't even mentioned.

In school, though, if you watched real close, you could tell Amanda was not like before. She didn't smile any more and when any of us spoke to her she would just barely answer, then walk away. With Ev she was even more so. A couple of times I saw him try to stop her in the hall, and she walked on by as if he wasn't even there.

If her brother noticed she was different, he never let on. He just went on being a wise guy and making the rest of us look like we didn't belong in the same grade with him. Like when Miss Carmody would ask a question, he'd be the first to yell out the answer. Or when one of us would be doing a math problem at the blackboard and would make a mistake, he'd jump up and start waving his hand like crazy.

"Okay, this has gone far enough," Ev Neilson said one day at recess in the schoolyard. "We got to have that snarf hunt."

So at our next meeting, which happened to be at my house, we told him.

He kind of rolled those froggy eyes of his and looked at us like he suspicioned something. "What's a snarf hunt?" he said.

"You know what a snipe is?" Ev asked him.

"Well, sure, a snipe is a bird."

"You got it," Ev said. "Only around here we call 'em snarfs. So Saturday we're going snarf hunting."

"Where?" Gordie asked.

"To the woods out past the old quarry hole. That's where we always go. It's kinda scary, though. Maybe you'd rather drop out of the club?"

"No, I don't want to drop out," Gordie said.

"Okay, then," Ev said. "We'll meet at my house at six A.M., rain or shine. Wear some old clothes because it's real rough in those woods. And the right kind of shoes, 'cause you'll be doin' a lot of walkin'."

"Six o'clock at your house," said Gordie. "Right. I'll be there."

Well, I set an alarm clock when I went to bed that night, because I don't usually get up so early. And when I looked out the window at quarter to six A.M. I never thought Gordie Hasler would be at Ev's house when I got there. He might be a brain, but he was no superman and would probably chicken out, I figured. Because it had rained most of the night from the looks of things, and even though it wasn't raining then, the low spot in our yard was full of water. The woods were bound to be sopping wet.

I got dressed and went over, though, and there was Gordie sitting on the porch steps all by his lonesome. Then Ev came out, and one by one the others turned up, and off we went.

It's two and a half miles out to the quarry on the old back road, and of course we had to walk it because none of us was old enough to drive a car even if we could have borrowed one. The road was under water in places and our shoes were soaked by the time we got there. But Gordie didn't quit like we half expected. He didn't complain any, either. Matter of fact, he didn't do near as much grousing as some of the others.

At the quarry we turned off into the woods, and as soon as we did that it was like night had fallen again. I mean, man, it was *dark* in there after all that rain, and with the sky all gloomy up over the tops of those big trees. It was just as dark as if we'd been doing this at night, the way the older kids in the Warlock gang do it. I could hardly see Mario Fusto in front of me, even though he was almost close enough for me to reach out and touch.

About thirty minutes in from the road we got to the clearing, and it was like nobody had set foot in there since we were there six months before, when we initiated our last new member, Jay Pekram.

"Okay, here we are," Ev said, turning to Gordie. "You ready, or do you want to rest a while?"

"I'm ready," Gordie said. "What do I do?"

"You take this." Ev unzipped his jacket and peeled off the bag, which was wrapped around him underneath. It was a big white laundry bag that I borrowed from my house the first time we ever did this, and my mom never has figured out where it disappeared to. Ev opened it up and showed Gordie how to close it by pulling on the cord at the top. Then he opened it up again and handed it over.

"What you do, Gordie, is stand here in this little clearing and wait for us to scare up the snarfs and run 'em at you. They don't fly too good, I guess you know, so what will happen is, they'll come floppin' and flappin' in here and you have to grab 'em and stuff 'em into the bag. You got it?"

"Is that all?" Gordie asked, like he was disappointed it was going to be so easy.

"Well, no, that's not all. Because this place is a hangout for more than snarfs," Ev said. "Isn't that so, guys?" He looked around at us—we were standing in a kind of circle with Gordie in the middle—and naturally we said yes, that was how it was.

"There's a thing in here we don't know what it is," Ev went on, talking in a low voice now in case the thing might be close enough to hear him. "We've only seen it a couple of times, and we don't even know what kind of a thing it is, but it sure is scary. If *it* should come busting out of the woods here instead of snarfs, you run for your life, you hear?"

"What's it look like, this thing?" Gordie asked. "If I don't know what it looks like, how will I know what to run from?"

"Well, it's an animal, sort of. Right, gang?" Ev looked around at us again.

All of us nodded, solemn as a bunch of choirboys in church.

"It's an animal like a big yellow cat or a tiger," Ev went on, "but it has a head like nothing you ever saw in your whole life, with rows and rows of godawful long sharp teeth. 'Course, none of us ever saw it up close—only when it was creeping through the trees here like a shadow. But, hey, the way you're able to talk to animals, it won't scare *you* none." He sort of cocked his head at Gordie and grinned.

"You saw this thing yourself?" Gordie asked, peering up at him with those froggy eyes.

"Sure, sure, we've all see it one time or another."

"Then it has to be real. I mean, anytime you believe in a thing, you *make* it real. Real for *you*, that is. You want to remember that."

"Okay, we'll remember. Won't we guys?" Ev was trying so hard not to laugh, his face was like a balloon about to pop. "So you just stand here with the bag, Gordie, and catch the snarfs when we scare 'em in here. And when we figure you've got the bag full, we'll quit and come back for you. All right?"

"All right," Gordie said.

"So c'mon, gang," Ev said. "Spread out and let's go."

We knew what to do, of course. We'd done it all before. Leaving Gordie there holding the bag, we took off into the woods in different directions, then circled around and met up again and hiked on home. That was all there was to it. Pretty soon we were all back at Ev's house, laughing our heads off at the thought of that smart little pipsqueak with the froggy eyes holding the bag out there in those spooky woods, waiting for snarfs to come so he could catch them and hoping that that other thing, the monster Ev had warned him about, wouldn't show up before the hunt was over.

We hung around Ev's house a while, telling each other Gordie Hasler wouldn't be such a pain in the neck after this. Then we went over to the schoolyard and shot baskets and talked about it some more, and to Quik Snak for hamburgers and fries and kept right *on* talking about it. We even took bets on how long it would be before Gordie wised up and came back. I bet he wouldn't show up until the middle of the afternoon, at least, and I won because that was when he did come. It was after three when he came trudging around the corner with his head down on his chest and his hands stuffed in his pockets.

"He left the bag," Ev said right off. "Should we make him go back for it?" He looked at me because the bag had come from my house, so by rights it belonged to me.

"No, never mind it," I said. "Just look at him—he's real beat. We can get another bag."

Then we just sat there on Ev's porch, not saying anything, while Gordie Hasler trudged up the walk to the foot of the steps and took his hands out of his pockets and held them out to us, palms up, and shrugged his puny little shoulders.

"I caught that thing you told me about," he said.

All of us, we just looked at each other. "What thing?" Ev said.

"With the big cat's body and the awful head. With the teeth. It was too heavy for me to bring back here alone. I had to leave it there. I didn't see any snarfs. I guess you didn't find any, huh?"

We looked at each other again.

"Why did you leave me there?" Gordie said. "You were supposed to return to the clearing when the hunt was over."

Still nobody said anything. He looked so pathetic standing there, I even felt sorry for him and I guess some of the others did too. Except Ev, of course. Ev could never feel sorry for anybody. He just looked puzzled.

"You say you didn't catch any snarfs but you caught the *thing*?" Ev said at last.

Gordie nodded.

"And it was so heavy you couldn't bring it back with you?"

"That's right. Yes."

"Where'd you leave it?"

"Right there in the clearing." Gordie shrugged his shoulders again. "Well, I guess I'll go home now. I'm a little tired after waiting so long for you guys to come back for me. I'm sorry we didn't get any snarfs." And with his hands in his pockets again, he turned and went back down the walk.

Nobody said anything. We just watched him until he disappeared around the corner. Then we all started talking at once.

"Hey, he said he caught the *thing!*" I said.

"What *did* he catch, you suppose?" Jay Pekram said. "A fox, maybe?"

"Naw," said Vern Gibb. "He wouldn't be quick enough to bag a fox, for Pete's sake. Most likely some dumb old raccoon waddled up to him and he scooped it up with the bag."

Ev Neilson shook his head, frowning so hard his eyes were almost shut. "Uh-uh," he said. "Gordie's too smart for that. He'd know if he caught a fox or a coon. Jeeze, what *could* he have caught?"

Nobody had any other ideas.

All at once Ev jumped up and said, "I'm going back there and find out! Who wants to come with me?"

Nobody volunteered. "Aw, hey, it's too late," somebody said.

"C'mon, c'mon, one of you," Ev insisted. "Somebody has to come with me. I'm not walkin' all the way back there by myself. You, Lamont. On your feet! Let's go!"

Well, Ev was club president and anyway, you didn't say no to him when he spoke in that tone of voice. I looked around at the rest of them, hoping somebody else would volunteer. But nobody did, so I said, "All right, Mr. President," just so he'd know how I felt, and I went with him.

So me and Ev hiked back to the clearing and there was the bag, just like Gordie Hasler said, and sure enough there was something in it—something so big the bag looked like it might bust open even before Ev got to it. But it didn't, and Ev leaned over it and yanked the top of it open, and what was in it flew out at him with a noise like—well, if you've ever heard one of those big round sawmill saws tear into a log, it was like that but even screechier.

And I can't even describe the thing that was *making* that godawful noise. About all I can say is that Ev Neilson came pretty close when he was telling Gordie to watch out for it. It had the body of a big cat or a tiger, like Ev said, and a head like nothing that ever lived, with rows and rows of long sharp teeth. And when it leaped out of the bag and grabbed Ev, I ran. There wasn't a thing I or anybody else could have done to help him. I just ran.

I never looked back, so I wasn't able to tell my mom what the thing did to Ev. But we know because she telephoned the police and they went out there, and it was in the newspaper, what they found. Not a photo—I guess no paper would ever print any photo that awful—but it said the body was "partly eaten" and "otherwise torn to pieces as if by some monstrous cat." When I read it, all I could think of was how Gordie brought his little black cat "Spooky" to school for show-and-tell, and it did everything he told it to.

All right. I guess I know what you're going to say. You're going to say if the thing was strong enough to do that to Ev, why did it just stay there in a flimsy old laundry bag until me and Ev got there.

Right?

Well, the way I see it, there's only one answer. Gordie Hasler must've *told* it to. Just like his sister must have told *him* what Ev did to her.

LADY IN CREAM-COLORED CHIFFON

by Elizabeth Anderson and Margaret Maron

As is too often the case, what ended in cataclysm began with the best of good intentions. Actually, it was Marshall Baxter's idea to spend Saturday afternoon at the park near the college where the three of them taught. He wanted to try out his new Nikon on the ducks that panhandled shamelessly beside the lake; but Helen, his wife, had insisted that her brother Thurston come along, too.

"It'll be just like old times," she said, even though the three of them knew it wouldn't be. Could never be again.

Not without Anne.

Even so, it was one of those glorious spring afternoons that enticed students from the college to wander hand in hand along the lakeside; a day that brought young parents out with their shiny new baby strollers, and sent rollerbladers careening along the upper walks toward the ice cream stand that lay near the carousel.

The May warmth had also brought out art students and weekend painters. A dozen or more had set up with easels, water color boxes, or sketch pads on a level stretch of grass halfway between the carousel and the lake. Some faced the water while others seemed intent on the colorful wooden animals whirling giddily through the sunlit afternoon.

As in times past, Helen and Thurston sauntered down the path, each savoring an ice cream cone. Helen had chosen strawberry while Thurston took a fudge ripple, his favorite since childhood. He always discussed the merits of blueberry vanilla or butterscotch almond and then invariably ordered fudge ripple.

"Old habits die hard," Thurston said when Helen teased him.

Marsh had forgone his usual butter pecan in order to keep his hands free for his camera. Had she been there, Anne would have ordered a coffee lemon or peanut butter lime or some other outrageous combination of flavors. Part of her charm had been her unpredictability, even in small things.

Helen glanced at her brother surreptitiously, wondering if Thurston were remembering, too. It had been a rough year since Anne drowned, but he had joined them today without arguing and even seemed to be enjoying himself, so maybe he was finally coming out of that dull gray fog which had enveloped him all these long months.

Followed by a carefree waltz from the carousel, they walked down to the water's edge and were immediately importuned by noisy ducks. As Marsh fumbled with the unfamiliar dials and knobs on his new camera, Helen and Thurston fed the ends of their cones to the ducks, then dabbled their fingers in the water to wash away the stickiness.

"Smile," said Marsh for the tenth time and Helen stuck out her tongue at him while Thurston actually made donkey ears.

A liberating surge of relief washed over Helen. Thurston had loved Anne so intensely and had talked such wild nonsense when she died that Helen had been terrified that he might do something crazy. Now, though—

Impulsively, she hugged him.

"What was that for?" he asked, smiling down into her eyes.

"Just because you're such an idiot," she said, her voice shaky with happiness.

"Runs in the family," he said lightly, but there was understanding and even gratitude in the brotherly squeeze he gave her hand.

Routed by the ducks who kept trying to nibble his camera, Marsh took a path that looped back up toward the carousel and past the artists. Helen and Thurston trailed along behind him, not really caring which direction they walked.

Other people paused at various points to look over the artists' shoulders and the three of them looked, too. They moved slowly from one easel to another, respecting the semi-circle of space maintained between painter and spectators.

One artist viewed the lake as a splashy post-modern explosion of light while the next one made cubist constructions of the ducks and a third copied the scene as literally (and as unimaginatively) as Marsh's camera.

"Hey! Look at her," Marsh whispered and immediately began to focus his lens on an old woman who sat apart from the rest of the painters.

Dressed in a man's pair of baggy gray pants and a faded blue plaid shirt, the elderly artist made a drab contrast to her colorful surroundings. Strands of white hair straggled out around the edges of a disreputable felt hat festooned with tattered fishing lures. The cuffs of her pants were stuffed down inside a pair of black rubber boots that seemed incongruous on such a warm spring day, as did her black rubber raincoat which lay wadded beside the rusty tackle box that held her painting supplies.

"Tugboat Annie meets Norman Rockwell," Thurston said wryly and walked on ahead to see if the old woman had painted ducks or wooden horses.

Helen held the camera bag while Marsh changed to a telephoto lens. As her husband refocused, she noticed the old woman's token concessions to femininity. A necklace of amber-colored seashells terminated in an artsy medallion shaped like a silver starfish. A silver-and-shell bracelet flashed in the sunlight as her sinewy wrist deftly guided the brush across the canvas before her.

Idly, Helen's eyes moved from the woman's stooped shoulders to her brother's face and apprehension gripped her. Something was wrong. Very wrong.

Thurston stood almost rigid, his hands clenching and unclenching at his side, and Helen was instantly reminded of the way he had stood beside Anne's grave, oblivious to everyone around him.

She slipped past the strollers and sightseers and hurried over to link her arm in his. If Thurston noticed her presence, he didn't show it, but stared straight at the canvas, a muscle twitching in his lower jaw.

Helen followed his gaze and gasped as she saw the painting up close and recognized the dark-haired figure in the foreground of the canvas.

Anne?

Somehow, acrylic paints duplicated the dead woman's essential beauty and appeal, right down to that brooding and sometimes reckless gleam in her eye when she was ready to take any risks and challenge the universe if dared. Even the chiffon that swirled about the figure's slender legs bore an uncanny resemblance to the expensive cream-colored dress Anne had worn the night she sailed the *Sea Dollar* to her death.

Appalled by the coincidence, Helen stared at the canvas. Here was no placid, duck-filled lake under a sunny blue sky. Instead it could have been the Georgia coast, just south of Sapelo, with a high tide surging on a stormy spring night; except that in this picture, the clouds were breaking up and the woman—*Not Anne!* screamed Helen's protesting mind—seemed to be coming back from the dark ocean, strings of seaweed clinging to her wet hair, her bare feet leaving deep prints across the moonlit beach.

In the gloomy distance, anchored right at the water's edge, was a green-and-white sailboat that could have been a duplicate of the *Sea Dollar*. An old man in a slick black raincoat hunched over the anchor line, his face hidden beneath the brim of a shapeless felt hat.

As Helen turned to Thurston, she was afraid of what she might find on his face; but he crossed the empty space behind the old woman and said, "How much do you want for it?"

Helen touched his arm, but he ignored her. "How much?" he repeated thickly.

The old woman dabbed at a wave with the tip of her brush. At Thurston's words, her head swung up and Helen saw her fully for the first time.

Well past seventy, the face beneath the hat was deeply lined and weathered to a leathery brown, a face exposed to the elements for most of a long lifetime. Her wide mouth was set in a permanent half-smile that hinted at secret knowledge rather than humor. But it was her eyes that sent a shiver through Helen and made her want to grasp Thurston's hands and drag him away. Something dark and ancient and compelling lurked in those eyes. Inky blue they were, like the depth of the ocean; but the intelligence that swirled there didn't just peer out at the world. It sucked the world into its depths.

And now those eyes were turned on Thurston. "Would ye be speaking to me, sir?"

Her accent sounded strange to Helen. New England? Irish? Surely she was coastal-bred? But not Georgia's coast—not that it mattered. How she got this far south and this far inland Helen didn't care. Right now she was too concerned about her brother.

"Come on, Thurse," she coaxed.

She realized that Marsh had come up behind them and she turned to her husband for help, but he was staring at the picture in astonishment. "What the bloody hell—! Is that Anne?"

Thurston ignored them both. All of his attention was focused on the old woman. "Please. The painting—is it for sale? How much?"

Something flickered in the depths of those blue-black eyes. She shook her head. "It's not for money this thing I do."

"Hey, c'mon, Thurse," Marsh said uneasily. "You don't really want this picture."

But Thurston impatiently shook Marsh's hand off and began to cajole the old artist as Helen could remember him cajoling their parents into later bedtimes, more dessert, bigger allowances.

"Please, ma'am. Surely you don't keep all your paintings? You'd run out of space. You must sell some of them once in a while, so why not this one?"

Beneath the brim of her shapeless felt hat, amusement flickered over that weathered face. " 'Tis charming ye are, lad, but few am I selling any more. My pretty pictures twist the heart too much." She shook her head again and the barbed fishing lures snagged in her hatband glittered sharply. "Nay, 'twould be wrong to be taking of your money."

"Now see here," said Marsh, coming to his brother-in-law's support. The picture struck him as morbid, but if that's what Thurston wanted—

The words died in his throat as those eyes met his

and he suddenly felt the need to put his arm protectively around Helen.

"Please," said Thurston, and there was naked anguish in his entreaty.

Absently fingering the silver starfish of her shell necklace, the old artist studied him a long moment.

"If ye'd care to be waiting till I've finished," she said finally, "perhaps we can set a price between the two of us." Her dark eyes pointedly swept over Marsh and Helen.

"I'll wait."

"Thurse," Helen began, but Marsh's arm tightened about her.

Thurston seemed aware of them then and of their concern. "It's okay, guys. I'll meet you back at the car."

"Are you sure?" asked Marsh.

"I'm sure," he answered and the easy smile on his face belied the grief so apparent only moments before.

Bewildered and reluctant, Helen allowed Marsh to lead her away.

By the time they reached the car and Marsh had fitted his new camera and all its lenses into the case, the incident had begun to take on sane proportions.

"God knows Anne attracted some weird characters in her time," Marsh said, "but that old gal takes the proverbial cake."

As Anne had occasionally lectured on art history for the college's continuing education program, Helen could only agree. Continuing Ed drew senior citizens from all walks of life and with varying degrees of mental competency. The dramatic story of Anne's tragic drowning had spread all over campus last May: a beautiful young art professor who had recklessly challenged the sea gods and lost. It was the stuff from which legends spring.

And evidently the tale had seized the artistic imagination of one of Anne's older students. It was just sheer bad luck that they had passed by her easel today. A year of grief therapy down the drain, months of watching Thurston slowly work his way through loss and loneliness, and now, when he was finally almost whole again—

"Instead of coming to this dumb park, we should have driven over to the Omni," Helen said. "Thurse doesn't *need* more grief."

Marsh hugged her comfortingly. "You worry about him too much, honey. He's over the worst of it. Maybe the picture will get him the rest of the way."

"Maybe," said Helen. But she didn't really believe it.

Nevertheless, she was relieved when Thurston came swinging up the hill with the canvas wrapped in a sheet of black plastic and tied with stiff white twine. He seemed no less cheerful than before they'd spotted the picture.

"Sorry to hold you up," he apologized, striding across the graveled parking lot.

"It's okay," Marsh said and car keys jingled in his hand as he started to unlock the trunk.

"Don't bother," said Thurston. "I can slide it into the back seat here with me."

Suiting action to his words, he clambered into the

rear seat and balanced the wrapped picture on the floor next to him.

As Marsh started the engine, Helen asked, "Did that old woman say if she'd taken one of Anne's classes?"

"Classes? I don't know. I didn't think to ask."

He tousled her hair with his free hand, a brotherly bit of mischief that used to send her up the wall when they were children. "I know you and Marsh think I'm crazy to want this picture," he said, "but thanks for not saying it."

Which effectively cut off further conversation on that point. Suspicious that she was being maneuvered, Helen twisted in the front seat to look at his face, but Thurston just smiled at her blandly and asked what she planned to cook for supper. "I *am* invited, aren't I?"

"You are not," she snapped. "Marsh and I are going to a movie. Alone."

"We are?" asked Marsh.

The apartment Thurston had moved into after Anne's death was in a new townhouse complex with a Georgian facade. Marsh drew up in front and held the painting while Thurston crawled out of the back seat. "See you tomorrow around 2:30?"

"Tomorrow?" Thurston asked blankly, his hands cradling the wrapped canvas.

"You can't have forgotten," Helen protested through her open window. "The Hudsons are coming. He wants to hear about your Civil War project and he's the new managing editor at—"

"I know who Bob Hudson is," Thurston reminded his

155

sister patiently. He looked from Helen to Marsh and then back to Helen again. "Look, I know what you guys are trying to do—what you've been doing ever since Anne. . . ." He swallowed hard and tried again. "Keep good ol' Thurse's dance card filled and maybe he won't notice that big hole in his life, right?"

"That's not fair!" Helen said indignantly.

"Maybe not." Sadness and love mingled in his voice. "But I've tried doing it your way, and it still hurts. Now you've got to let me try my way. Okay?"

"Okay," Helen whispered even though tears pooled in her eyes.

Thurston leaned through the open window and kissed her. "I'll be fine. I promise."

An art theater near the campus was showing a Marx Brothers double feature, but *A Night at the Opera* was almost over before Helen stopped needing to cry.

The phone rang promptly at 2:30 the next day just as Helen was crossing the porch, trying to balance an ice bucket, a bowl of potato salad, and a bottle of tonic water in her arm. She dumped her burdens onto Marsh, who was adjusting the flame in their gas grill, and hurried back inside to answer on the fifth ring.

It was Thurston. No "Hello," no "How are you?"—just "Helen, I'm sorry."

She tried to keep her tone light. "You dirty rat! Does this mean you're not coming?"

"Sorry, honey," he repeated.

"You wouldn't have to stay long," she wheedled.

There was silence on the line and Helen knew she

was babbling, but she couldn't help herself. "Look, Thurse, I know you think I'm not minding my own business, but you're my only brother and I love you and I can't bear to think of you sitting over there in that apartment all alone when—"

"I'm not alone any more."

"*What?*"

"I mean, I'm not lonely," he said, quickly correcting himself. "And I'm not just sitting here. I've got things to do."

"What things?" she challenged.

"Term papers to grade, exams to draw up." He hesitated. "And there's the painting to hang."

The timer bell rang on the oven. "I've got to run, Thurse, and this is a hellish week coming up, so if I don't see you, are we still invited for Friday night? Answer quick before my pie turns to charcoal."

He laughed then and sounded almost like his old self. "You know you are. I ought to have the *Lady* up by then."

She could smell her pie self-destructing, but Helen frowned and said, "Lady?"

"*Lady in Cream-Colored Chiffon,*" he explained. "That's what the old woman called the picture. Suits it, don't you think?"

Before she could answer, Marsh hurried past her to the kitchen. "Is something burning?"

"Oh, God! The pie! See you Friday."

She hung up the phone and hurried out to see Marsh transferring her cherry pie to a cooling rack. The crust was three shades browner than she liked, but technically not burned.

Marsh looked at her quizzically. "Something wrong?"

"That was Thurse. He's not coming."

"So?"

"So he's going to sit around all afternoon staring at that damned painting."

Marsh rolled his eyes. "Thurston Mosely is a grown man, Helen. If he wants to sit around staring at a painting all day, it's his—" He caught himself and finished quietly, "It's his business. Right?"

Sadness touched Helen's eyes. "You started to say funeral."

The doorbell rang, announcing their first guests.

Marsh took a deep breath. "Look, honey, I know Thurse taps the earth mother in you, but you've got to ease off. He'll get over Anne, but you forget how joined at the hip they were. It takes more time for men like Thurse."

He touched her face and bent down for a quick kiss. "Pay attention to *me*, okay? I'm the guy you promised to love, honor, and whatever till death do us in, remember?"

The doorbell chimed again, louder this time and more urgent. "Coming, for God's sake, coming!" said Marsh, heading for the door.

Helen followed more slowly. "Part, Marsh," she whispered. "Till death do us *part*."

With graduation ceremonies only three weeks off, campus life turned into a three-ring squirrel cage. As usual in the second week of May, seniors suddenly realized that if they didn't pass their finals, their parents would be staring at a row of empty seats come Graduation Day.

The new department head had added the duties of Senior Adviser to Helen's already full schedule, so it was her phone that rang every time a marginal scholar's head-on collision with academia turned into a personal crisis.

As Dean of Students, Marsh was just as busy. He was also acting head of the campus news service and had been asked to write President Hewlett's welcoming address, so their dining table was now piled high with books and papers and Marsh sat there every night writing and swearing under his breath.

Racing along on her own little treadmill, Helen kept thinking she ought to call Thurston, but, still smarting from Marsh's gentle lecture and her brother's own silence, she decided to let it ride until Friday. If Thurse needed them, he knew where they were. That's what family was for, wasn't it?

The Baxters had kept a regular Friday night dinner date with the Moselys for nearly eleven years. Anne's death and Thurston's subsequent move to the townhouse on Verdin Street did nothing to change the ritual, so Helen and Marsh were both confused and a little irritated when they arrived on Thurston's doorstep Friday night and found his curtains drawn and the windows dark.

Marsh pressed the bell a third time. "Where the hell is he?"

Helen shook her head. It was inconceivable that Thurse had forgotten or made other plans without letting them know. It would be like forgetting to brush his teeth or put on his pants. She made a fist and rapped loudly on the door. "Thurston? Damn it all, Thurse—"

A rattle on the other side of the door interrupted her. It opened and her brother stared at them in confusion. "Marsh? Helen? What—" He slapped his forehead. "Good lord, it's Friday! Come in, come in."

Helen glanced at Marsh, not trusting herself to speak. In the hall, out of habit, she swung left toward the study, but Thurston blocked her path, grabbing the knob and firmly pulling the door shut.

He laughed nervously. "I'm doing a little reorganizing in there. It's a total mess." He gestured down the hall. "Let's go in the living room."

Helen ventured another glance at Marsh, who shrugged, clearly as puzzled as she.

Hurrying into the living room ahead of them to snap on the lights, Thurston pointed them toward the bar while he swept up scissors, twine, and a roll of masking tape and crammed them into the credenza across the room. He shut the drawer so fast that it came off track and, for some reason, this seemed to embarrass him as he jiggled the drawer back into place.

"Drinks!" he said, turning back to them with the air of a football coach calling a strategy session.

There was an awkward silence.

"Well, now! So you're here!" He laughed again, a

strained, high-pitch sound. "All I can do is apologize because I haven't planned—wait, I know. There's plenty of frozen pizza and—"

Helen took a step toward him. "Where were you, Thurse? You had us worried. And why were all the lights off?"

"I was ... well, I ... I was in the back bedroom. Up-stairs. I've been ... I told you. Reorganizing, boxing up some things for storage, that sort of stuff. Guess I forgot all about the time. I'm sorry."

Marsh raised his hand. "Hey, forget it. We can try that new Cajun restaurant."

Thurston shook his head. "No, no, really. It won't take a minute." He smiled at his sister. "It'll give me a chance to use that microwave you said I couldn't live without. Fix yourselves a drink and I'll be right back."

He disappeared through the dining room door and Helen faced Marsh. "Will you please tell me what's going on?"

Her husband let out a deep explosive gust of air. "Who the hell knows?" He went over to the bar. "Scotch?"

She nodded mutely and a moment later, he handed her a glass. Sipping the amber liquid, her gaze circled the room. "Wonder where he hung it?"

"Hung what?"

"Don't be cute, Marsh. The painting, of course."

"Helen, please. Give the guy a break, will you?"

She sighed and wandered over to the bookshelf be-hind the piano. There were gaps in the collection.

"That's odd," she said. "The Churchill books—the leather ones with the gold lettering—they're gone."

The six-volume history of World War II had been a Christmas gift from Anne and they knew how much Thurse cherished it.

Marsh came to stand beside her. The years had made Anne's and Thurse's bookcases almost as familiar as their own and he ticked off the empty spaces. "Anne's set of van Gogh letters, Donne's sermons, the anthology of Yeats' poems— Thurse wasn't kidding about reorganizing, was he?"

But Helen was moving about the living room. She had thought there was something different about it when they first came in and now she realized that there were other things missing besides the books—small things that held personal significance: the silver cup he and Anne had won at mixed doubles the year before they were married, a brass toy cannon their great-great-grandfather had played with during the Civil War, a purplish conch shell Anne had brought back from Indonesia, a watercolor of their cottage at Sea Island where the *Silver Dollar* was in drydock. On the wall over the couch was a glass-fronted case with Thurston's collection of Civil War coins. Two of the spaces inside were empty now, spaces that had held two gold coins.

As Helen ticked off one item after another, a sense of unease crept over her, an unease made all the worse because she couldn't stick a label on what it meant.

"Marsh? What's he up to? Thurse loves these things. Anne loved them."

Marsh put a cautioning finger to his lips as his

brother-in-law swung through the door carrying a tray of pepperoni pizza and a stack of napkins.

"I'd invite you into the dining room, but you might see the kitchen, and then my reputation as a neatnik would be permanently damaged," he said brightly.

It was evident to Helen and Marsh that he was trying very hard to act naturally, but somehow the trying only made it worse. Suppressed excitement seemed to ooze out through his very pores and his eyes had a feverish look that worried Helen.

They ate in almost total silence. Marsh tried to keep the conversation going, but every topic fell flat.

Helen's eyes kept going back to the coin case behind her brother's head. Finally she could stand it no longer. She pushed away the paper plate of half-eaten pizza and said, "What happened to those ten-dollar gold pieces? They weren't stolen, were they?"

"Those?" Thurston turned and examined the case almost as if the time he'd spent painstakingly building the collection no longer meant anything. "No, I used them to pay for the painting."

"*What?*"

He shrugged. "That's all the old woman charged. Two pieces of gold she said. They were the first thing I thought of."

"That's *all?*" Helen began incredulously. "Those coins were worth—"

Marshall interrupted her protest. "So when do we get to see it?"

"See what?"

"The painting, of course. You did hang it, didn't you?"

Thurston took another sip of beer and carefully set the glass back on the table before answering. "Well—yes."

"So, are you going to show it to us or not?" asked Helen.

"Sure. If you want." Again that high, artificial laughter. "But why bother? It hasn't changed any since Sunday."

Helen peered into his glazed eyes. Was he coming down with something? "Come on, Thurse. Pictures always look different after they're up. Show us."

He didn't like it. She could tell that, but there was no graceful way out. He came to his feet slowly and led them upstairs.

The painting, now framed in heavy carved wood, rested on an easel at the far side of the spare bedroom. The room was dark except for an overhead spot focused on the painting. Helen reached for a light switch, but Thurston shook his head, his face somber now, like a choirboy approaching the altar.

Helen glanced about the room uneasily. Thurston had set up Anne's antique brass bed in this room when he first moved in last summer along with some family pieces they'd inherited, an oak chifforobe, a rocking chair, Anne's dressing table, but he hadn't bothered with bed linens or curtains.

Now soft cream-colored organdy curtains billowed with a warm evening breeze at the open windows. Anne's antique lace bedspread covered the bed and a pile of her crocheted pillows rested at the head.

Thurston had even laid out Anne's gold dresser set on top of the dressing table amid a familiar array of cut-glass perfume bottles and the china pin dishes that Anne collected. The room breathed of Anne's presence now, and she seemed to be watching from that picture, her dark eyes thoughtful as they had been in life, and, yes, slightly wounded somehow, as if hurt by something they had seen once and couldn't forget.

Thurston stepped toward the painting. "She's beautiful, isn't she?"

Helen linked her arm in his as Marsh peered over her shoulder and said, "Funny. I don't remember that she was that far into the foreground before. Did you cut the picture down to fit the frame or something?"

"No," answered Thurston. "It's the same."

Helen leaned forward, her own memory now prodded by the background. "No, it's not. She *is* closer to the front and look! What's that in the boat? That wasn't there last Sunday."

She pointed to the stern of the boat where a black tarp was tied around a stack of boxes. Helen frowned. "And the old man looks different. Wasn't he on the sand? Now he's in the bow."

Again Thurston shook his head. "You're mistaken. It was just as you see it." He smiled teasingly, the first halfway normal thing he'd done all evening. "You were so busy trying to save me from myself, you never really looked at the picture."

Helen felt a little sheepish. He was right about the first part.

"Well," Thurston said heartily. "So there it is. Coffee, anybody?"

Helen started to refuse. She still wasn't satisfied about that second figure. Nor about the tarp-covered boxes, but Marsh cut her off. "We'd love some," he said firmly.

The painting was not mentioned again that evening. Campus politics, student inanities, and end-of-semester craziness carried them through coffee in the living room. Thurston's earlier agitation gradually subsided. By the time he walked them to the door, he seemed almost his old self.

But as soon as they were in the car, Helen turned to Marsh. "I didn't imagine all that about the painting, did I? It *was* different, wasn't it?"

At the wheel, Marsh shrugged. "I thought it was, but maybe Thurse was right. We did have our minds on other things last Sunday. Memory's a pretty poor tool when you get right down to it. Ask any student."

Helen grimaced. "Maybe, but I could have sworn that old man was on the beach and I'll be damned if I remember any pile of boxes in the stern."

Marsh was silent, his eyes on the road. She touched his knee. "What do you think about Thurse moving all Anne's stuff in with the painting?"

"I think it's none of our business, honey."

She sighed and watched the lighted storefronts along College Street. It had begun to drizzle and the sidewalks were slick and wet. A boy and girl strolled by hunched together under one umbrella. They made her remember something her grandmother used to say:

*"Mind out who you give your heart to, girl, because even
if you do get it back, it'll never be much good to you
again."*

Too bad Gran hadn't warned Thurston instead.

Although term papers had piled up on her desk and
every senior student in the department seemed determined to arrange a final conference with her, Helen
managed to meet Thurston for lunch in the cafeteria
on Wednesday. If she was ready to pull her hair out, he
seemed even more distracted. His voice kept trailing
off. Twice he failed to respond to a direct question and
once, right in the middle of a sentence, he interrupted
her to ask what date it was.

"Eat your salad," Helen told him worriedly. "Are you
getting enough vitamins?"

He looked around the noisy cafeteria. "It's just school
. . . all this. God! I don't think I can take much more of
this, Helen."

She patted his hand comfortingly. "Sure you can, kid.
Ten more days of chaos, then graduation and three
whole months of peace. Maybe you'll even finish your
book on the Civil War this summer."

"Maybe," he said dispiritedly.

A student rushed up for Helen's signature on an
IBM grade sheet and when she looked back, Thurston
was gone.

On Friday, he left word with the departmental secretary that he'd be unable to meet them for dinner. Helen
tried to call him all weekend with no success. Nor was

she able to catch him in when she stopped by the History Department on Monday afternoon, but Jennie Oglethorp, who'd been History's secretary since God said, "Let there be light," was glad to see her.

"Dr. Mosely turned in all his grade cards even though he's still got two exams to go," she told Helen. "And he forgot to enter half the grades for his 402 class and they're due tomorrow. Will you be seeing him tonight?"

"I hadn't planned to," Helen said. "My husband and I are scheduled for Dr. Dodd's retirement dinner tonight, but give me the cards. I'll drop them off on our way over."

She and Marsh were already five minutes late by the time the car slid into Verdin Street. Marsh waited at the wheel, the engine running. "Do not give him advice on food, health, sleeping habits, or paintings, okay?"

"Okay, okay!" she said impatiently, slamming the door.

It took Thurse forever to answer the bell. She'd already begun to stuff the grade cards through his mail slot when she heard the tumblers turn in the lock.

"Helen? Oh, lord!" Thurston said. "Don't tell me I forgot dinner again?"

Exasperated, Helen gathered up the scattered grade cards and thrust them into his hand. "Dammit, Thurse! It's only Monday, not Friday. You forgot to put down all your grades and Jennie Oglethorpe's going crazy."

Thurston looked at the cards as if they were some strange artifact. His khaki pants and shirt were dusty and his hair was disheveled, but his eyes glittered with laughter. "Grade cards!" he snorted. "I thought I was finished with them."

"You're losing touch with reality, kid. One more week to go till we're *all* finished with grade cards, so kindly—" Abruptly Helen realized that Thurse had stopped hearing her and instead seemed to be listening to something almost out of hearing.

"What was that?" she asked.

"Hm?" His lips seemed to quirk in secret amusement.

"That sound," she said. "Like a sheet flapping in the wind."

It was a warm still evening. Music floated through the window of the next apartment, a dog barked in the distance, a car door slammed down the street. Thurston cocked his ear in exaggerated pantomime. "I don't hear any wind."

Out at the curb, Marsh raced the motor and flashed his lights. As Helen started to leave, she saw in the hallway behind her brother his old khaki duffel bag with his navy blue mackintosh folded neatly on top. On the floor beside it rested Anne's canary yellow slicker and two pairs of black rubber boots.

Helen's eyes met his and a cold chill went through her. "Thurse?"

The question hung there between them, then he laughed. "As soon as I finish with school, I'm off to the coast. Guess I'm as bad as the students."

Out by the curb, Marsh lightly tapped the horn and Thurston leaned forward to kiss her forehead. "You've been a wonderful sister, Helen. This year's been almost as rough on you as it has on me, but you can quit worrying now, okay?"

She stood on tiptoe to return his kiss. "Okay. Talk to you soon?"

Marsh opened the car door. "Honey, please?"

"I'm coming, I'm coming!" she called, hurrying down the walk; but halfway to the retirement party, she remembered that Thurse hadn't answered her last question.

As she tossed and turned in bed that night, the thought made her feel oddly empty and, yes, afraid. She knew Thurse through and through. From childhood she'd seen him sick, depressed, exhilarated, worried, angry, grief-stricken, drunk, hungover, and a thousand other emotional states in between. But she'd never seen him in quite the mood he'd been in tonight, unless . . . she had a sudden memory of long-ago Christmas when Thurse was hoping desperately for a puppy. There was something of that same happy restlessness in him tonight—as if time would never pass quickly enough before something wonderful happened.

"Oh, my God!" she said and sat bolt upright in bed. A sudden vision went through her head of Thurston looping a rope over the exposed beams in his living room. Was that what he'd meant about being finished with grade cards?

"What is it?" Marsh said sleepily as she clicked on the lights and began dialing Thurston's number frantically. "What time is it?"

"Get up!" she cried. "Oh, Marsh, we've been so stupid! He was miserable for so long—then the picture—and now he's happy and talking about going away—he's going to kill himself. I know it!"

She slammed down the receiver, tore off her nightgown and threw on a pair of jeans, shirt, and sneakers.

Infected by her terror, yet trying to calm her, Marsh quickly slipped on pants and shoes and raced out to the car with her.

Even College Street shuts down by four *a.m.* and they tore through the deserted section of town in record time. Helen was out of the car before Marsh could turn off the ignition, racing across the wet grass with her spare keys jingling. Her hands shook so badly that it seemed to take forever before the right key turned in the townhouse lock.

She threw open the door and ran down the hall to the living room, switching on lights as she ran. Half sobbing, she burst through the living room door and halted.

Overhead, the exposed beams cast innocuous shadows upon the sloped ceiling. Gasping for breath, Helen hurried through the dining room to the kitchen testing the air for the smell of gas.

All was immaculately neat; the oven door was closed.

They backtracked to the hall stairs and there they saw what they had missed before.

"Look," said Marsh.

The duffel bags, boots, and rain slickers were gone, but scattered on the polished tiles like buff-colored confetti were the IBM grade cards Helen had given Thurse earlier.

Marsh took the stairs two at a time and flung open the bathroom door at the top.

The bathtub gleamed empty and white.

Beyond, the master bedroom was equally deserted except for the dresser top. There Thurse had carefully laid out his wallet, his credit cards, and the last five years of IRS returns, a pathetically modern gesture that drove home a chilling message.

They turned and slowly, fearfully, approached the second bedroom.

Inside, the shades were drawn. Except for the spotlight on the painting, the room lay in semi-darkness, but it took little light to see that this room, like the others, had been stripped of its most meaningful furnishings.

The lace bedspread was gone now, the dressing table empty except for a light layer of dust. Nothing much remained besides the furniture and other things people leave behind when traveling light could make a difference between getting there or not.

Numbly, they turned to the painting as comprehension swelled up along the edges of irrationality like a rising tide.

There, in the middle of the painting, almost at water's edge now, their faces turned to the sea, were Thurston and Anne. Hands clasped, their navy and yellow mackintoshes flapping in the wind, their boots kicked up sand behind them as they ran toward the waiting *Sea Dollar*.

In the stern, the boxes under the tarp rose twice as high as before and suddenly Helen knew that if the wind should tug aside one of the lids, she would see leather-bound books, a purplish conch shell, perhaps an old-fashioned toy cannon.

As for the old fellow in the boat, he stood in profile now, his face set in a smile of welcome for the two who hurried toward him.

"Wait!" Helen cried, reaching for the ornately carved frame.

She fell back with a cry as the eyes of the old man seemed to turn on her with full force and she realized that it wasn't a man at all, but the stoop-shouldered artist from the park. The old woman's necklace of amber shells and silver starfish hung low on her sagging breasts, the silver-and-shell bracelet gleamed beneath the sleeve of her rusty black slicker as she dropped two gold coins into her pocket. Her inky blue eyes dared Helen to touch the picture and Helen knew she lacked the courage to defy that warning.

Somewhere, way off, she heard Marsh speak and tried to answer, but her lips refused to move.

A sound not unlike the flapping of a canvas sail broke the silence; and, as they watched, the *Sea Dollar* ran with the surging tide and disappeared into the distance, sails billowing. The three occupants in the bow faded in a blur of midnight blue.

A whiff of salt air swirled around Helen and Marsh; cool breezes riffled their hair. Another crack of the sails and suddenly the waves stopped moving, suddenly it was just another badly executed seascape of empty painted waves and canvas sky.

Bereft, Helen clung to Marsh, torn between grief and terror.

Equally shaken, he held her tightly and made soothing noises. Yet, even as his mind rebelled against what they had just seen, he couldn't help thinking, *And all this time, I thought Charon was a man!*

THE PRAYING LADY

by Charles L. Fontenay

She was praying.

The man standing before her with his back to Breck concealed her except for a wedge from her right shoulder to her left waist. The startlement of coming in upon the scene flooded the lounge of *The Lermont Daily Spectator* with an eerie, timeless aura for Breck: the hushed room, one of the few carpeted areas in the newspaper building, the cushioned sofa and chairs, the water cooler in a corner—and Melody Schaeffer, partly seen, her hands folded and upheld to the male figure looming over her.

Momentarily Breck thought he had stumbled in on an incipient rape attempt and Melody was pleading for mercy from her attacker. But her big violet eyes upturned to the man before her were serene and there was no fear in her face.

He must have intruded on some private religious ceremony, Breck thought, and started to back out quietly. But the door squeaked.

The man started violently and half-turned toward Breck. Simultaneously Breck recognized him as Tommy

Knowles and realized Melody was kneeling on the sofa, skirt hitched up to her waist, wearing no underpants, thighs parted. Oops! No rape, folks, just a little private hanky-panky on the side.

With Tommy's movement Melody caught sight of Breck in the doorway. Dismay crossed her comely features, she scrambled off the sofa, smoothing down her skirt, and fled through the back door of the lounge, leading outside. Before she slammed it behind her Breck caught a glimpse of a panel truck backed up to the building, its back doors open.

"Sorry I interrupted," Breck apologized to Tommy.

"Guh?" inquired Tommy. Breck was struck by his expression: like a man coming out of a trance, not completely reoriented to his surroundings.

"Broke in on your playhouse," Breck explained. "I came in here to check over some notes on my martial arts feature without interruption. I didn't have any idea you were in here making out with Melody."

"Making out?" Tommy seemed to be struggling to gather his wits, the meaning of Breck's words sinking in on him gradually. "*I* wasn't propositioning the girl! And where'd she go? We stopped by here for a drink of water on our way to the cafeteria."

"Oh? How come your pants are unzipped, then?"

"What?" Tommy seemed genuinely surprised to find it true. "My God! They are! I hope Melody didn't notice!"

"How the hell could she *not* notice, when your fly's flapping open and your dong sticking up like a signpost

176

on the road to perdition?" Breck demanded dryly. "It's pretty clear what was going on."

Tommy hastily restored his apparel to a socially acceptable state and resorted to that common alibi of the guilty: "I don't remember."

"You don't *remember*? You don't remember *what*?"

"Damn, Breck, you're not going to believe this but I don't remember what just happened! I mean, Melody and I came in here like I said and then . . . well, everything's blank till you were there saying something to me, and she was gone. I didn't even notice her leave!"

Breck had no reason to disbelieve Tommy's disclaimer. The two young men had known each other for a long time and Tommy, *The Spectator*'s political ace, was known for his aptness at dallying with pretty young courthouse secretaries. If Tommy *had* been succeeding in what it looked like he was succeeding in as facilely as it looked like he was succeeding in it, he would have been inclined to boast about it a bit, not deny it.

Melody Schaeffer . . . now that was another matter. Discovering her all ready to go a round with Tommy on the lounge sofa wasn't quite as much a surprise to Breck as Tommy's strange lapse of memory—Breck didn't know her as well as he knew Tommy—but it ran a pretty close second. Coming to *The Spectator* only three months ago from somewhere out West, she was unmarried, though the mother of a young daughter, and exotically attractive enough to have drawn the vain attentions of the newspaper's stable of always-eager studs. But, while friendly enough, she was inclined to stay to herself, turning aside all invitations to a date.

The lounge was rarely occupied except during luncheon and supper breaks and while the staff was waiting for proofs to come up the tube, but people did wander in occasionally. Melody's reserved demeanor hardly fit the image of a woman who'd hike up her skirt and put out on the sofa in broad daylight when there was that much risk of being caught at it.

Breck could come up with no good explanation for what he had seen: Melody Schaeffer *praying* on the sofa, her skirt pulled up, and Tommy Knowles, his trousers unmasted and claiming to remember nothing of it. It was bizarre, unreal. Oddly, it brought to his mind an experience from his childhood.

When Breckinridge Forrest was six years old, his Uncle Joel conned him into tasting sheep shit.

The droppings of the Southdown sheep are round and black and about the size of one's fingernail. They look like little black berries and when Breck, observing a scattering of them in the short grass of the woodlot, asked Uncle Joel about them that's what Uncle Joel said they were.

"They're goopie berries," said Uncle Joel with a straight face. "They're good. Try a few of them."

Breck didn't actually eat any of the "goopie berries"—the foul taste when he bit into the little pellets made him gag and spit them out in a hurry. He despised Uncle Joel after that, as much for laughing at his discomfort as for fooling him in the first place. But the most profound effect of the experience was its disorienting jolt.

Accepting the evidence of his eyes and Uncle Joel's

words, Breck's comfortable conviction of his world as a predictable place was thrown into disarray by the revelation that not only were these berries not palatable—as he had been assured by an *adult!*—they were of a totally different order and class from that which they appeared to be. It was a strange and unsettling emotion for the boy, which he never forgot.

He felt the same sense of displacement from the sight of Melody Schaeffer praying ... and Tommy standing there with a hard on, not even aware of what was going on.

The incident had the effect of stirring Breck's interest in Melody Schaeffer, out of curiosity if nothing else. *The Lermont Daily Spectator's* city room was a spacious rectangle from one end of which the city desk supervised the multiple rows of the reporters' computer desks, and Melody's desk was two rows ahead of Breck's and a little to the right, convenient for casual observation but less so for conversation. The few words they found occasion to exchange at lunch or when he passed her desk aroused his interest further—he gained the impression she was an intelligent and sprightly young woman—but he was given no chance to promote these encounters into anything else. Tommy Knowles, once he realized how close he had come to scoring, made a determined play for Melody and she appeared to go along with his pitch willingly. They were dating two or three nights a week and, under the circumstances, the only thing surprising to Breck was that Tommy claimed he wasn't making out.

Breck was further nonplussed that this lack of carnal

success didn't cause Tommy, the man who boasted a near-100% seduction record, to drop Melody rather promptly and turn his eyes to some more promising prospect. He began to get an inkling of the reason for this deviation, on both sides, when Tommy confided somewhat sheepishly that an annoying attack of romantic sentiment was disrupting the normal process of his lust.

Well, well, Tommy Knowles was falling in love! And Melody obviously was encouraging it. She was undoubtedly holding out on him for the prospect of something more serious and permanent. That struck him as a most fortunate development which could settle Tommy down and make a decent, faithful husband out of him at long last. One of these days, he contemplated, such might even happen to *him*.

The only odd thing about Tommy's bright prospects was that just as Breck got the impression from Tommy that Melody was on the verge of yielding to his insistent importunity, Tommy vanished.

"Vanished" was the only word for it. It happened the night, or the day after the night, Tommy confided to Breck that Melody was farming out her daughter, Angelica, and promised an exceptional dinner prepared with her very own hands that evening.

"*I* don't know what got into the guy," complained Sid Pointer, *The Lermont Daily Spectator*'s city editor, when Breck pumped him on the matter. "Christ, he was drawing down top salary and I thought he was happy here. Didn't even bother to check out with me before he left, no two weeks notice, nothing, just a computer printout in the mailbox saying he'd gotten a job on another newspaper he couldn't turn down, and he was leaving."

"What newspaper?" asked Breck. "He didn't say anything to *me* about leaving for some other paper when I talked to him yesterday."

Pointer surveyed him from the status point of the battered city desk swivel chair. Pointer fancied himself the tough, hard-nosed city editor favored by the movies and occasionally smoked a foul cigar but was actually pretty soft-hearted with his staff when it counted.

"Now, you *would* think he'd tell us that, wouldn't you?" Pointer asked in an aggrieved tone. "But he didn't. Hell, I don't know where to send some of the junk he left in his desk, stuff I'd think he'd want—unless he gets in touch after he's settled in his new job."

Naturally, since they'd been dating and were supposed to have had a date the previous evening, Melody came in for some intensive questioning from both Pointer and Breck and probably from others on the staff when she came in to work.

"I don't know, he never said anything to me about another job offer," she said, appearing genuinely distressed. Melody had a soft voice, musical and hypnotic. "We were supposed to have dinner at my apartment last night and he never showed up—or called or left a message or anything. Do you suppose something's happened to him, mugged or something?"

"If he'd been mugged, he wouldn't have left that note

in the mailbox," Pointer pointed out. "If he wrote it. It wasn't signed, just the printed name."

"It was written the way he'd write it," said Melody. She had read the note. "But maybe he just didn't want to write a suicide note, Sid. He'd been depressed for several days. He wanted us to get married."

She didn't say whether or not she had accepted Tommy's proposal but the implication of the "suicide note" suggestion was that she had not.

"Tommy wasn't the suicidal type," Breck contributed. "I never figured him for the marrying type, either. Not belittling your unquestionable charms, Melody, but Tommy's had his heart broken before, several times, and he always goes out and gets drunk and has a new one on the string three days later."

"If he did himself in, it wasn't at his apartment, anyhow," said Pointer. "Just in case, I got the cops to check that out. He did leave all his clothes and stuff like his TV set there when he took off, but they won't go for a missing persons report because of that note. He doesn't have any relatives to get upset, and the police take the attitude he'll probably come back and get his stuff when he gets settled. They're probably right."

"Let's hope," said Breck. "If he does, maybe he'll be decent enough to stop by the office and say good-bye to all of us."

And so he did . . . except he didn't, exactly. A week later there was another computer printout note in Painter's mailbox, ostensibly from Tommy. In it he said he'd sailed through town to pick up his possessions but at an hour when no one was in the office. Tommy

182

would still have his ID card giving him access to the building, but none of the security people recalled seeing him go in or out—probably, each one said, on somebody else's shift. However, Tommy's stuff was gone from his desk and, on checking, so were his clothing and other belongings from his apartment.

"The invisible man," said Pointer wryly. "I wonder what he had against us?"

That seemed to dispose of the suicide theory, which Breck hadn't believed anyhow. It was his conviction, knowing Tommy, that Melody *had* accepted his marriage proposal, probably slept with him to seal it— which was the only thing Tommy had had in mind in the first place. As Breck had told Pointer, Tommy wasn't basically the marrying type, and Breck believed that as soon as Tommy realized the commitment he had made, he got cold feet and got out of there.

Since his friend Tommy had left Melody at the altar, so to speak, Breck felt it behooved him to comfort the deserted bride—a benevolent deed he had been ambitious to perform ever since that glimpse of Melody with her skirt hiked up, except Tommy had beaten him to it. A little to his surprise, Melody proved readily amenable to being so comforted. He asked her for a date a few days after it became clear Tommy wasn't coming back, she accepted, and they went to dinner together.

Melody got off work a couple of hours earlier than Breck and they met at the King Wan Restaurant, which claimed to offer authentic Cantonese, Szechuan, and Hunan dishes. The exotic Oriental motif of the place

harmonized fittingly with the mystery that had clung to
Melody in his mind since their first meeting.

As they ate sweet-and-sour chicken and Hunan pork
at a corner table beneath a pastoral scene adorned with
big red characters meaning, "good fortune and many
sons," Melody proved an even more diverse person than
his brief conversations with her had led him to suspect.
She confessed a preference for the Atlanta Braves and
the Dallas Cowboys on the sports scene, for mellow
and semiclassical music, and for science fiction and
entomology as reading fare.

"Entomology?" he asked. "I can understand the science fiction. I used to read the stuff myself when I was
a kid. Did you have entomology in college or something?"

"No, I'm interested in bugs," she said. "Sort of out of
character for a girl, isn't it? But so is my mother. You
see, insects differ from vertebrates in fascinating ways,
in structure and chemistry . . . and behavior patterns."

There was a curious inflection to her voice when she
said that, an ambience Breck couldn't place.

"Behavior patterns?" he repeated. It had never occurred to Breck that insects had any "behavior" worth
mentioning, just a matter of flying around or scurrying
around pretty much at random.

"The prevailing opinion is that it's exclusively genetic, not learned, but some insect behavior patterns
are complex," Melody told him seriously. "Especially
their mating patterns."

"Any favorites?" he asked. "Like bees or ants?"

"No, I'm more out in left field than that. I'll show you, sometime."

That wasn't a real strong signal, but it was encouraging. If she kept pet bugs, she wasn't likely to bring them to the office to show them to him. But if she was going to invite him to her apartment it wasn't tonight. When he escorted her to the restaurant parking lot, she led the way to her white Acura, thanked him for a pleasant dinner, and bade him good night.

"I thought you drove a panel truck," said Breck.

"What on earth gave you such an idea?" she asked with a quick, surprised look at him. "Who drives panel trucks, except for business?"

"That day I stumbled in on you and Tommy in the lounge," he explained. "Wasn't that your panel truck parked outside?"

"Oh, that," she said and laughed. "I rented that for the day, to haul away the carcass."

The unexpected words struck such a deep shock into Breck he was speechless. He stood staring at her, holding the door to her automobile open for her. Once again he experienced that sense of displacement like when Uncle Joel flummoxed him and he discovered that appearances and smooth adult assurances can be tricks to lure a boy into unpleasant and embarrassing situations.

"Ca . . . carcass?" he stuttered.

She looked into his face and laughed again, mischievously.

"What do you think I'm talking about, Breck?" she asked. "I bought a quarter of beef that day and rented the truck to take it home. I have a large freezer in my basement."

With that she leaned toward him and startled him totally by reaching back to caress his butt, briefly but firmly. Then she got in her Acura, smiled at him, and drove away.

He was hooked, of course. It was not the first time a good-looking woman had fondled his ass slyly but always before it had been after they'd been sharing sack time pretty regularly. Breck interpreted this as a *very* favorable omen.

The next day at the office he asked her out again that night, she accepted again and the next thing he knew they were seeing each other almost every night just as she and Tommy had been. And he discovered, or thought he did, some of the reasons independent Tommy Knowles had become attached to her so deeply and so quickly. Melody was not only bright, a good companion with a delightful sense of humor, she was the first woman Breck had ever met whom he could call genuinely *sweet*. She was thoughtful and considerate, seeming always in tune with his mood and responding to it. He was genuinely in love with her before the first week was past.

It was not long before Melody invited him to come to her apartment for a drink after their meal. He was making progress apace and all he had to do was continue playing it by the established rules and everything would fall into place nicely for him. By now he had come to the conclusion Melody was his ideal if he had ever seen her, and his memory of that strange tableau of Melody and Tommy Knowles in the lounge had dimmed to the point that when he thought of it he wasn't sure he hadn't imagined a great deal of it.

Melody's daughter Angelica was farmed out for the night with a sitter, she informed him as they took the elevator up to her spacious apartment. Melody established Breck at the end of a sofa and went to a bar in the corner of the room to fix their drinks.

Breck glanced around the room curiously. For an ordinary reporter on a median salary she lived comfortably. The tables and chairs were tastefully matched, the large painting of a fawn beside a clear pool on one wall looked genuine and the sofa was long enough, wide enough, and well-stuffed enough to have made a comfortable bed.

His eyes fell on the sofa end table and beside the telephone that sat there encountered a sight that brought him to his feet with a yawp. He looked around frantically for a newspaper or something to dispose of the weird sticklike insect, some two inches long, sitting near the phone and turning its knobby head to follow his movements with huge eyes. Breck hadn't known an insect *could* turn its head.

"No! Don't!" exclaimed Melody, the drinks in her hands, as he rolled up a copy of *Discover* magazine and raised it carefully. "It's one of mine!"

"Oh," he said, lowering the magazine. "You said you keep pet insects. What is it?"

"A praying mantis," she said. "I have about a dozen of them."

187

"A 'praying' mantis? What does it pray for?" Breck asked, looking at the insect.

She laughed.

"Its prey," she said. "It holds up its front legs like it's praying and sits very still, but there are sharp hooks on the inside of its arms. When another insect wanders close, thinking it's a twig, it strikes. I think the hooks contain a paralyzing narcotic. It really ought to be called the 'preying' mantis, with an E."

Odd pets Melody preferred, Breck thought as he looked again at the mantis. It was tilted on its haunches now, its forelegs raised in that praying posture Melody had mentioned. It reminded him oddly of Melody praying in the lounge that time.

"I let the mantids run free," Melody said. "They keep the place clear of bugs. I keep some other species caged up to study."

She led him into a small adjoining room where a number of glass cases stood around on tables, each case containing a number of different kinds of insects.

"Mimicry's one of the qualities developed by some insects for predation or defense," she said. "A predator may set a trap for its prey by resembling a harmless flower, for example, and some insects imitate objects like twigs."

She indicated one of the cages.

"Would you say all these butterflies are the same species?" she asked.

"Well, yes. Some are smaller than others, but. . . ."

"They're not," said Melody. "These little ones are Danaine butterflies, *Amauris altimaculata*, which have such an offensive taste that birds leave them alone. The others are a variation of the African swallowtail, *Papilio planemoides*, quite palatable to birds, but they've adopted the Danaine coloration so birds avoid them, too."

An odd thought flitted through Breck's mind. Maybe sheep shit could mimic berries to lure little boys into tasting it. Except there'd be no survival value to that, would there?

Melody chuckled and surveyed him with some amusement.

"An interesting aspect of insect mimicry," she said, "is that in butterflies it's confined to the female. The poor males are considered dispensable."

They returned to the living room and, instead of taking a chair or sitting at the other end of the sofa, Melody sat close beside Breck and after a bit she snuggled up to him and then turned her face to him and he embraced her and kissed her for the first time. It was a wonderful kiss, soft and sweet as a marshmallow, yet with a touch to it of that alien flavor of goopie berries and Uncle Joel.

Breck was subject to those extravagant hopes common to the male human when treated kindly by an attractive female of his own species, but his hopes did not deceive him to the point of unrealistic expectations. He did not really anticipate his first night in Melody's apartment developing into anything intimate nor did it. He felt sure Tommy had discovered Melody to be one of those women with whom one must be optimistically patient and so was he prepared to be. Since

Melody's behavior toward him on their subsequent dates was consistently affectionate, Breck refused to be discouraged.

He did not hesitate to make his ultimate objective known, however, nor that he desired the attainment of that objective as soon as she was willing. Breck had learned from experience that women usually appreciated such honesty.

"Look, if it worries you, I don't have AIDS or anything," he assured her. "And we can take precautions against you getting pregnant."

Her smile at him was amused.

"Procreation isn't the only biological use of sexual attraction," she said.

Soon afterward Melody took Breck to meet her mother.

"Sounds like she's got marriage in mind," suggested Chris Burson, the police reporter, when Breck told him about it at the office that afternoon before he went out with her. "Don't people take their significant others home to meet their families when marriage is in the offing?"

"Neither of us has mentioned marriage," demurred Breck. "She hasn't been married, her daughter's the product of a brief affair. Tommy Knowles wanted to marry her, but she never has said whether or not she accepted him."

Melody's mother did not live in an apartment but in a small house not nearly as elegant as her daughter's apartment. She was named Maureen and wanted to be called that, not Mrs. Schaeffer. She was a pleasant woman who looked much like Melody might look in another twenty-five years, fuller-bodied but middle-aged attractive. Maureen and her daughter were obviously very close; a wordless understanding lay perceptibly between them.

"Melody tells me you read science fiction," Maureen said over drinks.

"I did when I was a kid," answered Breck. "I used to wonder what an alien from some other world would look like."

"Fruitless speculation," she said. "An alien from some other planet probably couldn't live in a terrestrial environment. Mr. Forrest, have you ever thought there may be unrecognized 'alien species' right here on Earth?"

She gestured. As at Melody's apartment, Maureen had a collection of mantids and several were visible in the room, crawling on tables or clinging to curtains and turning their heads about.

"They mimic twigs and leaves by staying still and moving only their heads, to catch prey unawares," said Maureen. "But some insects resemble other species so closely the two species could live intermingled and you couldn't tell them apart."

Maureen proved herself a good cook. The roast was tender and tasty, with a faint sweetish flavor—Breck thought it was pork but didn't ask. Tommy would have enjoyed this meal, he thought; Tommy always did like barbecued pork.

"I see you're still using the big carving knife you had

when I was a little girl," said Melody as Maureen sliced off portions for them.

"Yes, it's served us well," said Maureen. "You may borrow it any time you need it for a special occasion, dear."

At dinner Breck met Melody's two younger sisters, Helen and Yvonne.

"They're all half-sisters, really," explained Maureen. "My husband died before Melody was born."

"Oh, you were married again?" he asked.

"No," said Maureen. She smiled. "Marriage can be so temporary. And it isn't really necessary these days for women who want children, is it?"

Breck thought he got it now. Melody's mother had established a family pattern of using men as studs . . . and probably tricking them into supporting her and her children economically. Maybe that was the symbolism of the mantids of which Melody and her mother were so fond: men were *their* prey. The question that arose in Breck's mind was whether Melody had been imbued by her mother with the same kind of motivation.

"You worry too much, darling," she said later that night when, back at her apartment, he referred obliquely to the matter. "I wouldn't take you for child support if I did get pregnant from you. I appreciate you too much for that, in a very different way. And Mother's not living off my sisters' fathers."

"Oh? Did they run out on her?"

"They died," said Melody. "Like my father."

Well, he thought, she was hardly likely to get pregnant from him unless she accepted him as a lover. By now he was too deeply involved emotionally with her to worry about such possibilities, anyhow. They got along beautifully and he had gotten acquainted with little Angelica and found he liked the girl very much. She was quiet, talking little, and sometimes when she looked at him Breck thought her gaze contained an element he also discerned in Maureen's, a certain calculation. Both of them, he thought, were assessing his potential as a mate for Melody.

Then one day Melody didn't come in to work. Sid Pointer said she had phoned in sick. Concerned, Breck telephoned her at home.

"It's nothing," she said. "I just didn't feel like coming in to work today. I want to spend the time preparing for a special meal. I still expect you to come over tonight."

Breck got away early. When he let himself in with the key she had given him, he was confronted with a major surprise: Melody was in negligee. Oh. *That* was what was special enough about tonight for her to stay home and make special preparations. The negligee made it almost a certainty, she had decided this was the night she'd accept him as her lover.

Alluring in the almost-transparent peach-colored garment, she welcomed him with a warm hug and escorted him to the sofa. Breck was moved to note how suitable this sofa would be for lovemaking.

"Angelica's home tonight but she's staying in her room until I call her," she said, bringing him a drink. "There's no hurry about dinner. It's going to be a special meal tonight."

Breck took a stiff slug from his drink and turned to

set it down on the end table. One of Melody's mantids was there, a big one. It was holding something between its upraised elbows, casually gnawing its head off.

"Your friend's got himself an insect," Breck said, repelled by the sight. The unfortunate victim twitched but seemed incapable of struggling.

"Herself," corrected Melody. "It's a female. She's just finished mating. They're like some spiders. They eat their mates afterward, sometimes while they're still copulating."

His sanguine assumption was correct. After their first drink, Melody prepared refills for them, then slipped off the negligee. Exquisitely naked, she climbed up on the big sofa beside him and knelt facing him, folding her hands together as though praying to him for relief.

"I desire you so much, I can't wait any longer!" she murmured, honey-sweet, half-closed eyes on his face. "Make love with me, Breck!"

His blood pounding in his veins, Breck stood up and divested himself of his clothing. Turning back to her, he realized she wasn't going to lie back on the sofa as he expected: she was still kneeling, her hands clasped devoutly before her face and her eyes completely closed now. Well, whatever strange way she wanted to do it suited him. He clambered awkwardly onto the sofa, knelt facing her and took her in his arms, moving his head aside to avoid the praying hands.

As soon as he embraced her, Melody leaned heavily against him, pushing *him* backward to a reclining position, and moved up astride him. Her hands still clasped above him before her face, she lowered herself upon him and engulfed his flesh. He succumbed to her in an ecstatic haze of surrender.

He was in her, enraptured, she moving rhythmically upon him. Gazing rapturously up the white column of her body, he thought he never had seen such beauty as glowed in her entranced features. As she whispered intimate endearments to him with closed eyes, all at once the violet eyes flashed open, she smiled sweetly upon him and ran her tongue over her teeth, and her climax shuddered voluptuously through her like the tumult of a storm wind.

"Come to me, darling!" she sighed, undulating, and she parted the praying hands to throw her arms wide like the spreading of wings and leaned far down over him.

Then he saw the long, deadly spikes, hinged at the elbows, unfold from the flesh of her forearms. He arched in orgasm even as the spurs struck deep into his sides at the waist. A paralyzing numbness seeped through his nerves.

Breck felt neither pain nor fear. He felt only that sickening let-down of aggrieved disbelief that the appearances of his secure world had deceived him ... like the goopie berries ... bitter-tasting sheep shit.

He was conscious, but he could not move. Melody, clutching him lovingly to her soft, warm body by the hooks that pierced his vitals, muttered greedily "Ahhh!" and lowered her open mouth to the side of his neck. Dimly he heard the phone ring and was aware she gingerly disengaged one of the hooks to reach over to the table and bring the instrument to her ear.

"Hello . . . Mother?" she mumbled through her feasting. "Why don't you and the girls join Angelica and me for dinner tonight?"

THE CURE

by Phillip C. Jennings

"A Fellowship of Young People Centered in Christ."
Making her way none too swiftly from Parking Lot D,
Dean Mohr's wife slowed even more. Her pedestrian
eyes lingered over the black-on-yellow sign; a hand-
lettered arch over the LSA Building's large picture
window.

A hundred times she'd driven her husband to campus, and always the same amazing words, always the
same brief sadness. Wendy was addicted, and weary of
her life's addiction. No doubt other people *were* centered outside themselves. *She* was the freak, so used to
her strange obsession she no longer found it hard to
deal with.

She no longer fought it, but still nobody knew. Nobody would *ever* know! Autoerotism carried to an ex-
treme. . . . Perhaps there were athletes who pranced
before their mirrors, but at least *their* weird kinks drove
them to discipline their bodies.

Not so for Wendy. *Her* peasant face, *her* mouse-
brown hair, *her* cellulite; therefore a perfect turn-on.
Her body could do no wrong. Not yet thirty, she

watched it bloat toward hefty matronliness with lewd delight . . . and a sense of moral defeat.

The feel of pantyhosed thighs slipsliding with every step . . . "My lover is always with me," she whispered. Intellectually she knew it wasn't enough, but she was hopelessly shackled to her special carnality. If all she could enjoy was her own abundant flesh—well, then, life was too short to waste!

Life was short and she was here. "I'm sorry," she announced to Mrs. Argenta of the committee. "I said yes to you over the phone, but I looked through my schedule afterward and I'm afraid it's just impossible."

"Really? We're *very* flexible. . . ."

Wendy suppressed a giggle. "They've asked for a huge block of time—you see, I'm going into Professor Neustrom's tank!"

Which was true. Blenwick University was a tight-knit community. Bad tactics to lie to someone who could easily check up on you.

Nevertheless Wendy fudged in describing the sequence of her obligations. She was tired of phoning and clerking, tired of the volunteer busywork expected of otherwise unemployed Blenwick wives. A great load lifted off her shoulders as she left Rosehill Hall and popped into the Student Union for a morning snack.

I hope he doesn't expect an empty stomach, Wendy thought as she nibbled her eclair. In a world filled with hes and shes she rarely identified the people in her thoughts. In this case the mental tag was an image of her in a wet suit, descending into tepid water.

A tight, slick wet suit. Part of her mind pursued this

crotic vision, another half comforted her doubts. Hunger had no place in a sensory deprivation experiment. In fact she should make sure of things beforehand, eat well, visit the bathroom.

Eat well. Punish myself with another eclair! Make myself so fat—Wendy had long since given up *opposing* the evil inside her, but sometimes she bent that evil to attack herself. *Good people must be very simple,* she thought, *because I'm so terribly complex!*

And hypocritical. She wouldn't buy that eclair here. Someone might keep track. Union Street was fast food row, and the Psychology Building lay down the other side, not far from where she'd parked the car.

More walking, and always that internal voice to keep her company. *Another form of narcissism, always analyzing myself as an exotic mutant!* Wendy wondered if a job might lift her out of wearisome egotism, but she was too lazy to look seriously for work.

Chinese or Greek? Greek food. Baklava. She halted by the newsstand and looked at her watch. The experiment began at one. She had a long meal's worth of time to kill. *Me in wet rubber! Wires and electrodes— will they weigh me? Sure, a whole physical exam!*

My 166 pounds bulging out of a wet suit! How can I get one if it turns out fun? I bet they cost money, and I've already shot my clothing budget. Feed a Haitian family of twelve on what I spend on clothes. There! All right to be selfish because I always let my conscience dump on me, and it's safe to do that because I never pay attention . . . God! More convolutions! Kill me, God! Stop this internal chatter!

Wendy began to have misgivings. Kids had sugar fits after too many sweets. She wondered if she was experiencing a spiritual sugar fit, even more psychic noise than normal. What would happen inside the tank? She could lose herself in all these multi-elemented dialogues!

And is it autoerotism after all? she pondered. *With so many voices, so many souls—one of them controlling my probing hands while another rules the rest of me? I may very well be the wrong kind of subject for Neustrom's study. Utterly and catastrophically wrong!*

Calm down! Yet despite herself Wendy pursued these thoughts right through dessert. *There's a male me with eager eyes and probing hands, the one with picture-images: me in a wet suit! And there's a female me, vain and spendthrift, deluded into thinking she's beautiful—the one who enjoys all that tickle-and-slap before the mirror. . . .*

It made sense. Wendy entered the Psychology Building. As she took the elevator to the seventeenth floor, two more identities came to light. *The peasant-wife me. No, she's not important. The only me who isn't selfish, but maybe that's because she doesn't exist. Except in my husband's mind?*

Isn't there another unselfish me? The sad, would-be Christian? Wouldn't SHE say I have an immanent loving God in me who can rescue me from all this hairsplitting?

In through door 707. Ahh, and the complex, psychological, hairsplitting me who's temporarily in control—Control of WHAT?

"You seem distracted," Professor Neustrom interrupted. Wendy was startled to find herself expeditiously shunted from office to lab. "I don't think you heard. I asked how long you wanted this first session to last. We can make it as short as forty minutes."

"No," Wendy answered, remembering Mrs. Argenta. Forty minutes would louse up her excuse. "Isn't there a two hour option?"

"A bit ambitious, but if you like." Professor Neustrom shrugged and turned, and found his clipboard. "Now just a few measurements, and then sign this release."

Wendy had so much to do those next minutes that she abandoned her soul-searching. The wet suit *was* a delicious novelty, if thick and ill-fitting, but she had no time to admire herself. Professor Neustrom was sandwiching her between other obligations, and eager to hurry along.

And finally, the wires, the pool, the lid . . . darkness!
Yoo-hoo! Anybody home inside?
OM MANE PADME HUM! OM SHANTI SHANTI SHANTI! I should be trying to meditate . . .

. . . two hours! Give it up! Even during my yoga days I never made it more than fifteen minutes!

Wendy pondered, wondering if her brow was wrinkled. Did she even *have* a brow? What was her body now except a theoretical base, a sensorium without sensation?

A substrate for all these identities. How many did I count? Six? Add one more, the weary, lazy, morally defeated me who tells me I can't meditate worth a damn!

And how different is she from the self-despising, secretive, judgmental me?

The fearful me?

That eclair this morning! Who am I mostly? A pleasure-loving, food-loving liar; a glutton-slut? Or the self-punishing me who eats for a different reason? Aha! Alliances! The despiser needs the despicable, or she's out of a job!

That makes the glutton-slut more basic, more real. The most horrible of possibilities! But no, it's the hyperanalytical me who just now created her!

Oh, God, am I going to be nattering like this for the whole two hours? How much time has gone by?

She had no way of telling. Outside the tank Professor Neustrom's graduate assistant walked in and was greeted by a curt nod. He picked up his books as the academician vanished back to his office. The clock read 1:18.

Inside the tank Wendy was rapidly becoming a hypothesis, a mathematical set—no, that was a little too vague. She was a set of *identities*, and identities had to have behavioral quirks to distinguish themselves. What might do the trick? Floating in water . . . of course! She was a ship, the good old Ship of Fools!

Down in her art-deco dining hall her glutton-slut character was having lunch; waddling along the groaning buffet table, plate loaded with hors d'ouevres. And who was her enemy? The waiter, snooty and French. *"May I suggest the '87 Cabernet, madam, to go with your Cheez Curls and malted milk balls?"*

Next to the Purser's office a door marked "Chaplain"

cracked open. Reverend Sadchristian drifted out, graying and weak of chin, pained by all the wealth and color around him. He raised his basset-hound eyes. *"Tut, tut, Wendy, you have two hours, two precious hours, and better ways to spend them than in mere fantasy!"*

"So abandon ship! This is madness!" added her fear persona—oh, God, that phobic nuisance! *"Purser, keep that maniac off the bridge, take her to the ship's doctor and put her under sedation."*

The performance stopped, characters froze in place. *Well now, who should play purser?* Wendy lacked a truly clerkish persona, someone who kept track of valuables and remembered people's faces and names. She sorted through and decided to give her male aspect the job. Maybe Purser Happyhands would cop a feel as he wrestled terrified Mrs. Ditherfit down to the clinic!

. . . Where Doctor Hairsplitter stood waiting with the syringe. *"Not again, dear? You're really far from the strongest voice among us! This should put you away for the duration."*

"Doctor, you've got to know! If you're here, then there's nobody on the bridge! Nobody's sailing this ship! Nobody's steering it from the breakers!"

Doctor Hairsplitter administered the anesthetic and watched Widow Ditherfit slump onto her gurney, her emaciated torso enmeshed in a loosely-woven black shawl. His lips tightened in thought. Perhaps the woman was right. Would Wendy's lazy, defeated Lieutenant Spiritless bother to steer the ship?

He left the clinic and found Spiritless boozing it up in the Cabaret Lounge. The bar stood at one end of the long nightclub, at the other Wendy's female aspect paraded about the stage in feathers and boas, practicing her striptease.

"*You're needed up on the bridge,*" Doctor Hairsplitter whispered to the morose drunk in the white uniform. "*Captain's orders.*"

"*Ain't no Captain,*" Spiritless answered, bringing his eyes into focus. "*The company offered me the job, but I don't want it.*"

"*Somebody's GOT to be Captain,*" Hairsplitter retorted. "*No, wait a minute. Cancel. That can't be me, it's not my voice.*"

"*It's mine,*" growled the intercom. "*What a bunch of shits, just moping around: Get off your ass, Spiritless—if you know how!*"

"*Who—where are you?*" asked Hairsplitter.

"*Radio Officer, but don't bother to come see me. I'm the secret Wendy. Secret, self-despising, judgmental: I'm not sure I deserve a name! In any case I'm not staying aboard this Ship of Fools five minutes longer. I'm heading for the lifeboats!*"

"*See?*" moaned Lieutenant Spiritless, pouring himself another drink. "*His job to goad me to action, and he won't even stay around to do it!*"

Doctor Hairsplitter heard a giggle and turned. On the stage Purser Happyhands joined the stripper and they danced together, close and tight. Wendy lost track of how much time she spent whirling in her own close embrace, but finally she achieved a moment of ecstasy that turned immediately to ashes.

Reverend Sadchristian dropped to his knees in his

small chapel, not so much to pray as to deplore: *"Again, again!"*

Wendy paced from room to room, taking dizzy inventory. Not far away in the dining hall Mrs. Glutton-Slut wiped her face, smearing her chocolate cheeks. She was significantly fatter now; the seams giving way on her muumuu. *"I'm still hungry!"* she whined, and her mock-waiter came, tray laden with yet another series of desserts.

The radio room was empty. Yes, the nameless officer was gone, never more than a ghost. The thought reminded Wendy of that empty Captain's bridge, and of Widow Ditherfit down in the clinic.

Except Mrs. Ditherfit *wasn't* in the clinic any more! Her anesthetic had worn off!

Oh, dear! Wendy sent Doctor Hairsplitter scurrying. Lieutenant Spiritless was no use, but *somebody* had to keep the old widow out of the Captain's bridge!

No problem. Doctor Hairsplitter was vigorous, while Mrs. Ditherfit still tottered from the drug. Except . . . *What was this? Reverend Sadchristian?* "Get out of my way!" Hairsplitter shouted. *"Out of the way, you old fool!"*

"No! You're the fool to interfere! You want to continue like this all your life? A prisoner on our ship's barren course? Do you really want to cling to such a poor existence?"

He had some gumption after all! They scuffled, then broke and began to swing clumsily. Sadchristian's blows delayed Hairsplitter until Mrs. Ditherfit reached the bridge. She moved to the Captain's mike. *"NOW*

HEAR THIS! NOW HEAR THIS! ABANDON SHIP!
ALL HANDS ABANDON SHIP!"

From port to starboard and stem to stern klaxons began to whoop. Startled from post-coital bliss, Purser Happyhands grabbed the stripper and they puffed urgently through curtains and up stairs, flapping and bouncing their overdeveloped pink way toward boat deck, naked as the day they were born, and a good deal steamier.

Widow Ditherfit watched from her coign of vantage in the captain's dinghy, and saw the long-legged waiter run to join the naked duo, a new expression on his face, boggled eyes instead of a sneer. The three tore off the tarp and clambered into their boat while her davit swung her out. Lowering to freedom, she noticed the radio officer already far at sea.

Meanwhile Doctor Hairsplitter and Reverend Sadchristian stopped their useless fighting, and dashed off toward open air to save themselves. WHOOP! WHOOP! Behind them the grotesque Mrs. Glutton-Slut puffed, barely able to waddle, her pudding-arms loaded with plates.

"So hungry—will there be food on the boat? Is there any food? Won't anybody tell me?"

The ship's alarm drowned out her words. Lieutenant Spiritless wove into sight, hands over his ears against the blare, and blinked. *"Too much! Well, I'm certainly not going to be left behind with YOU!"*

Lurching through the bulkhead onto the deck, he noticed three empty davits and shook his head. *"What's the use of a boat?"* he mouthed at the faces looking up from the bobbing craft below. *"What's the use of life at all?"* He climbed onto the railing and casually let go, a white ragdoll making an arms-out tumble into the waves.

Even as he fell, the alarm cut off suddenly. In another universe Professor Neustrom's graduate student set down his book, picked up his clipboard and punched the shutoff bar. After noticing the time he drew the shades, moved to the tank, and lifted the lid.

He looked inside and his polite smile faded. Dean Mohr's wife closed her eyes against the muted light; a form of reflex, but when she opened them again, they seemed strangely unfocused. Her whole face had a dreamy vacancy. "Are you okay?" the psych student asked.

No answer. "Mrs. Mohr?" he asked again, reaching for her hand. "Time's up. Your two hours are over."

Wendy looked at the young man. After a long pause, words finally came. "Such peace! I feel so empty, so purged, so totally *unified!* This . . . this tank has changed my life!"

The student helped her stand, and climb out of the tank. "No anxieties? Some people have a hard time."

Wendy shook her head. "A little, toward the end. I remember wanting to get out, to get away, but that was because of the alarm. And I seem to recall little pest voices buzzing in my head, but now they're gone. I tricked my demons into leaving me and now I feel such *peace!* You can't *imagine!* I'm the only one inside my mind, and it's like I'm a new person!"

With these words Wendy climbed out clumsily, and accepted a towel. *Peace, Transformation, Unity—'only one inside my mind'* the graduate student penciled. "Professor Neustrom would like a post-session interview," he reminded her, looking up as she headed for the dressing room.

He frowned, wondering at her exaggerated waddle. "Oh, dear, right away? I'm *so* hungry," Wendy answered. "Do you have any candy with you? Is there a grill in this building?" She smiled to wheedle the student out of the last of his M&Ms. "You see, I've just *got* to have something to eat!"

STILL WATERS

by Barry B. Longyear

Benjamin Waters sat at the far end of the counter in Izzy's Deli on East 74th Street sipping his coffee. The pin-striped fellow to his left asked for the salt and Benjamin pushed it gently in the man's direction.

"Thanks," said the suit.

Benjamin didn't answer. The man looked and smelled like a lawyer. Besides, Benjamin Waters was fully engaged in studying the perfectly pear-shaped buttocks on the waitress behind the counter. She was new.

Suzie was usually behind the counter at noon. This one's name was Nola. Benjamin felt his lips grow dry. He did not moisten them with his tongue, however. Too revealing. Instead he sipped his coffee and used Izzy's decaf to provide the necessary moisture.

The way Nola moved. The way she moved beneath that sheer yellow uniform. It was obvious how she was making him do it. The way she jiggled forced Benjamin to lean over the counter, grab her hips with both hands, lift her high in the air above his head, and begin biting. Biting through the phony lace apron strings, biting through the yellow polyester, biting through the black knit panties he just knew were beneath, biting deep into the creamy pillows of her buttocks, the feral cries coming from his throat, the hot blood drowning the cries, the warm wetness of it running down his chest onto the floor—

"Would you like me to freshen that up?"

The waitress, Nola, had ripped into his thoughts. Benjamin pulled his mind back from his imaginary cannibal feast and glanced up at her. Nola's lips, touched with the color of ripe peach, were parted in a smile that revealed a slight overbite. In her hand was a half full pot of coffee, its orange plastic handle branding it as decaf.

Benjamin looked down at his cup as he felt the heat rise in his collar. "Please," he answered.

The heat, he knew, was the last vestige of an alien feeling called embarrassment; a feeling that suspected that others might be able to see what he was thinking, and might catch him thinking it.

He knew no one could see what he was thinking. No one could tell, no one could react, accuse, or punish. He almost had the feeling entirely conquered. Once his victory was complete, he could experience his chosen realities at will, while continuing to travel within the one that contained Izzy's Deli, East 74th Street, and the Merit Literary Agency where he held down a desk and attempted to sell literature to baboons who were only interested in purchasing "another." Another *Godfather*, another *Carrie*, another Ninja damned turtle rapping Muppet heap of horseshit.

"You're Benny Waters, aren't you?"

"Benjamin." He looked up at her. She was still smiling. "How do you know me?"

"Suzie. She told me all about you." The outside ends of her eyebrows were turned wickedly up. Her eyes were greenish blue.

"She told you what about me?"

He felt light-headed; his skin tingled. Trapped. She's got your number, Benjamin Waters. It's all over for you. Your secrets are everyone else's idle gossip. The cops are waiting outside the deli door.

Suzie had done some time in Benjamin's fantasies, although he never before suspected that she suspected. Her suspicions could have only been in the general, he reminded himself. After all, the specifics had been rather lurid, involving at times several partners, and once a well endowed Clydesdale, straight off the beer wagon.

"Suzie said you're a literary agent."

"I work for one," said Benjamin. "The Merit Agency, around the corner."

Why did her eyes seem to speak a different language? She had knowing eyes. Sherlock Holmes had eyes like that. "It must be interesting work," she began, but was interrupted by another customer who wanted coffee. As she left, Benjamin glanced down at his watch. It was approaching time for him to end his lunch break. He looked up and allowed his eyes a moment longer to continue their exploration of Nola's buttocks.

Someone was watching him.

The cop sitting facing him from one of the tiny imitation wrought iron tables near the street window had a face like a shark: white, dead, and full of menace. The officer was looking at him, his thick lips curled into a sneer. "You have to do it with your eyes 'cause you can't get one in your hands," said the patrolman's look.

Smart said let it go. Whoever listened to smart?

"Why don't you write a book about it, asshole?" Benjamin shouted across the deli at the cop. Everyone, eyes wide and mouths open, looked first at Benjamin, then at their immediate surroundings to determine who Benjamin had been addressing. The cop, his brow knotting into a storm, rose to his feet and cocked his head as he tucked his thumbs behind his gun belt.

"What did you say?"

"Don't tell me you're deaf as well as stupid, you butt ugly, blue-fuzzed flatfoot asshole you." Benjamin closed his eyes, put back his head, and laughed at the officer.

"I said it," he shouted, "I said it, and I'm glad I said it, I tell you! Glad! Glad!" He laughed again.

When he opened his eyes, he saw that the officer's gun was out of its holster, aimed in his direction. The gun jumped, the concussion smacking every eardrum in the room, as it fired.

Benjamin quickly grabbed the lawyer, and using him as a shield, pushed his way toward the enraged cop. He felt the lawyer's body twitch violently each time one of the officer's slugs tore into it. When he was a step from the cop, he shoved the lawyer's lifeless form into the officer and disarmed him.

Once he had the gun in his hands, Benjamin blew

the cop away, turned, and smoked a customer who attempted to help the officer, and pulped the face of the customer behind the first just for good measure—

"Here's your check," interrupted Nola.

"Thanks," answered Benjamin as he looked to see the amount.

He pulled out three dollars for the tip. He usually left two for Suzie. Nola was different. Special. It was the eyebrows. The mouth. The eyes.

On his way to the cashier, Benjamin passed the patrolman. The cop was halfway through a lettuce and tomato sandwich. "Still watching the calories, Tony?" Benjamin asked the cop.

"Yeah. The doc wants fifteen more pounds off by the end of next month. Hey, Benny, how do you stay so skinny?"

"Surgery, seltzer, and celery. And that's Benjamin."

Tony the cop laughed. "Yeah, sure. Later." He went back to his sandwich as Benjamin handed his money and check to Julio and stepped into the chill that was whistling down the street. He pulled up the collar of his coat against the wind and turned the corner. There, huddling for warmth in a doorway was that same damned bum that whined at him for money every time he passed. The same damned army blanket for a coat, the same damned red stocking cap with the holes in it. The bum did it again.

"Hey, buddy. Can you spare a couple of bucks? I'm really hurting. Can ya, buddy? Huh?" The begging in his voice was not matched by the look in his cold gray eyes. The eyes said, I know I got you. I got you right by the guilts. You got a job. I can see you got a job. The world can see you got one and I don't. The money is mine. I got a right to it. You *owe* me.

"Owe you? I *owe* you?" Benjamin stepped into the doorway and faced the derelict. "Here, you son of a bitch." He reached beneath the bum's blanket and pulled out a three-quarter-full bottle of muscatel. "Here's your god, you bug-infested piece of shit! Ask *it* for money! Ask *it* for a place to sleep!"

The bum grabbed for the bottle. Benjamin took it and shoved it neck first into the derelict's mouth. He smacked the bottom of the bottle with the heel of his hand, driving it down into the man's throat. As the bum choked, Benjamin kicked the bum's legs out from beneath him. Down he fell, smashing his head on the concrete landing, the bottle still caught in his throat, the cheap wine filling his esophagus. Benjamin hauled back his foot and swung the toe of his jack boot at the bum's chin, shattering the glass as it struck—

"Thanks, Benny," said the bum as he took the two dollars Benjamin had given him and tucked it away beneath his blanket coat. "Give those publishers hell."

"Sure, Freddy. Take care of yourself."

The bum hid his hands beneath his armpits and stamped his feet against the cold as he looked past Benjamin for the next touch of the day.

"And it's not Benny; it's Benjamin," he muttered.

On his way back to his office, Benjamin Waters forced a middle-aged matron to eat her own poodle's feces, followed by the poodle. He left her hanging in a tree by her dog's rhinestone studded leash. In addition, he tore out the tongue of a loud cabbie, jammed a coin pot up the ass of a bell-ringing Salvation Army sergeant, cut the throat of a pushy flower lady, and had sex with a cover girl model in the back of her maroon limo.

Just before he entered his own building, he decided that he had had enough. He was fed up and he wasn't going to take it anymore. At that moment the Chrysler Building imploded, sending the entire column of rubble down to the street in a choking cloud of mental dust. Prior evacuation of the building had not been a particular concern of Benjamin's, since allowing oneself to work in such a structure in effect condoned the thing, compounding the crime.

Before his desk at the agency, Benjamin Waters mentally flipped a coin. Heads he would call his therapist. Tails he would call the next editor on his worksheet. The mental coin, as it always did, came up tails.

The editor was Colin Dean, a dribbling case of arrested mental development who couldn't tell Voltaire from a voltmeter. Dean might be interested in the new Roger Parish novel, but Benjamin had been warned in advance not to expect anything near what Roger had gotten for his first novel. Times are lean, budgets are tight, and that's how that song is played.

Benjamin was convinced that Colin Dean had spent his entire perverted youth watching *Baretta* reruns. And that's the name of that game.

At Grover Hill, Dean's secretary put Benjamin on hold. His ear filled with Bobby Darin's rendition of

"Mack the Knife," Oh, the shark bites, with his teeth, dear, scarlet billows, eek, eek, etc.

Benjamin hated being put on hold, particularly when he knew it was only for effect. He could see Colin Dean, that eternal smirk on his pasty face, looking at the telephone as he left his office to gab with someone or to take a leak.

Enough was enough. It wasn't all games, deals, and hey baby on the telephone. Roger Parish needed to eat, too. His family needed to eat. No one can spend four years writing a book only to get a fifteen thousand dollar advance and expect to live and support a family.

Put Benjamin Waters on hold. He's only second string at Merit. A little cool down time on hold will set the proper tone for negotiations. You give us the book; we give you squat. Have a nice day.

Benjamin lowered the receiver to his desk, grabbed his coat, and in moments he was on the sidewalk hailing a cab. How long would he have on hold? The last time Colin Dean had kept him there sixteen minutes. The time before it was closer to twenty.

The cab pulled up to the curb before a familiar structure on the row. Throwing a twenty at the cabbie, he rushed into the lobby and took an express elevator to the twenty-first floor, the home of Grover Hill, Ltd. They used Ltd. instead of Inc. because they thought it lent a touch of class to a publishing house keeping itself afloat through cookbooks and soft core porn. Benjamin pushed his way into the lobby and past the receptionist into a door-lined corridor. Reaching a tee, he turned left. He knew the way to Colin Dean's office, and he marched toward it with the resolve of a professional assassin prepared to risk all to settle a matter of the deepest honor. "I do not purchase regret at such a price!" he cried.

"Hold it!" shouted a voice from behind. He kept marching until he heard the distinctly metallic click of a gun being cocked. He froze, turned slowly, and looked at the security guard advancing upon him, his pistol held in regulation dual, stiff-armed fashion. He had been hired during the Salmon Rushdie scare because Grover Hill had a Middle East cookbook on the stands with a cartoon of a camel on it. In later editions the Middle East became Manhattan and the camel became a couple of home boys munching baklava and collard greens.

"Stay cool, buddy. Whatever it is, we can talk about it. Okay? Just stay cool." More late night, *Hill Street Blues,* I-can-talk-him-down, crisis intervention dialogue.

"Death to baklava!" Benjamin screamed as he sprang to his left through an open doorway. As he did so the guard's gun barked, the slug splintering the door frame. In the office there was a middle-aged woman in jeans, plaid flannel shirt, and bifocals sitting at one of four desks in the office. Her desk was piled with book manuscripts: wrapped, unwrapped, rewrapped. The hopes of countless pitifully naive writers who wanted nothing more out of life than to share their visions, touch a piece of fame, and eat once in a while. The woman had long stringy brown hair, wide frightened eyes, and incredible body odor. Her feet were up on the desk, and

217

the manuscript she had spread on her lap slid to the floor as she held her hands to her mouth.

Benjamin felt there were some things he should say to her on behalf of the manuscripts and their authors, but they all jammed in his throat at once. How many times had she ditched a promising writer's career because her stomach was upset, or a cabbie was rude, or her PMS meter was off the scale? How many careers and lives had been trashed because the author's pages had not contained the politically correct slant, the cause of the moment, the verbal wash-and-wear fad of the hour? There was simply too much to say. Bending over, Benjamin took the dull-edged letter opener off her cluttered desk, thrust its point through her left eye and out the back of her head. She hadn't even had time to scream. Her mouth was open, a single string of drool hanging from her astonished lower lip.

Withdrawing the letter knife from her head, Benjamin whirled and faced the door. Across the hall was the closed door of Colin Dean's office. His name was on the door's frosted glass pane.

"I'm coming for you, Dean!" he bellowed. "Do you hear me? I'm coming for you!"

It would be simple. Run, leap across the hall, dive through the glass panel, and take Colin Dean and throw him through his own office window. That accomplished, he could then shout after him, "If you can't do the time, Colin, don't do the crime!" After that it wouldn't matter what happened.

Taking a deep breath, Benjamin braced himself against the dead reader's desk and—

"Sorry to keep you on hold for so long, Benny." The sounds of "Mack the Knife" had been replaced by the words of Colin Dean. The editor's voice was soft and articulate. Benjamin looked at the receiver in his hand as though it had appeared there through magic. He turned and looked around his office: the desk, the filing cabinets, the birch paneled walls. He rubbed his eyes and shook his head as he listened on the phone. Part of him was still across town trying to kill Colin Dean. As he sat in his office he could hear the glass shattering, Dean's screams as his body hurtled toward the sidewalk.

"If you can't do the time . . ."

And Dean was talking in his ear about the Roger Parish manuscript. Grover Hill's editor was still alive. Despite that, the day turned out rather well. The final figure on the Parish novel came in with a broom strapped to its bowsprit. Simple really. Colin Dean kept interpreting Benjamin's stunned silence as someone who could not believe the crap he was being offered and was about to take a walk. They eventually settled on an amount for Roger's manuscript that was almost triple the author's previous advance. In addition, Dean gave Benjamin Waters the biggest compliment an editor can give a literary agent. He said, "You're getting to be a real pain in the ass, Benny. I won't be so easy next time."

After the talk was ended and Benjamin had hung up, he collapsed on his desk in tears. He was listening to the sirens as the crowd on the sidewalk gathered around Colin Dean's bloody smashed corpse.

"You are the one who asked for this session, Benjamin," said his therapist. "I had a devil of a time getting hold of someone to cancel to make a hole for you. Now that you've got it, what's the emergency? You're just going to sit there?"

Don Franklin was tweedy, bookish, and blinked large blue eyes through oversized lenses. He looked like a bass who taught comparative literature at Columbia. His foot twitched impatiently. "Well?"

"Thanks for the support, Don."

The therapist grimaced, took a deep breath, and nodded as he let it out. "Okay. I'm steamed. This wasn't the most convenient emergency you've ever had. Anyway, I apologize. I know you can't pick your moments. But I did say they'd get worse if you quit therapy."

"It takes real class not to say I told you so, Don."

Don Franklin's eyebrows went up. "Look, you can either tell me what's the matter, sit there like a post, call me names, or whatever. You're going to be billed for the time all the same."

Benjamin leaned forward, rested his elbows on his knees, and felt the tears well in his eyes. "It's really getting out of control. It used to be fun. It still is fun a lot of the time. I get to do things, say things, that a lot of people would secretly like to do—"

"No," interrupted the therapist. "You do *not* do those things, and you do *not* say them. It's all in your head. It's all fantasy."

"I hear them. I see them. Hell, I even smell them."

"No, you don't, Benny. You don't see them, hear them or smell them. . . ." Benjamin listened in astonishment to the therapist. He couldn't remember why he had called the idiot in the first place; his superior attitude, his lies, all of his own unresolved issues. The man was being paid to infect his clients with his own disease, and now finally it had come out. Don was totally out of touch with reality.

After all, he had just called Benjamin Waters "Benny." Everyone in the world knew about that. Benjamin sprang out of the chair, whirled about, and struck Don Franklin in the head with his naked foot. The therapist fell backward over his chair and scrambled to get to his feet. Again the ball of Benjamin's callused foot struck his head, again, and again until Don Franklin's body was still, the blood from his nose, mouth, ears, and eyes pooling on the hardwood floor.

"Benny, are you all right?"

Benjamin lifted his head from his desk, opened his eyes, and looked up to see Alex Merit's concerned face peering in the door. "I was resting my eyes, Mr. Merit. I guess I have a bit of a headache." Benjamin decided against calling Don Franklin for an appointment. What would be the point? The man was hopeless.

He tapped his fingers on the papers in front of him. "I just finished talking with Colin Dean at Grover. We have an offer on the new Parish novel."

"Oh?" Alex Merit pushed his way into the small office and took the papers from Benjamin's outstretched hand. His florid jowls quivered as his quick eyes scanned the worksheet. "Excellent," he murmured beneath his breath as his eyebrows went up. "Excellent," he said out loud. "I'm proud of you, Benny. You've done a fine job here. Take your headache and go home, son. You've earned yourself the rest of the day off."

"Thanks, Mr. Merit. I might do that."

"You've been here long enough, Benny. Call me Alex."

"Only if you call me Benjamin."

Alex Merit laughed and nodded. "That's right. Benjamin. Okay, Benjamin."

After Mr. Merit left his office, Benjamin waited to see if some trailing feather of fantasy might make him a junior partner in the agency or bring the entire building down in flames, but nothing materialized. Anyway, he did have a slight headache, and he felt emotionally drained. Benjamin decided to grab a bite to eat at Izzy's and head on home.

At the deli he and the waitress Nola were the only occupants. Julio, who usually manned the cash register, was in the back. Benjamin had barely started undressing Nola to take her upon the counter when she placed the hot corned beef on rye in front of him. "Here you go," she said, her wicked smile hovering beneath those wicked eyebrows. "I made it just the way Suzie said you like it." She leaned her elbows on the counter as Benjamin lifted the sandwich and took a bite. It was delicious. Better than delicious, it was erotic. As Benjamin chewed, Nola's full bosom strained against the front of her uniform.

"So, how do you know Suzie?" Benjamin took another bite and mentally sank his head between Nola's heaving breasts.

"We've been roommates for a few weeks."

Benjamin took a sip of decaf and positioned his sandwich for another bite. "And what's Suzie been saying about me?"

"She calls you Still Waters. That's your last name, isn't it? Waters?"

He nodded.

"She says you never reveal anything about yourself, but your head is smoking every second."

He shrugged and took another bite of his sandwich. "They can't put you in jail for what you think."

Nola nodded, picked up a slice of pickle from Benjamin's plate, and placed it upon her tongue. As she slowly chewed it she said, "That's why no one will go to jail for all of the murders that happened in here today."

"Murders?" Benjamin frowned and studied Nola's wicked eyes. "All of them?"

"Dozens. One customer was chainsawed to pieces just two stools down from you."

Benjamin glanced at the gleaming silver stool and returned his gaze to Nola's eyes. "I bet you had a time cleaning up."

She lowered her voice. "Of course. We had to lock up the place and remove our uniforms to keep from getting blood all over them." Her voice came deep and breathy. "I didn't have time to shower. There's still some blood on me."

Benjamin stared at the waitress until he realized he had been chewing the same mouthful for minutes. He swallowed and spoke. "Nola, do you think I might call you some time? Maybe we could go to dinner and take in a movie."

Nola nodded, her hooded eyes not even blinking as they fixed Benjamin to his stool. "I'm done here in another half hour, Benjamin. How about tonight?"

He sipped his coffee, nodded, and said, "Call me Benny."

MESSENGER

by Adam-Troy Castro

The Messenger's arrival in her life would have been impossible in the summer. In the summer, when the sun was a blinding flower in the sky and the ocean was packed solid with the laughing forms of tourists, Tricia avoided the beach: there were so many people there, living so many different lives with such little show of effort, that it was impossible for her to wander among them without feeling like a despised visitor from another world. In the winter, the beach changed character, becoming the perfect habitat for a person like her: the sky was gray and the water frigid and the vast stretches of sand abandoned by everything except the flocks of mad shrieking gulls. In the winter there were no loud radios blasting songs about the love affairs she'd never have, no beautiful young people playing volleyball with the beautiful friends she'd never share, no lifeguards mocking the urges she felt every time she looked at the endless expanse of pitiless ocean. In winter she had the beach to keep her company, and in winter, she roamed the water's edge, searching for something she did not have the wit to name, and touched only by the waves that obliterated the foot-prints she left in the sand.

Tricia was a thin, owlish woman, with short black hair and watery blue eyes magnified to the size of sau-cers by her coke-bottle eyeglasses. She looked much older than her years: not the kind of old that an-nounces itself with wrinkles and gray hair, but the kind that expresses itself with the pursed lips and hesitant speech of those who have been taught to constantly apologize for themselves. It was the kind of old that made people her own age overestimate hers by a dec-ade or more: the kind that made customers who'd fre-quented her tiny bookshop for years still have trouble remembering her name.

She hadn't really meant to visit the beach today. It was too damn cold, even for her: the wind chill factor had combined with a killer cold front to turn the air into something capable of instantly draining the heat from her bones. She'd meant to spend the afternoon at home, catching up on her reading. She'd even looked forward to it: it had been weeks since she'd managed to read anything. Normally she loved books—she lived for them—and normally she loved the winter precisely be-cause it made evenings spent reading at home so com-fortable and cozy. But as this latest, unusually brutal, winter shot down from the north to totally eradicate the last remaining warmth of the fading summer, decipher-ing the words on the printed page had become impos-sible. For weeks, every time she'd tried to read she found herself turning page after page without absorbing any meaning from the words. Today, sheer stubbornness got her all the way through one chapter when the music she was playing reached the end of the tape, leaving her suffocating in a tiny room where the only sound was the soft hiss of her own breath. Before she knew it, she'd thrown on her coat and fled out the front door to the dubious comfort of the beach, and was hugging herself for warmth by the time she traveled half a mile.

The Messenger arrived in the form of a bottle a breaker deposited in the sand by her feet. She wasn't surprised; the Atlantic is filled with garbage, and bottles compose much of it. Once or twice she'd even found empty champagne bottles, tossed corked into the ocean for her to find: taunting messages, from unknown revelers, that somewhere people other than her had something to celebrate in their lives. But this bottle was gallon-size, and it was delivered to her by a wave that reached out with a will of its own to place it gently at her feet.

Tricia had always prided herself on her cold rationality. The world as she understood it was made of concrete and right angles, with no loose corners to put anything that didn't fit. But there was no doubt in her mind, as the bottle glistened before her in a festive gift-wrapping of seaweed, that the ocean had deliberately placed it there for her to find. She felt a surge of vertigo. She wanted to flee the beach and let the seas find another poor soul to bless with unwanted gifts. Instead, moving with a will not entirely her own, she kneeled, picked up the bottle with both hands, and peeled off the concealing seaweed, revealing the contents: a tiny but perfectly formed human fetus. It was a boy. His face was pink, his eyelids almost translucent, his expression filled with an all-consuming peace that made her heart ache just to look at it.

It looked almost old enough to be born. The vessel was just barely large enough to contain it. The corked opening was way too narrow to explain how anybody had ever managed to get the fetus in there. For a moment she even wondered if someone had simply blown the glass around it.

She turned the bottle over in her hands. The printed label on the other side was discolored by seawater, but the single word was still easily readable. It said MESSENGER.

It was a pun. A sick pun at that. MESSENGER in a bottle.

She scowled to think of the kind of person who could dream up such a thing, and examined the baby's face again, to determine just what kind of person this unnamed creature would have grown up to be, had he lived. His expression no longer looked peaceful. His brow was furrowed slightly, giving him the look of somebody disturbed by all the problems in the world.

She lifted the bottle closer to her face.

He opened his eyes and blinked at her.

She didn't scream out loud, but only because she was too stunned. But she did drop the bottle, did see it fall, did see it land precisely the wrong way on a rock half-buried in the mud, did see it explode into a thousand pieces.

She thought of razor-sharp glass slicing through infant flesh, and with a muffled gasp knelt to grasp the baby lying calm and collected amidst the shattered glass. She was so sure he was cut to ribbons that it was a second before she registered the total absence of blood. There wasn't a mark on him, not even a bruise. She picked him up, running her hands over the smooth flesh that felt so so much unnaturally warmer than her own. The needles of glass peppering his skin simply fell from his body like snowflakes. There didn't seem to be enough of them to comprise the remains of an entire bottle, and as she watched she began to see why: now that its job was done, the glass was simply melting. Within seconds the shards were all gone, the places where they had been marked only by slight indentations in the sand.

She half-expected the baby to disappear, too. But no: he was real. And he regarded her with genuine recognition. It wasn't the simple recognition of a child for its mother, but the purposeful gaze of somebody who'd come from someplace very far away to tell her something very, very important.

"Messenger," she whispered.

The baby blinked and—impossibly—nodded. Too young to understand the word, he still recognized his name, and his purpose.

And then he did the first normal thing she'd seen him do. He sneezed.

Only when he started to tremble, like any other naked body exposed to the January chill, did the meaning of that sneeze penetrate the shock caused by his arrival. Then she bundled him inside her thick winter coat, next to the warmth of her body, and hurried him home.

For almost three hours she sat on the edge of her bed, watching him lay on her rug before the heat of the fireplace that until his arrival had been the only warm thing about her little home. By the end of those three hours she knew that she couldn't simply turn him over to the authorities as an abandoned baby she'd discovered lost and unloved on a freezing beach. It would have been the easiest thing to do. It would have left the daily pattern of her life untouched and unsullied, its rhythms as predictable as those of a sturdy old clock. But he and the unknown message he carried had obviously been meant for her and her alone. Giving him up to strangers would be a crime. Pretending he was her own would be equally impossible: faceless as she was, friendless as she was, there were still way too many people around town who would know she hadn't been pregnant with him.

No, she'd have to move. Just like that. And it was shocking, now, to realize how easy it would be. There were no cords to cut, no connections to break, no sloppy emotional good-byes to make. There'd just be a long afternoon of packing, a large bank withdrawal, and a quick drive to the interstate. Even the sale of her most substantial possessions—the bookshop and the house—would be a cold, civilized thing, handled quickly and impersonally through brokers she'd never have to meet face-to-face. She could use the proceeds to buy herself an almost identical house and bookshop in another town. It didn't even matter which town, since in all her life she'd never found a place she could approach as more than just another stranger.

Something tugged at her shirttail. She looked down, and saw that he was no longer an infant. In the few seconds her eyes had been away from him, he'd become a toddler, old enough to stand and walk and gaze up with an expression of deliberate purpose that made a lie of his physical age.

"Messenger," he said.

It was a child's high-pitched voice, the tone not so much that of a child groping toward speech as that of an adult announcing his business as he entered a room.

She found herself smiling, like any other mother confronted with her baby's first word. "That's right. Messenger. Can you say that again?"

"Messenger."

"That's very good. You learn fast."

"Messenger," he repeated, pointing at his own chest.

Then it hit her. He wasn't just saying his name for the first time. No. He was explaining himself to her. He was saying, *This is what I am, this is what I'm here to do.* She felt the kind of dizziness that came from standing too quickly after too much time kneeling to stock the bottom shelves of her store. The blood burned in her ears. "Yes, I know. That's what you are, all right."

The tiny hand swung away from his chest and pointed at her. "Messenger."

After a few seconds of waiting for her to understand, he relaxed with a gesture resembling a shrug and indicated that he wanted to be picked up. In a flash he was curled up in her lap, protected by her arms, and watching the meaningless dance of the flames in her fireplace.

Tricia found herself trembling. Up until now she would have sworn the reaction was totally alien to her. She never felt fear. Not waking fear, at any rate. She'd used up her entire lifetime's supply of that long ago, when she was eight years old and running from the angrily shouted sound of her name. These days she was afraid only in the dreams she only knew she had when she woke up with a rapid heartbeat and sweaty sheets. She'd always been able to keep the terror safely imprisoned in those dreams. But not now. Now, with the heat of the fireplace, and his breath the soft hum of a child entirely content to stay where he was, the distance the years had placed between her and the crawlspace of her childhood vanished, and she found her heart pounding just like that frightened little child who'd learned the hard way that there was nobody willing to help her. For the first time in years, she felt it again: the ground beneath her feet becoming a bottomless pit, leaving nothing between her and the molten center of the Earth but a neverending fall that would leave her awake and screaming every foot of the way. It was all wrapped up in the child on her lap: like mother and father and everybody else she'd ever foolishly allowed into her life, he had come from his far forbidden country only to attack her and hurt her and forever sign his name in the scars he left behind.

Tricia wanted to fling him away from her and run from the house screaming.

He placed his tiny hand on the back of hers, and said "Messenger" a fourth time. With particular emphasis.

The panic popped like a soap bubble, replaced by tears. She felt them streaming down both cheeks, leaving burning trails, from her shame at ever suspecting him of traveling such a long way just to hurt her. "I'm sorry," she said, her voice breaking.

He rested his head against her breast and lay still. In minutes he was asleep, and she was staring into the fire, searching in vain for the comforting patterns something inside her insisted she should have found there.

When Tricia awoke the next morning, with no memory of actually crawling off to bed, the boy was standing nude in the open doorway, watching her sleep. He looked around ten now; his hair had come in, taking the form of ragged black bangs. He wore an expression of calm, unhurried interest, and he nodded only slightly when her sleepy eyes met his.

She sat up at once, too shocked by his appearance to allow herself the usual luxury of waking up one lazy inch at at time.

"You talk in your sleep," he said.

Tricia pulled the covers up to her chin, and held them there like a shield. They felt ludicrously flimsy. "W—what did I say?" she managed, after three separate attempts at speech.

"It's always the same word," he told her. " 'Please.' "

She wasn't surprised, but even so, her next words came out harsher than she intended. "Is that what you came here to tell me?"

His eyes darkened, becoming the color of the sea during a storm. "No, it's not." He turned away and left the room.

Maybe five minutes passed before Tricia found the nerve to leave her bed. Even then, she forced herself not to follow him right away. Instead, she crossed straight to her bathroom and took what comfort she could in the rest of her morning rituals: brushing her teeth, showering, choosing one functional set of clothing from all the others standing in her wardrobe. Only when all her armor was in place did she actually take a deep breath and leave her bedroom.

Messenger was sitting at her kitchen table. The table had come with two matching chairs; she always sat at the one closest the refrigerator. He sat in the other, making this the first time the chair had ever been used. He looked perfectly at home in it, and his keen interest in every move she made was enough to make her turn away and start rummaging through her cabinets. She faltered for something to say: "Uh . . . do you . . . do you want me to make you anything?"

"No," he said.

"You haven't eaten anything since I found you."

"I don't eat food."

"Do," she swallowed, "do you mind if I make something?"

"Do anything that makes you comfortable."

Hands shaking, she put two slices of wheat bread in the toaster, set it for DARK, put up some coffee, took another deep, shuddery breath, and sat at the table opposite him. "I thought you would stay a baby," she said, mostly because she couldn't think of anything else. "I thought . . . I was expected to raise you or something."

The sea-green eyes bored into her own. "Are you disappointed?"

Tricia looked down.

His laugh sounded like breakers crashing against a rocky beach. It was a frightening laugh, not because there was any cruelty in it, or because it threatened any harm, but because she heard in that laugh all the power of all the world's oceans, complete with an echo of the tidal waves capable of wrecking ships and drowning entire populations. She shivered.

"No," he said, a genuine affection flavoring his words. "I'm not here to place that kind of demand on your time. Not when I can do what I came here to do within twenty-four hours."

"And what's that?"

"Deliver my message, of course. You should get that."

Tricia was about to ask, GET WHAT? when the toaster popped up. She jumped at the sound, hurrying across the room to escape him, grateful for the excuse the toast provided. Messenger seemed to understand that, calmly watching as her trembling fingers fumbled with the butter knife.

Halfway through the second slice her hand spasmed, flipping both slices off the plate. They fell to the floor and landed butter side down.

She flinched. *You Clumsy Little Idiot! Do you think bread is free?*

I'M SORRY, DADDY. IT WAS AN ACCIDENT!

Sorry isn't good enough. You're going to pick it up, and you're going to eat every single crumb!

BUT I CAN'T EAT IT! IT'S DIRTY!

Are you talking back to me, girl? Is that what you're doing?

She closed her eyes so tightly they hurt, turned her hands into fists, and pounded the side of the counter with the helpless, impotent anger of a child.

"It's all right," the Messenger said. "You're not hungry anyway."

Without opening her eyes or turning to face him, she demanded, "How the hell do you know? How do you know who I am or what I'm feeling?"

"I know everything about you," he said. "I know the entire story of your life, from the day you were born to the moment you found me. It's why I came."

Tricia looked at him.

He was no longer naked. He'd grown a goose-down coat with a hood. Thick corduroy pants. And mittens. The clothes looked almost incidental on him; they were there not because he was seriously worried about suffering from the cold—he wouldn't—but because if he accompanied her outside he'd need to dress like a normal child to avoid the stares of distant strangers. He'd even made himself a little pair of round eyeglasses. They magnified his eyes, making them look comical and owlish. Just like hers.

"Let's go out," he said. "It's a sunny day."

* * *

It wasn't. Not really. The sky was an unbroken field of white. But enough light had penetrated to give the impression of sun; even the ocean itself seemed fooled, sparkling with a glow completely out of proportion with the light that shone down from above.

Tricia and the Messenger walked along the water's edge, holding hands and saying nothing. His hand was firm, and warm, and possessed a strength way out of proportion to his size. She held with it with the self-conscious, tentative grip of a woman who didn't know whether to squeeze tighter or let go and run away as fast as her legs could carry her. But it seemed he could read the strength of her panic right through her skin, because whenever she made up her mind to flee from the miracle walking by her side, his grip tightened briefly, assuring her he meant no harm; so instead of running she found herself holding on, determined to let him take her wherever it was they were both meant to go.

She failed to hear the vaguely familiar voice calling her name until the source was standing right in front of them.

"Hey, I thought I recognized you! You're Tricia from the bookshop!"

She felt a twinge—nobody knew her last name; she was always Tricia from the bookshop—and searched her memory for the name matching the familiar face. A second later she had it: Wendy something. She was a fairly popular painter, though Tricia had never seen any of her work. She always came in on Wednesdays, late in the afternoon, to buy poetry or books on fine art. They always exchanged sterile small talk as Wendy wrote up her check. "Oh, h–hi, Wendy. Didn't hear you."

"Tell me about it," the other woman said, with a short laugh. "The two of you looked so deep in thought I wondered if you were sleepwalking or something." She smiled at Messenger. "And who are you? I never met you before."

The silence that followed was so brief that Tricia might have been the only one to notice it; but to her it seemed to last eons, and when she finally spoke, her words felt false and heavy. "Oh, th–this is my nephew, ah . . ."

She drew a blank, then, but before the silence could stretch, the little boy supplied the next word: "Messenger."

"What's that?" Wendy said. "Messenger? That's a nice name."

"It's what I am," the boy said, simply enough.

"Well, it's nice to meet you, Messenger." She glanced at Tricia, obviously sensing the silence only temporarily held at bay by her attempts at small talk, and said, "Well, uh, nice seeing you, too."

Tricia managed a weak smile and nod.

As the other woman walked away, Messenger looked up at Tricia and asked, "Do you dislike her?"

"You know I don't."

"The woman's trying to be your friend. Why do you drive her off?"

"I'm not. I just . . . I just don't know how not to."

"I see." Messenger looked down the sand, as if expecting it to help him understand that. They continued walking. About thirty seconds later he asked, "And is that your problem with most people?"

"No. Most people stay away from me."

"I think they stay away from you because with every move you make you tell them to stay away."

She dropped his hand, and walked away. He didn't rush to catch up with her. Thirty paces later she slowed, stopped, and used her left hand to feel the palm of her right hand, the one that had been holding his. The skin there was tingling; it felt oddly empty, as if it had grown accustomed to the touch of another hand and was now protesting the way that touch had been taken away. She didn't have to turn around to know that Messenger hadn't hurried to catch up with her—that he was still standing in the place where she'd left him, waiting impassively as she fought the question taking shape in her mind.

"Why are you here?" she managed.

"I thought you knew. The ocean sent me."

She emitted a short, hysterical laugh. "It's just water! It's not alive!"

He walked around to face her with dark and emphatic eyes. "It's more than just water. It's everything that lives and dies in that water, everything that swims on or under that water, everything that needs that water to live. How can something that big not be alive? How can it not feel?"

"How can it feel ME?"

"How can it not? Every day you walk along this

shore, you bleed your pain into the sand, and every day when the tide comes in, it swallows up some of that pain, and brings it back out for the waters to taste. There are any number of creatures who speak to the ocean that way. The ocean tastes them all, with each ripple that touches the shore. And once in a great, great while, perhaps once a century or more, when the taste is sufficiently special, it decides to send a message back."

Her throat was dry. "But WHY me?"

"Your unhappiness was different. It never changed. It never got better or worse. It was the same day after day, season after season, without respite, and it was always unnecessary."

"Is that your big message?" she asked, bitterly. "That I should cheer up?"

"No. It's just the answer to your question." He reached up, took her hand, and pulled her back in the direction they'd been walking. "Come on. There's something I want to show you."

He brought her to a place about a quarter of a mile farther down the coast, hidden from the beach itself by two huge outcroppings of rock. Anybody sitting on the beach would have thought the rocks just plunged straight down into the sea on the ocean side. But no. Centuries of assault by the tides had carved a narrow cleft in the rock, wearing it down to a narrow strip of sand sheltered by the two great walls on either side. Messenger showed her the easiest place to climb up and over, warned her away from slippery patches of seaweed; then motioned for her to stay where she was and hopped down to the freezing wet sand.

His clothes were gone, again. There was no longer any reason for them. Nobody except Tricia could see him here.

Flashing an expression that might have been a naughty smile, he knelt in the freezing mud and began digging a trench. He pulled great heaping handfuls of the stuff toward him, making a brown mound on the ground at his feet. Only when he started a second trench, and added the freshly excavated mud to the top of the mound, Tricia realized he was not even remotely interested in digging trenches; the trenches were just scars left by his real project, which was gathering together the raw material for a sand sculpture. She hesitated—it was cold, after all—and then descended to the sand herself, to watch the creation taking shape beneath his graceful hands.

The mound was his own height by the time he began molding it. His fingers moved like lightning then, rounding off the top, then creating a slight indentation about eight inches down.

The indentations grew deeper. Smoothed out.

His hands flew. Became blurs.

His speed dizzied her, so she turned toward the horizon. There were usually some cruise ships out there, taking their fat, complacent passengers away from their warm, comfortable homes to places so warm they had never known a winter. Sometimes she wondered bleakly how many of them were looking back at the gray skies and deserted beaches she'd claimed for her own, and congratulating themselves on finding a better place to go. But there were no ships today; today the water had arranged for them to be elsewhere. Today there was just the ocean, rolling up and down the way it always did.

She remembered what the Messenger had said about bleeding her pain into the ground, and thought, *What are you getting from me now?*

Tricia looked back at Messenger, to see how much of his sculpture he'd completed. And froze. Because in the minutes since she'd turned away he'd transformed the mound into a startlingly realistic sculpture of a little girl. The attention to detail was so exhaustive that Tricia could read the pattern of the little girl's dress, but that wasn't as important as the unbearably forlorn way the little girl was standing: hands locked together in front of her, head bent, looking down at her inwardly pointing shoes. When Tricia looked closer, she could even tell that the little girl was crying. The face was . . .

No. God, no.

Tricia's throat went tight. "Please . . . Messenger . . ."

"Please what?"

"Please don't . . . don't do this."

"You're too late," he said, deftly adding a few finishing touches to the sculpture's anguish. "It's done."

He stepped back . . .

. . . and the sculpture exploded with uncontrollable sobbing.

The cries came from somewhere deep inside its chest, and burst outward with a force that shook its entire body. It rocked back and forth, rhythmically, seemingly unaware that it was moving at all, but too frightened by the force of its misery to release the grip its hands had on each other. Tears of sand rolled down its cheeks, clung unsupported to its sandy chin, then shook loose and fell to the sandy ground. In seconds, the sobs exhausted whatever the poor creature used for breath, and the sounds pouring from its mouth grew even more ragged and lost.

Tricia couldn't move. She whispered, "Stop it. Stop it. Stop it."

"I can't stop it," Messenger said. "Only you can stop it."

"Please don't make me."

"I'm not. If you want, you can just let her continue crying."

Tricia stood then, fully determined to just walk away from here, leaving Messenger and his obscene creation alone with nothing but each other for company. But even as she took her first step she found herself horribly certain that she couldn't end it that simply. If she walked away now, the horrible miracle would stay here forever, refusing to be melted away by the tides or the rains or even the sheer unbearable weight of its own pain. It would be a living monument to unhappiness, doomed to last long after Tricia, its model, was reduced to unfeeling dust.

Tricia damned the Messenger to hell with a look.

He responded with a shrug.

And no longer caring that he was manipulating her, Tricia raced forward, wrapping her arms around the little sand-girl, pressing close until their cheeks touched, repeating, "Sssshhh, sssshhhh, it's all right" over and over again, like a mantra. And it did not feel like a creature made out of wet sand scraped from a winter beach; it felt warm, and dry, and deeply wounded, exactly like the little girl it had been sculpted to resemble. The wracking sobs never stopped—but as she held it in her arms, and it convulsively clutched at her arms in return, the character of those sobs changed. They contained just as much pain as they had before, but they were no longer hollow, hopeless sounds, endlessly echoing against each other because there was no other place they'd ever be heard. No. Now they were the sobs of somebody who knew that another person who understood that pain was here to listen, and comfort, and make it right.

"No one's going to hurt you any more," Tricia said. She felt an uneasy sense of displacement, as if she was not quite sure the words were coming out of her own mouth, or somebody else's.

It sobbed: "Thank you," and again she felt strangely displaced, as if she was saying the words herself, to the nice stranger lady who'd just done a kind thing for her.

They released each other. And as Tricia moved away, she was not surprised to see that the sand sculpture was now only a sand sculpture. Oh, it was still shaped like a little girl, but now it was only a crude approximation of one. Merely the sort of thing that could have been fashioned by any reasonably talented set of hands.

She was also not surprised to realize she was trembling. She faced the little boy, who was sitting quietly on the rocks, and demanded: "Was that it? Was that the message you were sent to give me?"

"No," he said. "That was my own idea. I thought you'd like it."

"Then what's the Message?"

He just shrugged and threw a pebble into the ocean. The splash was almost too small to be noticed. The waters healed over immediately, keeping their own counsel, saying nothing.

Overcome with frustration, she cried: "It's just a sick game for you, isn't it?"

He didn't look up.

She began climbing the rock wall that would take her back to the beach. It was much more slippery going up; she almost fell twice. But in less than a minute she made it back to the top, and stood there, shivering horribly as she faced the deserted beach.

She didn't know why she felt so cold. She normally liked walking in the cold. But her time with the Messenger seemed to have removed all her tolerance for it. The frigid temperatures had penetrated all her layers of clothing and sucked all the strength from her limbs. She tried to tempt herself with all the cold-weather remedies that usually made her feel better, on those rare occasions when the winter actually forced its way past her thick skin: soup, hot chocolate, even a nice steaming bath. None of them appealed to her at all. The way she felt now, she didn't think they'd ever appeal to her again: the chill had penetrated so deeply into her bones that those time-worn solutions would only make matters worse, by reminding her what warmth was like.

She tried to tell herself that walking away would be The Right Thing To Do.

The EASY Thing To Do, yes. She'd built a life out of walking away. She hadn't been to a party in years, ever since she'd learned that parties were something she simply had no talent for, but back when she still occasionally made an effort, it always ended with her turning red and panicky and silently escaping through the nearest door. It had always been Easy. Nobody had ever noticed she was gone, because nobody had ever noticed she was there . . . except that one time, when, wandering quietly through the two dozen conversations taking place on either side of her, she heard a neighbor say, "Look there, the zombie came out to play." Tricia had whirled, certain that the words were directed at her . . . and saw the woman who had said it, grinning with the cruel satisfaction worn only by those who are glad to be overheard. It had been a bad moment. But that was pain caused by staying too long, not pain caused by leaving too soon. It was easier to just leave earlier, and spare people like that woman the blood their wit demanded.

But walking away was just one step removed from staying away. And it ended with her home alone, facing an empty fireplace, with nothing but chill in her bones and nothing but the four walls for company.

Not to mention a lifetime of wondering about the message.

She climbed back down, and crouched in the sand beside him.

He looked older now—maybe 15 or 16. He was drawing circles in the sand. They were all perfectly round, and they linked at the edges, forming a chain. He didn't look up from his work: "I'm glad you're back."

"But not surprised," she said.

It wasn't a question, but he answered it anyway. "No."

"Nothing I do surprises you, does it?"

The corners of his lips twitched. "You can walk away whenever you want."

"You know that's no answer. Not until I know what the message is."

Still avoiding her eyes, he heaved a long sigh and stared out to sea. "If curiosity is the only thing keeping you here, you're going to be disappointed. It's not as profound as you seem to think it is. It won't cure disease or solve world hunger or end a single unjust war. At the very, very MOST, it'll just affect you and a few scattered others. So if that's what you're worried about, you're free. You can go home now, and return to the life you've chosen for yourself."

Despite everything, it was a tempting thought. "And you?"

"I'll go back where I came from. And maybe someday, if the conditions are right, the ocean might decide to send somebody very much like me to deliver another message." He abandoned the circles locked together in the sand, and faced her with a look bright enough to pierce the darkness at the bottom of the Marianas trench. "But it won't be the same messenger. And you won't be the one to receive him."

Tricia touched a finger to the sand. "And this message—is it something bad?"

"You might think so. I don't. It's always been precious to me."

He stood, stretched, and faced the line where the gray winter ocean met the gray winter sky. It was clear that he'd said all he was going to, for the present.

And for no reason at all, Tricia thought of the day her parents had died. It had been a car wreck three hours into the New Year they had just come back from celebrating. A drunken driver doing ninety in the wrong lane had killed not only her mother and father but three innocent pedestrians who'd been unlucky enough to be standing on the sidewalk when the two vehicles somersaulted twisted and flaming off the road. She'd been fourteen at the time, just old enough for all the lessons they'd taught her to get firmly embedded under her skin, and when the police had come to tell her what had happened it took her a good four hours to understand why she was crying. It wasn't just that she'd loved them, despite all the abuses they'd heaped upon her. No. It was the certainty that for as long as she lived, she'd never, ever have anybody else.

Until Messenger, she'd never had any reason to feel otherwise.

She didn't have to say anything to make her decision known. He smiled. "Come on. There's one last thing I have to show you."

* * *

They strolled dry and warm across the freezing ocean floor.

For all her fascination with the sea, she hadn't gone swimming since high school. She couldn't, not when she only braved the beach in freezing weather. And she knew she'd never be able to consider this visit an exception, because while they were IN the water, far below the surface, they were never quite TOUCHED by it. They breathed, without seawater rushing in to crush the life from their lungs; they walked, without being slowed down by water pressure or feeling their native buoyancy pull them toward the surface; they spoke, and understood each other perfectly, unbothered by even a single bubble distorting the sounds of their voices. It was like walking through warm air. She felt its eddies and currents the same way she'd feel an errant breeze blowing against her skin.

She wasn't sure she liked it. Oh, it was exhilarating enough, at first. Admittedly, the visibility down here was not as good as she would have liked—in part because the sun was hidden behind clouds today, but also because so many of the sights were veiled by silt stirred up by the current—but there were still plenty of sights to see, ranging from the mysterious shapes popping up all over the sea bottom to the shifting patterns of light that represented waves seen from below. But the farther she traveled, the more it seemed wrong to stand totally enveloped by that which had created so many miracles for her, without even momentarily permitting herself to feel it.

Tricia mentioned this to Messenger. He said, "Would you rather drown?"

"No. Of course not. But I don't even feel like I'm really here. It's more like I'm watching it on a movie screen or seeing it through the window of a moving car."

"I feel the water. Do you want me to tell you what it's like?"

"Please."

"Right now . . ." He closed his eyes. "Right now it's like being attached to everything in the world. There's the water immediately around us, of course—which happens to be very, very cold; you would not be able to stand it—and beyond that, the water this water touches, and beyond that the water THAT water touches; and beyond that the beaches and everything that touches them. That's what it's like. I can feel all of that, through the water touching us right now."

Tricia, who had lived her entire adult life without ever once feeling like she was a part of anything, merely shivered forlornly. "I wish I could feel that."

"I can't help you there," Messenger said, squeezing her hand. "Not with water, at least."

It had all the feel and delivery of an exit line, and as soon as he said it he dropped her hand and stepped away, disappearing into the murk.

The abandonment was so abrupt she didn't even have time to feel fear. She just turned in a circle, searching for his form in an undersea landscape suddenly filled with shadows. He could have been five feet behind her and she would have missed him utterly. She whirled, sure that that was the case. But no. There were just the swirling clouds of silt, puffing about her like the smoke from an unseen fire.

She tried to terrify herself that he wasn't coming back: that he was just going to leave her here until she starved or suffocated; that the Message was just a sick joke dreamed up by a world intent on amusing itself at her expense. She tried to persuade herself that the ocean around her was a vast and impersonal thing, interested in her only in the same way that sadistic schoolchildren are interested in pulling the wings off flies. She tried to believe that the Message was one she'd already firmly believed all her life: that trust was a game for fools, and that people who actually brought themselves to rely on others were only placing their trust in enemies eagerly searching for a place to stick a knife.

When all of that failed, she tried to torture herself with the memory of the crawlspace under her house: a dark, forbidding place, filled with scurrying noises, protruding pipes, and spiderwebs lying in wait for the touch of her face. She'd always tried to stay near the sliding door that barred the way back to the basement, since, even when Mom and Dad locked her in, the crack of light along the floor was just enough to keep away the menacing shapes that leered at her from the darkness. But she'd always had to move around just to keep warm—and when she moved, she invariably strayed too far into the darkness and found herself unable to feel her way back. She was always reduced to sobbing, *Mommy, Daddy, let me out.* She forced herself to remember all of that in the most clinical detail, and tried to tell herself that the exact same thing was happening now, that the ocean was just reenacting the petty cruelties of her childhood on a much larger scale.

None of that worked, not even for a moment.

Because her hand still tingled from the way Messenger had squeezed it before he left.

And so she calmly waited, in this cold and lonely place, so much like that crawlspace, for him to come back. She didn't know how long it took, since there was no way to gauge the passage of time. It felt like minutes; it might have been hours. But she did not allow herself to feel fear. She didn't even allow herself the temptation. And knowing that she was able to stay here, alone, without once shouting for help from the parents she feared almost as much as the darkness— not to mention her discovery that it was downright EASY—was such a liberating sensation in and of itself that she would not have been surprised to find out that this was the whole of the Message he'd been sent to bring her.

It wasn't.

Because, eventually, somewhere off to one side of her, Messenger grunted, rustled around a bit, and announced, "I'm finished."

And as suddenly as a light being switched on, the water around her just . . . focused.

She shouldn't have been surprised the ocean was able to do this. After all, it had already bathed her in miracles. It had sent her a Messenger, animated sand sculptures, and taken care of her under circumstances that should have choked the life from her body—but when all the silt dropped to the ground and all the shadows came alive with light and all the distorting effects of the water disappeared, leaving everything in her line of sight as clear as air, the shock of what was revealed almost drove her to her knees.

Messenger had brought her to a valley whose walls sloped up all around, creating an underwater amphitheater. Hundreds of sculptures rose from the walls: men and women of all shapes and sizes, all of them totally unfamiliar to her. Some were walking with each other; others were sitting alone in chairs; one was lying in a bed; there was even one—a young woman wearing an expression of intense concentration—sitting on a chair playing a guitar. There were at least half a dozen children. Two were tossing a beach ball, which the sculptor had impossibly frozen in mid-flight between them. The other four were playing alone, running or doing handstands or, in one case, making a sand sculpture of her very own. There was even one of Messenger himself, or somebody who looked very much like him, sitting cross-legged and impassive on the ground halfway up the wall.

The real Messenger stood patiently just a few feet away.

"What do you think?" he asked softly.

"I'm—" She hesitated, not entirely sure how she was supposed to take this. "I don't know. I'm overwhelmed. Did you make all of these just now?"

"It wasn't hard. They're just sand sculptures. I'm sure making the real people was harder."

"They're all based on real people, then?"

He nodded. "As many as I had time for. I know them all, you see; they've all walked on a beach, at one time or another."

"Is there one of me?"

"No, you're already here. If you weren't here, you couldn't ask that question."

She was unable to tell whether he meant that as a joke. "What do they have to do with me?"

"At this point . . ." He spread his arms. "Absolutely nothing. But they're all people you could have known. People who tried to reach out to you, or would have responded if you'd reached out to them."

She looked up at the motionless figures filling the ampitheater around her. "I don't recognize anybody."

"There aren't many you would. You've gotten very good at avoiding them. But if you look around, here and there, you'll find a few actually know. That woman we spoke to this morning, for instance."

"Wendy? Which one is she?"

"The one in the bed," Messenger said.

Tricia felt a surge of dread then, deeper than anything she'd felt in years. She looked at him for reassurance, found none in his carefully impassive expression, and for one endless moment tried to talk herself into letting the matter drop. But eventually she hurried up the slope to the place where an emaciated figure lay in a hospital bed, the outline of her bones clearly visible through the sheet her skeletal arms hugged to her body. It was impossible to recognize her. She had lost all of her hair, and her face had collapsed in upon itself, the sunken cheekbones and haunted eyes reduced to land-marks on a relief map of agony. It could have been the sculpture of a woman eighty years old, or ninety.

She looked for Messenger, found him quietly stand-ing beside her, and asked, "How long?"

"Eight months," he said. "Cancer. The pain's already started, but she doesn't realize it's anything serious. In a couple of days the doctor will give her the bad news. After that, she'll go downhill quickly."

"Can you help her?"

He shook his head.

"Then why the hell—" (her voice trembled with rage), "—did you bother showing me this?"

"Because you could have helped her," he said. "When she finds out, she's going to turn to her friends and family for the strength she needs to get through it. You could have been one of them—and believe me when I tell you that you would have been one of the most important—but it's too late for that now. Just as it's way too late for her to help you. Your last opportu-nity is gone. From here on in she's going to be way too busy to make new friends."

"And is that your damn message? Something you just wanted to taunt me with?"

He shook his head. "No. It's only one of the reasons it's important."

A fury rose in her then: thirty years of repressed rage, bubbling upward all at once. She couldn't believe she'd brought herself to trust him so implicitly. Now she knew that if she let this continue he'd just go on torturing her with hints until she said stop. It was time to say stop. She said: "I've had enough of this. I don't want to know it any more."

His eyebrows furrowed. It seemed she'd finally succeeded in surprising him. "You've already said you—"

"I don't care what I said, don't you understand that? I've changed my mind. I just want you to bring me home and go back to wherever the hell it is you came from!"

He straightened. "All right."

And they began the long walk back, without exchanging even a single word until they emerged on the beach later that afternoon.

When they hit dry land, only a few yards from the place where his bottle had first washed up on shore, the glow of the setting sun was just beginning to flare over the far horizon.

The instant she and Messenger emerged from the water, the ocean rescinded its protection, and she began to feel the temperature again. If anything, it had gotten colder. Shocked by the sudden change, she hugged herself for what little warmth her own arms could give her. Still, her teeth chattered. The night was going to be even colder than the day had been. It might even be too cold to leave the house. Maybe she'd just build a fire, fall asleep, and go back to living what passed for her life.

He asked, "Can I tell you something?"

It was the first thing he'd said since she'd announced her intention to wash her hands of him. She refused to look at him. "Will you . . . please . . . go?"

"I will. I've already said I will. But I have to tell you something first."

She glanced at him, meaning to argue, and saw that he now looked old. Not the kind of old that announces itself with wrinkles and gray hair, but the kind of old that she saw in the mirror every morning: the kind of old that comes from knowing that she was no damn good for anything.

"I don't have much time left," he said. "I would have had to leave just about now anyway. But I can't let it end like this."

"You should have thought about that before you started with the mind games. Now I've had all I can take, and I don't want to play anymore."

"Then forget the Message," he said, almost pleading. "I told you, that was always your decision. But I have something else to tell you. Something personal. I can't go back without saying it."

"You're going to have to."

He slumped in defeat, closed his eyes, and kneeled on the sand, so completely a portrait of failure that Tricia felt her anger knocked out from underneath her. She opened her mouth to ask a question, then shut up, knowing it would only insult him.

After a timeless interval he spoke, in a voice that sounded like it was coming from a great distance underwater. "I know everything about you. I know about the things they said to make you feel worthless, and what they did to you when you cried. I even know what your father started doing when you turned twelve. I know things about you that you don't even know yourself. I've felt everything you felt, thought everything you've thought, suffered everything you suffered. I'm only sitting here now, in this form, because you needed me."

She started to move toward him.

He gestured her away. "No. Please. I don't have much time left. Let me finish it.

"This isn't the Message. Believe me, it isn't. It's just me talking. And I want to say that while I can't help hating your parents for everything they did to you, I can't understand why you've let them continue doing it to you. Why you've let them rob you of the world. And even worse, why you've let them rob the world of—"

He stopped in mid-sentence, perhaps afraid of saying too much, then looked down, trembling from the force of the words he'd bitten back.

She tried to tell herself it was just part of his act. And again, as when she'd tried to tell herself that he'd abandoned her in the sea, she couldn't. The breath caught in her throat, and she reached out to embrace him.

It was like embracing the sand-sculpture, only different. His substance wavered, and rippled, giving in ways that flesh couldn't give. He felt hollow. Less than real. Liquid. But for just a moment there, as he squeezed her back, he was just a child, crying alone on an abandoned beach.

"I never promised I wouldn't say the personal part," he said. "I love you."

Then he stood and walked into the water.

He was knee-deep in the surf by the time she realized he was finished: that he'd said all he could say without violating the rules she'd demanded of him.

"Messenger," she murmured.

The word was barely audible. If he heard it, he gave no sign. He just kept walking, neither hesitating or hurrying: just moving along at a comfortable walking speed, a little piece of him disappearing with every step.

And she found the strength to run after him, yelling "Wait!"

He froze.

The moment stretched.

She followed him into the water, ignoring the shock that ran up her spine as she splashed knee-deep in the freezing surf.

He took another step.

Then he gave up and turned around, a question in his eyes.

"I'm sorry for what I said before . . . when you showed me Wendy. I'm . . ." she swallowed, and forced herself to finish it: "I'm glad you came. You've been a good friend."

He nodded slightly, acknowledging that. "Thank you."

"And . . ." the words came out one at a time, slowed to a crawl by all the conflicting emotions they carried. "Uh . . . if there's time . . . the message. If you don't mind . . . I think . . . since it's what you came here to say . . . I think I really do want to hear it."

He smiled then. She saw that he was fully transparent now, a creature more water than skin. "You still don't understand, after all this time? You are the Message."

She blinked, uncomprehending.

The smile fell from his face, replaced by a look of wholly human uncertainty. For just one moment more he retained his shape, a humanoid pillar of water standing tall and alone at the edge of the sea. The setting sun reflecting against him filled him with fire and lined him with gold. Then gravity took over, and he rejoined the oceans that had given him life.

Tricia thought of the waves taking him as their own, blending and churning everything he'd been until he was evenly mixed with all the oceans of the world. Before long, it might be impossible to walk any beach anywhere on the planet without seeing a breaker that contained a piece of him. People would be wetting their toes in the surf without recognizing his special essence in the puddles on the sand.

The thought made her dizzy. She walked from the water—her soaked legs on fire from the cold—stumbled up the stairs to the boardwalk, and sat heavily upon the first bench she saw. Her eyes burned. She felt his absence, but she had no idea why he had come or what his last words to her had meant.

It was impossible to avoid feeling that in the end she'd failed him.

The sun was almost gone. She squeezed herself with both arms, to lock in the failing heat of her own body, and stared through blurring eyes at the boardwalk and the streets leading back to town. There weren't many people visible: just a few solitary forms, here and there, too far away to recognize. It was impossible to know who they were or where they were going.

Unless she went up to them and asked.

It was a useless thought. She'd never be able to do that.

But if she didn't, how would she ever know?

Maybe, she thought, that's what all people were: envelopes made of skin, carrying messages meant for the eyes of all others.

She thought of herself as a letter never mailed and therefore never received. A letter whose message was known only to herself, a letter that would forever remain incomplete until it was offered for somebody else to read.

And finally she thought of millions of other lonely forms, huddled in darkness all over the world, hugging their precious hidden messages to themselves, afraid of being heard, or being seen.

And at long last she understood what he'd been trying to tell her.

She looked out at the distant strangers and thought, I will hear you. I will see you. I will make you hear and see me. I will shatter your hard protective bottles even as I shatter mine and together we will learn how warm the beach can be in winter.

She stood—her legs freezing, but strong—and facing the ocean one last time, mouthed the words *I love you, too*.

When the tide came in, the next morning, she was gone. There was just the ocean, filling the horizon the way it always did: vast, and cold, but capable of reflecting much, much more than just the rays of the sun.

THE DUKE OF DEMOLITION GOES TO HELL

by John Gregory Betancourt

So this is hell, Big Jim Carnack, the self-proclaimed Duke of Demolition, thought to himself.

He remembered dying. He remembered the sterile smell of the hospital, with so many doctors and nurses looming over him, so many fruit bowls and flower baskets and potted plants oh-so-tastefully arranged around the room.

Reality had gotten a little weird at the end. He'd drifted through a painkiller haze as endless streams of relatives and business associates trooped through for one last look. They had no hope—he saw it in their eyes. They knew he was terminal. *He* knew he was terminal. Cancer was like that; it was just a matter of time.

Don Esmond—his junior partner in the construction and demolition business for the last eight years, the kid he'd brought in straight from business school to handle the financial side when the company got too big—shoved his young, tanned, sickeningly *healthy* face close to Big Jim's. "So this is it," Esmond whispered with a rictus grin. "I get it all, old man.

Hurry up and die, will you? My wife and kids are waiting in the car."

I don't deserve this, Big Jim thought, but all the arguments had long ago leeched out of him. He merely closed his eyes. When he opened them again, Esmond was gone.

That was the last thing he remembered.

The next thing he knew, he was walking along a twilit street. Victorian mansions with huge front lawns and wrought-iron fences faced him from both sides, looking not run down, but new, the way they must have been at their prime. The soft yellow glow of oil lamps spilled from their windows.

"So this is hell," Big Jim said again, this time aloud. He gave a low chuckle.

His fate had a certain ironic quality. These were the houses he'd torn down his whole life, decaying relics of bygone days when coal had been cheap and ten-room houses the middle class standard—huge, drafty, inefficient monoliths to a lifestyle which no longer existed.

He'd enjoyed destroying them. Was that his sin? He'd made a career in buying Victorian mansions. Abandoned by their owners, too rundown to renovate, they went cheaply at public auctions. His men moved in like a swarm of army ants, stripping everything salvageable. Big Jim had an eye for art: stained glass was a prize plum. Lead-glass fixtures, old tile, old brick, oak floorboards . . . it all ended up recycled into the new houses ("a touch of old-time class") his company built on the foundations of the old. He squeezed every penny out of a mansion's corpse before laying it in its grave.

In the old days, before he started his construction company, it had been just demolition and salvage. He'd worked fifteen-hour days with nonunion kids he hired at minimum wage. He'd operated the wrecking ball himself, and he'd *enjoyed* the work, *enjoyed* the slow, ponderous motion of the ball as it swung back, gathered speed, then slammed into a building with killer force. He'd raised demolition to an art form. Shattering walls without caving in roofs, loosening mortar without pulverizing bricks, knocking out windows one by one: it brought an almost sexual fulfillment, a sense of satisfaction like no other. Was that so terrible?

He thought back to his wife, to his son and twin daughters. They'd seemed happy. He'd given them everything they wanted or needed . . . a nice home, a swimming pool, Catholic schools, two dogs and a cat, a car for each of them. Sure, they'd had fights and arguments, but what family didn't? And when his son came to the hospital that last day, Big Jim could've sworn there were tears in his eyes. All past sins had been washed away, forgiven. They'd been friends.

And his wife . . . Big Jim knew it had broken her heart to see him in the hospital, slipping farther away each day. But that hadn't been his fault, had it? And his daughters, sobbing in the corner as he made lame jokes. If there'd been any other way . . . if suicide hadn't been a sin. . . .

Perhaps it had been his business dealings that brought him to hell, Big Jim thought uneasily. He'd tried to run an honest company, but he'd paid his share of graft. The construction and demolition business floated on under-the-table cash. Even so, he'd never stabbed any partners in the back (literally or figuratively), never stolen, never cheated on his taxes—never done anything *overtly* illegal. All he'd done was tear down old houses and put up nice new ones. What had he done to end up in hell?

What if it's not hell? he wondered suddenly. *What if it's all been a dream—my dying, everything?* He stopped and held up his hands. They'd been yellow-gray and liverspotted with age in the hospital. He'd been sixty-three, after all, not young anymore. But *these* hands . . . he turned them over and over in the dim light. These hands looked young, healthy, like the hands he'd had in school.

Reincarnation? he wondered. *Amnesia?*

Shadows flickered in the windows of the Victorian opposite him. Had a person moved inside, or was it a trick of the light? Big Jim hesitated. He knew he couldn't spend the rest of eternity wandering aimlessly. Better to check out the house than stand in the street and guess.

Having a plan made him feel better. He opened the Victorian's gate, strode up the brick walkway, then climbed the porch steps one by one. Stumbling on the top step, he almost fell—a loose board had caught his foot, he realized.

Be careful, he chided himself. He was used to Victorians; he knew how treacherous they became when they were old and decaying. Several of his workmen had fallen through rotted-out floors, or had walls unexpectedly cave in on them.

He knocked, paused a minute, knocked again. No answer came. When he tested the knob, though, it turned easily.

He pushed the door open with his fingertips. A needlelike pain jabbed his index finger, and he jerked his hand back with a startled cry. "Ahhh . . ." he muttered. *Damn splinter.* He pulled it out with his teeth, spat it away, then stumped in.

The place was deserted: not a stick of furniture anywhere. Varnished oak floorboards creaked underfoot. A cold draft touched his cheek. The place felt as if nobody had been inside in years, even though a flame flickered in the old-fashioned oil lamp hanging from the ceiling.

Big Jim shivered. It was cold in here.

Crossing to the huge, cast-iron radiator, he reached out cautiously. He didn't feel any radiating heat. When he bent to check the valve, though, it burned his hand. He leaped back, cursing out loud this time, nursing burned fingers.

Another draft touched him. The house seemed to exhale, as it it were alive. *Alive?*

Big Jim backed toward the door as dust began to sift down from the ceiling. The place seemed to exude hated, he thought, as though it wanted to collapse on top of him, as though it wanted to *kill* him.

He ran for the door, made it through, didn't stop for the porch steps but leaped over them. On the brick walkway he came to a sudden stop.

A wrecking machine now sat directly in front of him. It hadn't been there when he entered the house, nor had he heard it drive up. *It must be a trick of some kind, he thought*

He circled the machine cautiously. Its huge stabilizing feet had been lowered and locked into place, spread out in a huge X to brace against movements of the wrecking ball. The ball itself, a five-hundred-pound steel slug at the end of a chain, hung from a forty-foot-tall steel tower.

The door to the operator's cab had "Carnack Demolition" stenciled across it. Big Jim climbed onto the tractor tread, then the stepping rung. The cab door opened easily. He slid into the padded bucket seat, the smells of plastic and new rubber surrounding him.

A manila folder lay across the controls. He flicked on the cab's light, opened the folder, and began to read.

JAMES HOUSE (1884–1973)
December 8, 1884. Leaking roof ruined 473-book library.
January 14, 1885. Child broke leg on steps.
January 19, 1885. Clogged flue filled house with smoke.
February 2, 1885. Ceiling fixture fell, injuring woman.
March 17, 1885. Maid slipped on wet kitchen floor.
March 24, 1885—

It was a list of the house's sins, Big Jim Carnack realized. He leafed through page after page of petty annoyances. Broken pipes, leaking gas valves, rotting wood, lots of burns and splinters and minor injuries for the people who lived there. The house had even killed:

an old woman fell down the second-floor steps and broke her neck in 1904. It killed again in 1951, a teenage girl who slipped in the bathtub and hit her head on the sink.

As Big Jim skimmed the entries, he got a sense of the house's true nature. It wanted to hurt people, he realized, to make their lives as miserable as it could. He thought of the stumble he'd taken on the front steps, of the splinter the door had given him, of the burn he'd received from the radiator—even when it wasn't radiating heat.

The pettiness irked him. The house needed to be punished, he thought, and he was just the man to do it.

He turned the key in the wrecking machine's ignition. The engine purred to life. He changed gears; the steel ball began to swing back.

Big Jim knew then why he'd ended up in hell. It wasn't a punishment. He'd come to render justice. Throughout his life he'd specialized in destroying Victorians. *They must fear me,* he thought. *I must be their worst nightmare.*

He revved the motor.

The house began to scream even before the wrecking ball struck.

SALT

by P.D. Cacek

"Dammit, Henry, will you set the lantern down. You 'bout near blinded me."

"Mary, Mother of God will you look at that."

"Ain't natural, that's what it is. Just ain't natural."

The other men grunted in agreement. Old Tom was the oldest man most of the salt harvesters knew, and if he said a thing wasn't natural they were, by God, going to believe him.

With one exception.

"What ain't natural, ol' man?" the exception asked. "You find all sorts of interesting things when you drain a new pen. Hell, I even heard o' one man finding himself a gold watch. Natural as all get out, if you ask me."

Hands went into well worn pockets, salt-crusted boots kicked at the chilled ground, shoulders hunched beneath heavy wool. The small movements were like waves scurrying across the surface of the ponds right before a major blow, and each man prepared for the worst. Old Tom didn't take kindly to a challenge after he'd pronounced something as fact.

"Don't recall hearin' anyone ask you, new man," Old

Tom growled. "Besides, this ain't no gold watch, this used t' be a woman."

The new man, Lyle Jenkins squatted in the lantern's glow and tapped the body with a salt-hardened reed. The sound was like wood on leather. Boot heels clicking across a boardwalk. An empty, dry sound. He scraped harder and flicked a patch of crust off one of the dead woman's breasts. The nipple was erect— preserved in salt for all eternity.

Jenkins felt some movement of his own.

"An' a right nice one if she had a little more meat on her." He wrinkled his nose at the body and stood up. "I prefer m' women with more of the juice still in 'em. Salt all but sucked this one dry."

A few of the men chuckled softly. Lit low by the lantern, the shadows deepened across Old Tom's face as he frowned.

"Ain't right t' make sport of the dead, new man."

Jenkins ignored the warning by pretending to study the sunken features. Salt crystals as thick as a whore's makeup lay in the hollows of the eyes and cheeks. Death had given her a whore's smile as well—wide open and inviting.

If he squinted hard, Jenkins could just make out the tip of her tongue, salt-cured and prime as any he'd seen hanging in a butcher's shop window, poking out at him between her teeth.

He hawked up a lungful of salt-bitter phlegm and shot it into the nearest pond.

"She been dead too long t' make sport with, old man," Jenkins said, sticking the reed into the corner of his mouth and sucking loudly—smiling at the sounds the men made. "But you go right ahead if you're a mind to."

One of the harvesters, a big Mick from the city of New York, coughed a chuckle into his fist. Jenkins accepted the small victory over the old man as if it carried a twenty-dollar gold piece along with it.

"Well, we can't leave 'er here," Henry growled, hands on hips, feet planted close to his lantern. "I gotta be drivin' my team in here come sunup n' I don't want to be troddin' on no dead woman. Long dead or short."

The laughter came openly, easier now that Old Tom was no longer its intended mark.

"I say take her out t' th' locks n' toss 'er back in," Jenkins said, figuring he was on a roll, "ain't like nobody's looking for her."

Jenkins scraped off another patch of crust with the side of his boot. Less than three hours in the air and the salt was already hard as flint.

"Not like she hurt the flavor of the salt none, has she?"

He looked up expecting guffaws and leering grins. Instead, the reflective orange glow showed him something verging on disgust.

As was their tradition, the harvesters had scooped handfuls of rim salt from the draining pond to flavor their midday meal.

The body was discovered just before sunset.

Jenkins felt his own double helping sour in his belly.

"Well, what d' *you* think we should do with her, Tom?" Henry asked. "Ain't gonna leave her."

"Mabbe we better call th' sheriff," another, younger voice interrupted. "Mebbe she got herself raped an' throwed in t' drown."

Jenkins could hear the men shift uneasily in the darkness beyond the lantern light. Rape wasn't uncommon along the flats, but men generally stuck to killing each other. Women, even the ones who fought and scratched, were just too scarce to waste.

"Mebbe . . ."

"She weren't raped," Old Tom said matter-of-factly, as if he were choosing the winning pie in a county fair.

Jenkins spit the reed toward the bay. "An' just how are you so sure, ol' man? You know her personal?"

It suddenly got so quiet that Jenkins could hear the waves lapping on the other side of the seawall.

"Can't say that I do, new man, but I ain't so old that I can't remember that a woman gotta have her legs spread t' rape." Old Tom jerked his bearded chin toward the body. "This gal's legs been stitched t'gether."

Jenkins meal took another half twist as he dropped to his knees next to the body. They were there all right, thin strands of salt-jeweled rawhide snaking in and out of her legs from crotch to knee. It wasn't fancy needlework, just something done in a hurry . . . as if the woman had been alive and struggling while they sewed her shut.

It ain't natural, Jenkins conceded as the silence settled down over his shoulders.

"Be only right t' bury her, Tom," Henry said softly. "Only Christian thing t' do."

"Ah, now, an what makes ye think th' lady's a Christian?" the Mick asked, his voice sing songing through the darkness. "I've never in all m' days seen a Christian woman runnin' round stark naked."

"Then don't you be introducing me to any of them chippies you been ridin'. I like *my* whores buck naked."

There the unmistakable sound of a closed fist striking damp wool, followed by coarse laughter and lewd comments—mostly from one pock-faced boy who was speculated to have not gotten within pissing distance of a cat house.

The dead woman in the salt was all but forgotten. Except by Jenkins.

And Old Tom.

And one other.

"She weren't no Good-Christian," the other said.

All faces turned toward the source—a small man, dark skinned and darker eyed, hunched into a funeral black duster . . . a living shadow among the dead ones.

"You got somethin' t' tell us, do you, Joseph?" Old Tom asked.

The Ohlone nodded but stayed rooted to his spot near the edge of the circle. The Good-Christians at the Indian School, along with giving him a *proper* name and teaching him to walk in ill-fitting shoes, had given him daily lessons on his place in the white world.

Joseph still carried the scars of those lessons on his back.

"She weren't no Good-Christian," he repeated. "Do like th' new man says an' toss her back into deep water."

"She ain't no sackful o' kittens," the lanky boy

growled, his voice easing into a superior tone. "We can't just dump 'er."

Only the Indian's eyes turned toward the boy. "She were a witch. Long a'fore the Good-Christians come, my first people throw'd her in the shallows t' drown."

Jenkins watched the boy's jaw go slack and stifled a laugh. If the lad was green enough to believe in such rot, then far be it from him to deprive him of any enjoyment.

"Why'd they do it, Joseph?" Old Tom asked, quietlike, as if he were in church.

Jenkins could see the reflected lantern light glitter off the indian's eyes as they turned back toward the body. "She witched th' men of th' tribe an' forced 'em t' . . ."

"T' do what, Joseph?" Henry asked so loudly that some of the men started. "Hellfire, boy, now you got me interested!"

Joseph backed up a step, away from the light and men, his eyes never leaving the body.

"She forced them t' lie with 'er."

Jenkins looked down at the shriveled corpse and bust out laughing. More than half the harvesters joined him.

"Just like some godless savage t' get a little pleasurin' mixed up with witchin'. Damn me if the government didn't know what it was doin' puttin' you all on reservations like it done. Keep you from hurtin' yourselves." He rocked back on his heels and slapped both thighs. It was the best joke he'd heard in a long time. "Killin' a whore for doin' what comes natural . . . shit, that makes about as much sense as shootin' off a toe t' make your boots fit."

"Do seem like a waste," Henry agreed.

"But why'd they sew her like that?" the lanky kid asked, still not satisfied. "Why didn't they just run her out'a town like the Marshal done t' that whore with the pox?"

Jenkins settled back, as eager as the others for the answer.

"It wasn't like that," the indian said. "My first people say that after a man was with her he was . . . changed."

"Changed how, Joseph?"

"Couldn't hunt . . . couldn't do more'n crawl. His wife an' children could go hungry, but he'd go crawlin' back t' the witch like a dog after a bitch." Joseph swatted a wisp of salt-tangled hair away from his face and back up, away from the light . . . away from the body. "Soon all the hunters dead, dried up like scraped hides, an' the women an' children all but starved. When the little boys started crawlin' t' the witch, the women went an' got her.

"My first people said the women told her to get out, but the witch just laughed." Joseph melted back into the darkness, his voice barely a whisper above the off-shore wind. "My first people said that them starvin' little boys were crawlin' all 'round her legs like maggots, tryin' t' get in."

Jenkins heard dry rumblings coming from the men and felt his own spine hunker up at the thought. Glancing down, he studied the shrunken, lantern-yellow features and tried to conjure up the woman's living image. Without success.

Whatever she'd been, there was more horror than whore in her now.

"I'll take her," Jenkins said loud enough to make sure they all heard.

The sound of the bay got loud again. Jenkins could feel Old Tom's eyes boring into the top of his skull. Looking up, he met the old man's gaze and smiled.

"What the hell you mean *you'll take her?*" Henry snapped, snatching his lantern off the ground as if he thought that might be appropriated next. "Half a minute ago you were a' set to toss 'er."

Jenkins stood up slowly, working himself up to his full six feet by degrees; knowing the effect it would have on the scrawny chicken of a man.

He wasn't disappointed.

Henry backpedaled so quickly he almost dropped his precious light.

"Half a minute ago I hadn't reckoned on just how much she were worth."

Henry stared at the dead woman the way a kid would stare at a wagon-trodden dog.

"Worth? Hell, new man, she ain't worth the salt clingin' t' 'er."

"That's where you're wrong," he said. "She's worth more 'n any o' you'd ever guess."

Stooping suddenly, Jenkins dug his arms under the dead woman's shoulders and sewn knees, cradling her against the front of his jacket like a child . . . a very cold and stiff child. She smelled lightly of brine and the years in the salt had taken most of the weight out of her. Jenkins was surprised at how light she was. He was even more surprised by the way his skin crawled under his clothes, as if it were trying to distance itself further from the dead thing in his arms.

"You can't just claim a body like it were a sack of salt," Old Tom said. "The sheriff gotta be called in."

Jenkins let his smile grow teeth.

"To do what, haul her in for disturbin' the peace? Hell, she seems pretty peaceful t' me right now."

"You out 'a your mind, new man." Side-lit by the lantern, Old Tom's face looked as hard and lifeless as the woman's. "People 'round these parts used t' hang body snatchers."

Stiff tendons creaked against his chest like a two-dollar saddle.

"What the hell you dickerin' at, old man. I never dug her out 'o no grave. She's salvage, just the same as if she floated in from the bay. I know the law, and the law says a man can claim salvage if no other man objects. . . ."

Jenkins shot a warning glance into the silent crowd of men.

"So I'm claimin' 'er. And there'll be no more 'bout it." He paused, watching the men. "Will there?"

The haulers suddenly found things of interest near their boots.

"Well . . . whatcha gonna *do* with 'er, now . . . Mr. Jenkins?"

Mr. Jenkins. *Miss-ter* Jenkins. He liked that. Puffing up, he smiled down at the shrunken face.

"Gonna buy me a first rate coffin n' haul 'er into 'Frisco. People on that side o' th' bay pay good money t' see curiosities." He could already hear the twenty-dollar gold pieces jingling in his pockets. "Heard tell o' one man made 'nuff gold off cheatin' folks with a mermaid he made himself to buy a castle.

"But I got somethin' better. I got me a *real* Injin witch. There ain't nobody who wouldn't pay t' see that."

It was pure swagger . . . something to pull a little more wind out of the harvesters' sails. At least that's what Jenkins kept telling himself as he gave way to a sudden inspiration and pressed his lips against the withered mouth.

She tasted like stale kippers.

Jenkins fought down the urge (*need*) to vomit as he pulled away.

"Not bad." The voice he heard sounded thin, verging on hysteria. Jenkins cleared his throat until he felt a sharp scraping and looked up. "Might just forget 'bout showin' 'er off an keep 'er salted away. So t' speak."

None of the harvesters thought enough of the joke to offer so much as a nod. The Kid looked close to feeding a few fish on his own. Old Tom just looked.

"You're th' sickest son of a bitch I've ever seen," he said just loud enough for Jenkins to hear. "Nothin' good's gonna come of this."

"Plenty good, ol' man," Jenkins fired back, still feeling the rock-hard lips against his own, "I'm gonna be walkin' a golden road . . . an' she's gonna line every inch o' th' way."

"No."

All heads, Jenkins' included, turned toward the sound. Joseph was nothing more than a stain on the already black night. A *mouthy* stain, Jenkins thought.

"You gonna stop me, Injin?"

There was a tiny movement in the darkness surrounding him, as if he were glancing from side to side. Don't be expecting help from this bunch, Jenkins thought at the man, they ain't got th' brass.

"Well?"

The movement stopped.

"You have t' take her back t' deep water," the man said, "out where n'body'll find her. Like a Good-Christian."

Jenkins never felt less like laughing, but he bent his knees, tipped back, and let go a belly-buster that echoed halfway down the coast. The dead thing in his arms curled closer, nuzzling his neck.

"'Pears t' me that them *Good Christians* walloped the word o' God a little too hard into you, Injin." Jenkins shifted the weight into a more comfortable position and took a step forward. "An' I *am* bein' a Good Christian . . . I'm making profit off a poor heathen."

Any further comment was lost as Jenkins shoved past him. None of the others tried to stop him, but cleared a path as soon as his intentions were obvious. Only Old Tom had fixed him with an evil eye and a scowl that cut his face in two.

And Jenkins had dismissed both with a glance.

He left the pens whistling, keeping well to the center of the moonlit wagon path, fixing his eyes on the distant lights he knew came from their coolie shacks. Ignoring the swaying shape in his arms.

He stopped whistling halfway up the path and concentrated hard on just walking. The dead woman seemed to grow heavier with each step he took.

"Just cold," Jenkins said out loud because the night had gotten too quiet. "Shoulda known better than standin' out in damp salt, jawin' with a bunch o' jackasses like that. Sucks all th' strength out o' a man. 'Course you'd know more 'bout that than me."

He glanced down at the shrunken face bathed in moonlight, the half-open eyes like pearls, and felt his bowels twist into knots. Even when he looked away, he could feel the marble-hard eyes fixed on him.

Watching him.

"Stupider 'n a mare in a windstorm," he chided himself as gooseflesh crawled down his spine. "Nothin' here but a chance t' make a whole pitful o' greenback . . ."

Watching him.

". . . nothin' 't all."

Jenkins lowered his arms supporting the head, then shuddered at the crackling sound it made as it tipped backward. It reminded him of chitterlings cooking.

He passed the coolie shacks on the windward side, afraid of what the smell of their damnable cooking would do to his already anxious belly, then quickened his pace—aware that the others had had more than enough time to realize the opportunity they'd let slip through their fingers.

"Just let 'em try," he panted, scrambling up the side

of a salt-crusted berm. "They had their chance an' they lost it. If they're real lucky, we might just drop 'em a line from 'Frisco."

Tossing her unladylike to one shoulder, Jenkins patted her narrow butt (. . . feeling the naked flesh beneath the salt . . .) and walked toward a slat-sided equipment shed. There was no way on God's green earth that he was going to bring her into the bunkhouse, to be stared at and coveted. And stolen the minute his back was turned. No way. He'd sit up with her tonight, keeping watch. Then in the morning he'd take her into town and buy her the prettiest coffin he could find.

"Have pink satin linin'," he told her, working the door latch. The Crew Boss never locked the door, wouldn't have even if there'd been a lock. If anything turned up missing, he'd get a couple o' harvesters to go down and bust up the Chinks. Little, if anything ever got stolen . . . although things were known to have been "misplaced" during slow periods in the pens.

"Pink linin' an' silver trim, just like m' maw's had." He kicked the door shut with his boot and struck a match. In the wavering light he saw a pile of gunny sacks near the back and quickly carried her there. He'd keep it dark, he decided when the match burned out. There was enough light leaking through the cracks to see by, and he sure as hell didn't want any unexpected company busting in on them. "Maybe even have one o' them windows put in t' give all them rich folk a little peek . . . whet their appetites, so t' speak."

To demonstrate, Jenkins licked his own lips. There

was something more than just salt and brine clinging to them, something that left a bitter aftertaste. Something that made Jenkins think of bloated muskrats ripening along the edge of the pens. Spitting into a row of drying-rakes, he rubbed his mouth against the back of his sleeve.

The taste was there, too. Stronger, as if he'd been soaking in it. . . .

Jenkins turned his face toward the skeletal leg and sniffed. Nuzzled it. Touched the tip of his tongue to it.

And gagged.

The undulating cry that came out of his mouth didn't sound any more human than did the mourning cry of the gulls. He was still screaming as he flung her on to the sacks. She landed clumsily, head tipped back, arms flung wide, peaceful . . . the way an unconscious woman looks just before a man takes her. Only the crude (*cruel*) stitching kept her legs modestly closed.

The sound softened into a whisper and was gone.

Jenkins took a step closer. All he had to do was cut the threads and spread those legs open and . . . and stopped with the suddenness of a man slamming into a brick wall.

Not usually a man to shy away from the "rougher" pleasures of life, the image of him pushing into her (. . . *like maggots, tryin' t' get in* . . .) was enough to squeeze the contents of his belly up into the back of his throat. What the hell's the matter with me? She ain't much more 'n bones an' tanned hide. Hell, ridin' her'd be . . .

". . . like couplin' with an ol' boot."

The sound of his voice startled him. He hadn't planned on talking out loud, the same way he hadn't planned on thinking about the dead woman as if she were alive and wholesome.

But he kept doing both.

"First thing in th' mornin' I'll fetch y' over t' th' Funeral Home. Then we'll up and leave. Take the *Alma* into 'Frisco an' set up shop." Smiling, Jenkins walked over and sat down on the sacks next to her. "Them city stiffs'll take a right fancy t' you, they will."

He ran his hand slowly down the desiccated flesh on her thighs, gently plucking at the rawhide binding them together.

"Especially th' men."

Plucking them like a fiddle. It made a flat sound, like rain striking a tin roof.

"Yessir, those fine gentlemen'll come crawlin'," (. . , *like dogs after a bitch* . . .) "hands full o' money just t' get a look."

like dogs

Jenkins had his pocket knife out and locked back, admiring the feel of the blade against his thumb.

"Might as well give 'em somethin' t' look at."

The pickled rawhide cut like warm butter under the knife. Long frozen knees snapped as he lifted them. Salt-encrusted curls tickled the palm of his hand.

"Maybe I'll even invite a few o' em back . . . after th' show." The knife was lost somewhere in the folds of the rough cloth as Jenkins began exploring her with his fingertips. Beneath its concealing layer of salt her flesh was as smooth and firm as his.

"Ain't no one alive could resist you," he whispered, fumbling with the buttons on his suspenders. "Soon as th' word gets out 'bout our *special* shows, hell, we'll be rollin' in gold."

rollin'

. . . like a dog after a bitch . . .

Engorged a moment earlier, Jenkins felt himself shrivel as he pushed himself into her. From the cold, he thought, using his fingers to stuff himself in. Has to be the cold.

"Them fancy men'll drop their drawers, a'right." Something suddenly opened up inside her—like a warm mouth, sucking him deeper. . . . "If I let them. I—I may—just keep you t'—m'self."

She liked that idea. Jenkins could tell by the way she moved under him, opening herself to him. Drawing him deeper.

When the first spasm hit, he felt her legs wrap around his back, locking him into her.

"You don't need t' worry 'bout me pullin' out," he told her, as he brushed the salt away from her face and smiled into the shining eyes. "Wouldn't do that if I could."

She arched her back, clawed at his back with thick nails. She was ready to go again. Eager. Better than any five-dollar whore.

"Hell, you're better 'n any *twenty*-dollar whore," he whispered, the only endearment he knew.

Fingering her lips apart, he forced his tongue deep into her waiting mouth. She tasted like salt pork left out in the sun and honeycomb dripping with sugar. Jenkins lapped it up like a starving puppy.

When he pulled away to catch his breath, she was smiling up at him.

"Won't put you in no coffin, however fancy it is," he promised. "Get you a room at one o' them fancy hotels an' make 'em pay a hundred dollars a ride."

Yes. Make them pay. She arched her back, slid her long-nailed fingers into his ass, and pulled. Wanting him. Needing him. Demanding. *I'm free only to you. Only you.*

Jenkins felt his body respond to the challenge, meeting her demands with renewed effort.

This time he was whimpering—panting like an animal run to ground and willing to just lie there and wait for the hunter's bullet. He tried to explain it to her, but she wouldn't listen. She had years to make up for. Her demands were less subtle.

She ground his hips raw, clawed bloody furrows into him when he tried to pull out, forced a rock-hard nipple into his mouth when he opened it to gasp for air.

And their lovemaking went on.

And on.

And on.

Old Tom looked down at them and shook his head in a way that neither conveyed sadness nor judgment. Surprise, maybe. In his sixty-four years he'd figured to have seen just about everything. But he figured wrong.

"You don't think it's . . . I mean, it couldn't be."

Henry stood just outside the shed door, gaping like an air-strangled fish. "Could it?"

"Well, that 'pears t' be that long-coat he's so proud of, an' I 'magine that's a real good likeness o' his boots."

"But that ain't possible, Tom." He lifted the lantern higher, until the orange glow showed directly on the pile of sacks. And the two bodies.

The dead woman from the pen was flat on her back, legs spread, arms wrapped around the shriveled corpse of a man. The thick layer of salt covering them both glistened like snow in the reflected light.

"Jenkins left the pen not more'n an hour ago." Henry said, lowering the light. "That couldn't be him."

"Why not?" he asked. "Never heard o' a woman suckin' a man dry?"

For the first time since they'd heard the high-pitched screeching coming from the shed, Old Tom looked at the slack-mouthed men crowding the doorway and winked.

"'Course it can't be the new man. This is just his way o' funnin' us." Cocking his head, Old Tom was convinced he heard the man's coarse laughter on the night breeze. "Probably out there right now, brayin' like a jackass."

A few of the harvesters smiled. Most looked ready to string the new man up by his balls. The wild-eyed terror was gone and that's what the old man had been aiming for.

"Man was as close t' a grave robber as they come," he said. "Stealin' one more body t' play a mean-spirited joke wouldn't seem like nothin'."

SALT

Henry stepped to one side to let the old man pass. "What d' you think we should do with 'em, Tom? I don't like t' idea o' just leavin' em."

"Do like Joseph said an' toss 'em back t' deep water." Old Tom smiled at the indian. "It'd be the Christian thing t' do, wouldn't it, Joseph?"

The returning smile looked like a dusky white moth hovering in the darkness. "The very Good-Christian thing t' do."

"But what if th' new man comes back lookin' for 'em?" Henry could be as stubborn as a bulldog when he wanted to be.

Old Tom gave the bodies one more glance (the big one *did* look familiar) and stepped down into the night. The harvesters were already moving toward the bunkhouses.

"Doubt if he'll be comin' back, Henry. If he does, he can just go swimmin' for 'em." Henry listened to the sound of the old man's hob-nailed boots fade. "Just you don't get yourself attached t' that Injin whore, Henry—"

The voice was little more than a whisper.

"—can't afford t' lose—"

Henry chuckled as he turned. Old Tom sure knew how to keep a joke going, he glanced at the bodies and fell silent, even if the joke was more nightmare than fun.

"Well, better get t' 'er."

Swallowing hard, he hooked a hand under the male corpse and tossed it to the floor. It looked as long dead

287

as the woman—the exposed privates resembling a dried out, stomped on toad.

Henry couldn't stop the series of shivers that took over his spine. The man didn't look like he died easy.

"Gonna dump you an' your lady friend deep," he told the corpse, covering the distorted face with one of the sacks. "Take you way out past th' breakwaters an' sink you deep. Give ya both a good rest this time."

Turning, he focused the light on the dead woman. She seemed more comfortable with her demise. More peaceful. Henry let the light play over her body, taking particular note of the space between her open legs.

"You really musta been somethin' if they took it in their head t' sew you shut."

Smiling, he sat down next to her and ran his hand slowly down the inside of her thigh.

She didn't look half bad.

Not bad at all.

ALWAYS, IN THE DARK

by Charles Grant

It just slips away, doesn't it. So much time. Days, years, months . . . it all just slips away. People up there, the ones who've made it, the ones who don't have to worry about their bills, their food, they don't really know. Maybe, in the dark, when they're trying to get some sleep, they get a hint of some kind. But they don't really know about the rest of us, about most of us.

I tried, Maggie. I swear to God, I tried. And you'll probably never know, not really, just how much it all hurt.

Never know how many times I wanted to just quit, chuck it, light out for the territory, and get myself so damn lost I'd never find my way back.

When you're young, they call it the coward's way out; when you're old, they call it worn out; when you're somewhere in between, but closer to the worn out, they don't know what to call it because they're not there yet and they haven't got a clue. They haven't got one damned clue.

I saw him today, you know.

I didn't mean to. It was one of those things, you're

just walking along, minding your own business, checking on the neighborhood to see how things are going, see if anything's different from the last time you were around, and damned if he doesn't show up on the corner, coming out of the luncheonette. He didn't see me at first, and I almost made it by without having to say anything, but he did, and the look on his face was something else again. It damn near made me laugh, I have to be honest, and when I headed for the park without saying hello or good-bye or how's the wife and kids, he followed me. I didn't look around. I could feel him. I could hear him.

He hasn't changed, Maggie.

God. He hasn't changed.

He followed me, and I hurried through the gates and up the blacktop, past the ice cream kiosk, past the place where the kids cut through the shrubs to get to the playing field, and when I got to the old pine, that miserable-looking tree that should have died a hundred years ago, I turned off the path and made my way up the slope.

He followed.

I have to give him that—he still followed me.

So when I got near the top, I turned right and made my way through to the open, and sat down. There were people down there, a few playing ball, some little ones playing tag around the bandstand, a lot of them sitting in a circle doing something, I don't know what.

He came out of the trees a few minutes later, and I couldn't help it, I did laugh then. His suit was a mess, his tie was hanging to one side, and that precious ton of hair wasn't quite so perfect anymore.

He might have had a tan, I don't know.

I do know he was pretty damn pale.

Now wait a minute, Maggie, hang on there, I'll get to it, don't rush me, you know how I am and I don't guess I'm ever going to change. Certainly not now.

So he stands there for a minute, swiping at leaves and twigs stuck to his clothes, muttering to himself, saying God knows what until he looks up and sees me. He blinks a little, like he was trying to be sure it really was me, then he comes up and stands below me a little, so we're nearly looking eye to eye. His eyes are a little puffy, he's carrying some extra weight, and I think he was trying to decide if he'd maybe had just one too many back there at lunch. But I also know he doesn't believe that, because if he did, he wouldn't have come along.

Then he turned around and kind of flapped his hands and looked down at the playing field. Shook his head. Looked over his shoulder and shook his head again. I guess he figured there must have been a hundred things he could have said about then, and I'd bet he'd been practicing for years, just in case. Good things, bad things, a bunch of in-between things, but I don't think he'd planned on saying what he did:

"What the hell are you doing here?"

"Live here," I told him.

His face, kind of caught by the sun, got a little red. "You won't ever leave me alone, will you."

I smiled, but not much. "I'm not sure. Depends."

"Hey," he said, getting quiet like he does when he's going to lose his temper. "Hey, don't play games with me, Pop. I don't need that crap."

"Don't know what you're talking about," I said.

"Jesus, give me a break, huh? Just give me a break."

And then, Maggie, the damnedest thing happened—he moved between me and the sun, and just like that, he turned into a shadow. I couldn't see his face anymore, I couldn't see anything about him except, suddenly, the way he used to be.

Jesus, darlin', it slips away, doesn't it.

Eight years old and trying to catch a baseball, chasing that thing like it was Mexican jumping bean; ten years old and making faces at his cousins at someone's birthday party; fourteen and in what he thinks is love for the very first time, coming home and wanting to know why girls think he's stupid, he's not stupid, Daddy, he's not stupid, why do they always want to call him stupid?

I remember I told him it's just one of those things, son, just one of those things. Girls get smarter faster, grow up faster, and live longer; boys are boys from the day they're born until the day they die.

He cried, you know; I never told you that, darlin', but he cried.

Then he moved again, and he was as he is.

"You don't think . . . I mean, you don't plan on coming by the house, do you?" he asked, not really sure he wanted to hear the answer.

I plucked at some grass. "Maybe. Depends."

"Jesus Christ, can't you ever give me a straight answer?"

He stomped off, just like he always does when he doesn't get his way, and I laughed a little, but not enough for him to hear me. I figured he would go back to his office, yell a little at his secretary, and by the time he got home to Joanie, he'd call it a dream, or a bit of a bad shrimp, or part of the hangover he woke up with that morning.

I didn't care.

Just as long as he knew I was still around, I didn't care how he explained it.

In fact, I'm willing to bet a million dollars right now that as soon as he walked into the house—they're still out there on the Pike, that damn drafty place at least a hundred years old, I always hated it, you know—as soon as he got there, he told Joanie he had seen a ghost, and when she gave him that look, you know the one I mean, he probably said that he ran into his old man in the park and figured I must be a ghost because he'd given me up for dead.

A long time ago.

Now, now, Maggie, don't say things like that. He's not a poor boy anymore, he's a grown man.

And I'm not the villain.

Not anymore.

In fact, I'll make you another bet—that the one thing I'll never do is go to that house and ask him to forgive me. He gets old enough, either he'll understand or he won't, and nothing I say will make him go one way or the other.

So anyway, a couple of days later, after checking on our place to see what the new owners had done to it, I was back in the park, up there on the slope, and there were these children down there . . . oh, Maggie, you should have seen them. All these little guys in baseball caps and shorts and gloves that were too big and trying to run those basepaths, those little legs churning away like mad and they must have been making all of about two miles an hour. And all their folks just cheering them on and waving and screaming, you'd think it was the World Series instead of a quick game on a Saturday afternoon.

About halfway through it, the sun low enough to start poking in my eyes, he came back.

He was wearing scruffy jeans and some beat-up old sneakers, and his shirt was pulled out and looking a little ratty. Even his hair wasn't the way I knew he wanted it to be.

He looked like a grown man trying to remember how it was to dress like one of those kids down there.

He sat down a few yards away, pulled up his legs, tucked his chin to his knees.

"You're not going to believe this, but Joanie thinks I should ask you home to dinner or something."

I nodded.

"I don't think so."

I nodded again.

"The kids, Pop," he said. "They think you're . . . you know." He shrugged a little, just one shoulder. "It wouldn't be fair."

The wind came up then, a handful of dead leaves

tumbling down the slope, and when I checked, I could see a few clouds dark on the bottom scudding in from the east, behind us. I hoped it was going to rain a little that night. God knows the Station needed it, the lawns going all to hell, the crops out in the valley stunted and going brown.

But it didn't feel like rain; it felt hot, that's all. It felt hot.

Like that day.

Oh, Maggie, no need, no need.

I don't hate him.

He didn't know.

"Pop?"

"I'm listening."

He settled his chin a little, hugged those shins a little tighter.

Someone down below hit a ball, and the crack of it carried all the way to the clouds.

"I'm going to be fifty next week, you know."

I grinned. "Tell me something new, son."

He gave such a sigh, I thought he would fall over. "It's not going so well. At least, not like I planned it."

"Yep. It seldom does. Hardly ever, as a matter of fact."

"We sold Joanie's car and a lot of those savings bonds I had at the bank. Thank God, the kids got through school."

Home run down there, I think.

Lots of cheering, anyway; lots of running around and hugging and throwing caps in the air.

His hands dropped to the grass. "It's falling apart,

Pop. Christ Almighty, it's all falling apart, and I don't know what to do about it. I'm too old to get another job, too old to start over, at least that's what they tell me, and I . . ." He kind of laughed, kind of sighed. "I just don't feel like I'm twenty-one anymore, you know what I mean?"

He turned his head.

He looked at me.

"I'm tired, Pop. Jesus Christ, I'm tired."

But he wasn't sad, and he wasn't feeling any self-pity, not like some people who get to the place he was. I could see it in the way those sweet blue eyes turned damn near black. He was angry; he was furious; and he didn't know who he had to hit to let it all out.

Like he had hit me when you left, darlin'; like he blamed me for not taking care of you better, for letting you take that walk in that evening shower, when I knew that walking in a July shower day or night was the most favorite thing in your life. Helped you grow, you always said, but he never liked it, not even when he was growing up.

My fault.

It was my fault, according to him.

He thought I was God, Maggie; hell, I was only his father.

Now, damnit, Maggie, stop it, you hear me?

It wasn't my fault, no matter what he thought, and you know it.

He had his mind made up, there was nothing I could have said that would have changed it. He thought I killed you, that the pneumonia was my fault, and I decided he might as well hang on to that for a while, long enough for him to learn.

How was I to know he wouldn't, that he'd carry it with him like some kind of charm?

That's when he stood up; that's when he stood over me; that's when I could see that he'd finally found someone to hit.

"Fifty," he said.

I looked up at him.

I shrugged.

"I followed you, you know," he said, voice low, not quite trembling, little bubbles of spit frothing at the corner of his mouth. "Every year, you came back here around my birthday and spent days over in Memorial Park talking to Mom. You never came around to the house. You never wrote. You never called. You just talked to a goddamn gravestone. And then you stopped. Just like that."

He stepped closer.

"Why?"

I looked straight at him. "No need," I said. "I did what I had to, and then I didn't have to anymore."

That's when he hit me.

Or, at least, that's when he tried.

And when he realized that he couldn't, that I wasn't there, he kind of choked a little and backed away, looked around at the ground until he found a rock, and when he had, he threw it.

When that didn't work, he found a stick and threw it.

I didn't do anything, Maggie.

I just sat there.

Just like the afternoon I sat on the back porch of that place over to Darien and told my heart to knock it off, I was tired, I wanted to go.

You know, I never told them my real name. Not the doctors, not the other old folks. I'd signed myself in, told them my family was gone, and I just wanted someplace to put my head other than a park bench. And when they buried me, I decided it was time.

But you know what?

When I saw him running away down that slope, when I saw him fall, roll over, get up and run again, I knew I done it again.

I had made a mistake.

I wanted to tell him how it slips away, how he shouldn't let it, not if he could help it, not if he loved anyone the way I love him.

Too late again, Maggie.

I was too damn late again, he was running away just like he did the first time.

But today's his birthday, and I know what has to be done.

He's alone, Maggie; despite his family, my son's alone, and he needs me, I don't care how old he is, how many grandchildren I have, how many great-grandchildren on the way.

He's hated me for half his life, and he hasn't learned a thing about what it's all about. Well, damnit, I've given up trying to be the good old dad, the dear old dad, the understanding dad that's going to wipe his nose every time it runs and lead him by the hand over every goddamn pit and ditch.

It slips away, Maggie, whether we want it to or not.

So from now on, that fifty-year-old kid is going to know that he's never going to be alone again, because I'm going to be there now, for the rest of his life.

The sun's too bright; he won't see me anymore.

But I'll be there, in the dark.

Always, Maggie.

Always.

In the dark.

AFTERNOON GHOST

by Jack Dann and George Zebrowski

It was twelve o'clock. The secretaries were chatting and putting their desk in order. Michael Brown leaned across his desk toward the intercom. "Miss Manley, would you make a reservation at the Townshend Club for me? I think they can find me a table. Tell them I'm confirming a previous reservation."

Miss Manley did not answer. He got up and walked out to her desk and said, "Miss Manley." No response. "Miss Manley!"

She stared at him, took off her glasses, and laid them on her desk.

"Miss Manley, are you deaf and blind? *Answer me!*"

She covered her typewriter and called to her co-secretary. "Are you ready? Come on, it's getting chilly in here."

"Is this a joke or something?" he shouted as the secretaries left the room. "Damn you all, come back here . . . doesn't *anyone* hear me?"

He walked back into his office, feeling frustrated and impotent and angry. *Always a nothing, a nobody, even when he had money and an office, and a little authority.*

He stopped suddenly and stared at his desk. He saw his own body slouched over it, arms hanging over the front side; in a moment, it seemed, it would fall off the edge. Even as he watched it, the body fell gently to the thick green carpet.

He backed away from the desk until he was up against the wall next to the door. Then he was *inside* the wall. He screamed. He pushed vigorously until he floated back into the office. But he held back the next scream as he hovered over his body while rubbing his immaterial hands together.

"Help . . ." he whispered. "Someone please help me." He floated out the window and down to the pavement, but no one noticed Michael Brown. Very slowly he floated upright, a pale, paper kite. He tried to compose himself; if he did not get excited, he could imitate normal walking.

He walked up and down streets and avenues and alleys. He walked through people and building and eventually into the ladies' room of the Club Risque. He sat down on a pink couch and looked into an empty mirror.

Of course I can't see myself, he thought. I'm a . . . ghost. His fear seemed to melt away. It was as if the weight of the world had been removed from his shoulders. He felt light-headed and laughed and danced around the room. He was a ghost . . . he was free . . . he would live forever. Oblivious to his presence, a half-nude dancer continued to put on her makeup in front of a large illuminated mirror. Michael stopped and touched her shoulder. He concentrated. And after a while he could *feel*. He ran his hands down her back;

it was tight and smooth, and he imagined he could feel some of the warmth.

Now, he thought, no one can stop me. He was a man who could do as he pleased.

He sang three bars of "Stout Hearted Men."

He laughed as loud as he could and floated up over the sink.

There was an eternity of pleasure ahead . . . and it was all free.

Later he followed her home. He went into her bedroom and watched. She turned on the lamp by her double bed. She unzipped the back of her dress deftly. She kicked off both shoes, sat down on the bed, then lifted her leg to remove her stockings. She removed her bra and panties. She was all his now.

He hovered over the bed and crossed his legs in the air. He watched.

Her hair touched the pillow; her leg was bent at the knee and her face was in profile. She turned completely onto her back and her large eyes were wide open. She made no move to pull up the covers. Michael felt slightly embarrassed. He looked into her eyes for a long time, until she closed them. Then very slowly he floated down on top of her. He pushed one hand under her brown hair, and he circled her waist with the other. He concentrated, until he could feel her warm breath and skin.

He rested on her, waiting for his excitement to quicken, for the girl to come completely alive in his arms. But she only shivered and reached through him for the covers, which she pulled up to her neck.

And he realized that once again he couldn't do it. Even now when it didn't matter, when no one could be hurt, his past held him tightly and wouldn't forgive him. The thought of sin and transgression was too great. That was why he had *never* been able to do it.

Something tugged at his arm, but he couldn't see it.

There was a blinding flash of light, and he tumbled into what felt like a pile of sand. He opened his eyes. A cloud of dust floated around him, reflecting the golden sunlight into his eyes. He stood up and tried to walk.

He took two steps, and a voice said, "It's about time."

A squat little man sat at a huge desk in the middle of a desert. He thumbed through the lined yellow pages of his ledger in boredom. "Well, come over here! I have an appointment in five minutes. So tell me *your* story. You now have four minutes."

Michael Brown tried to speak but couldn't.

"Look, just relax," the man said. "Give me your qualifications and we can *both* get out of here . . . I'm just as hot as you are, but the new rule is that we can't make anyone comfortable until they pass the test."

"The test?" Michael finally managed to say. "Where am I . . . ?"

"Mr. Brown," the little man said. "You are in heaven."

"This is *heaven?*"

"Well . . . this is where it begins. It's much nicer inside. This is sort of the exam room. They don't want people seeing Heaven and then getting excited over something they might not qualify for." The man turned a page in the ledger. "You don't seem to be in such good shape. You just haven't done anything *really* worthwhile. Nothing to speak of. Don't get me wrong, I'm not saying you were *bad,* we don't like to say that about *anyone,* but your records are sort of well, blah, you know."

"I was a very successful businessman and . . ."

"No, please don't go through all that. I've heard the same spiel a hundred and forty-five times today, and I couldn't listen to it again. Just tell me something of value that you've accomplished. Anything at all. We're agreeable."

"Well, I can't remember *specific* incidents," Michael said. "You should have them in your book. But I went to church—"

"Don't even start with the church business . . . you know why you went to church. Just tell me what there is of value in you. Tell me about a good deed. Surely you can think of *something.*"

"Maybe you could ask my brother, he should be up here somewhere. He can tell you about me."

The man stifled a yawn. "He said you were okay, but he couldn't come up with anything either. You'd better hurry, we're running out of time."

Everything has happened so fast, Michael thought. I need time to think things over.

"You're a problem," the man said. "I just don't quite know where to fit you in. Look, walk that way, west, toward the large red dune, and see what happens. I'm only a clerk . . ."

The man and his desk disappeared.

Michael walked, but he didn't seem to be getting anywhere. The dune seemed to be as far away as when he'd started. He turned to retrace his steps back to heaven when he saw the clerk. He looked almost like the little man he had met before, except his hair was thicker and he was smiling. And his desk was not as big.

"Were you going back? That just isn't done, you know."

"I got lost. Am I supposed to see you?"

"I'm the man."

"Am I still in heaven?" Michael asked. He looked around, trying to discover some clue to where he was. But there was only desert as far as he could see . . . and the swirling dust-devils of sand.

"No, this is hell. It's sort of a border between domains. The main part of hell starts beyond the third dune there."

"But this looks the same as—"

"As heaven?" the clerk said. "Yes, it's almost the same thing, except we take the bad and they take the good. I suppose it depends upon which ethical code you commit yourself to. It's just division of labor. Well, let's get on with it. It's much too hot out here."

"Isn't hell *supposed* to be hot?"

"I just told you it's about the same thing as over there." The clerk pointed toward the boundary of heaven. "You don't really think that heaven is hot, so why should hell be hot? That's the propaganda they teach you down there. It's revolting. Look, no more questions until later. Let's see if we can use you." He glanced at his ledger. "Now tell me what you've done."

"You mean the *bad* things?"

"Yes, bad things . . . anything from theft to murder. And intention is important, too." He paused, concentrating on a page in the ledger. "You know, this book doesn't say much about you. In fact, it says almost *nothing*. There must be something I can enter into the book on your behalf."

Michael was embarrassed, but he would have to tell the man about what he had done to the nude dancer before he had been summoned away from the world. After all, he couldn't stay in limbo forever, walking back and forth across this endless desert. Hell was better than being nowhere. "I made . . . I watched a nude dancer while she was . . ."

"That doesn't count," the clerk said. "You weren't alive, remember? All the returns are already in. Everyone gets time to see their family or friends before they leave. You can do anything you want with the time, but it just doesn't count for anything. Anyway, I wouldn't be proud of it if I were you. You made a fool of yourself, and you didn't even finish the job. No, that's no good."

Michael became even more nervous. "I did a lot of underhanded things in business—"

The clerk closed the ledger with a thud. "You did what an average businessman would do. There was no malice involved. You never really caused any major problems for anyone, even your so-called enemies."

Michael had to think fast. "I had a girl when I was. . . ."

The clerk shook his head scornfully. "Your time is up and quite frankly I don't know what to do with you. You don't seem to be able to produce any substantial evidence on your own behalf. Your potential for malice and evil was always diluted. You weren't much of an individual, simply a bundle of conformities. Every time you were about to do something that we would consider worthwhile, you stopped because you were afraid of what people would think. You just pitter-patted. It's terrible that so much of this is going on in the world today. We never had this much trouble, not even with the Romans."

"Well, I'm sorry," Michael said. "What are you going to do with me?"

"Wait here until I return. I'm afraid this is going to involve a conference between both sides . . . and that usually means trouble." Then the man and his desk disappeared.

They have to take me, Michael thought. I have to be *somewhere*.

The clerk and his desk appeared as suddenly as they had disappeared. "I had a talk with the other side and we came to a decision," the clerk said. He was perspiring heavily. "Neither side can take you on. To coin a phrase, you haven't lived yet. So . . . you're going back."

"You mean I get another chance?"

"That's it," the clerk said. "Try again. Go out and murder someone, or something." Thunder suddenly rolled across the sunny sky. "Sorry, forget that. Remember, we have nothing to do with you once you return to earth. What you do there will be entirely up to you."

The desert faded away.

Michael found himself standing in a parking lot. He knew this place, the street, the stores, the people. He took a long deep breath. He was alive! He walked jauntily out of the parking lot. He nodded and beamed at perfect strangers, looked in shop windows, enjoyed the rush hour hustle and bustle of the streets . . . all the familiar sights and sounds and smells that he had never really appreciated before.

He was going to make something of his life now.

And he had a whole lifetime to do it.

He passed a corner candy store and on impulse decided to stop in for a candy bar. Life was sweet. Why not enjoy it? Michael picked up a Hershey's bar from a shelf and reached into his pocket for change. But he found nothing but his handkerchief and keys. He looked around. The proprietor was not paying any attention to Michael; he was making up a chocolate egg cream for a customer.

Impulsively, Michael put the candy bar into his coat pocket. His palms were sweaty and he was shaking and his heart seemed to be fluttering in his throat. As he left the store, he repressed the urge to run. He walked down the block and turned a corner.

He was safe. Finally, he had done something . . . and it was easy. He felt wonderful. He felt like a kid again, and this was only the beginning. . . .

Michael started to cross the street. But he was paying more attention to opening his candy bar than to the traffic.

He heard a horn blaring as a station wagon hit him. His head struck the pavement, and the world and all its opportunities disappeared.

There was a different man at the desk this time. Michael did not recognize him.

"Welcome back," the man said. "The big boys on both sides had a feeling there would be a lot of fellows like you, so we opened this middle-of-the-road office. It's for those who don't have the qualifications to go to heaven *or* hell."

"Look, I didn't have *time* to do anything more than steal a candy bar," Michael said, waving the sticky wrapper before the clerk. "Is that good enough?"

"Walk west," said the clerk. "Let *them* make the decision."

In a few minutes Michael stood in front of the hell desk again. The clerk carefully examined the Hershey's bar wrapper. "Well, you did steal . . . technically. But it's nothing to write home about."

"I couldn't help it if a car hit me by accident," Michael said. "I was just getting started."

"Well, I'll admit it wasn't fair to you. You were nipped in the bud, right at the start of a promising career. Of course we're flattered that you chose our side. Let me talk to the old man and see what he thinks."

Satan brushed the sand from his sports jacket. He was tall and had a receding hairline, a large nose, and an angular face. He stood dramatically in front of the desk and looked at Michael. "I understand your problem. Nasty business. "But *this*"—he pointed to the candy wrapper on the desk "—is not enough to get you into hell. It's a question of pride . . . and ethics. It's a shame we can't send you down again, but all this second chance business really louses up the natural laws."

"You mean I can't go back?" Michael said. "What's going to happen to me, then?"

"You've had an unlucky break," Satan said, sitting on the desk. "It's really a bureaucratic tangle now. You can't go back down and you can't come in here or . . . there." He gestured toward heaven. "So you'll just have to stay here."

"In the desert? Forever?" Michael was dumbfounded. "I *can't* stay here. I'll go crazy. This isn't fair." Michael started to cry. What did he do to deserve *this*?

"Please stop crying," Satan said, looking agitated. "I suppose the principle has been violated, and that's what counts. And the intent was there on your part. . . ." The clerk behind the desk was nodding vigorously.

Michael tried to compose himself. "You mean it's good enough? I can come in?"

"Yes, I suppose," Satan said. "You tried very hard, and it *was* theft. Yes, go on in. It's that way, toward the dunes over there," he said, pointing. "I'll catch up with you in a minute."

Satan adjusted his narrow tie. "These charity cases. I wonder how long it's going to take before all hell goes to. . . ."

The intercom on the desk buzzed. "I'll get it," Satan said to the clerk. "You go guide our new charge." The clerk nodded and left.

"Hello, hell."

"This is the middle-of-the-road desk. Another soft job just came in. I'm sending her right over."

"Oh . . . fine," Satan said, wondering about his decision. Sooner or later, he thought, these Michael Browns would have to be put into a clearer category, their status institutionalized, if only to prevent these rule-of-thumb decisions being overturned one day.

After all, being wishy-washy *was* a failure, and failure *was* a crime, wasn't it? He toyed with the idea of sending them into the nothingness of limbo. Plenty of room there. No, that would be ideologically untidy, as was all non-being. Too much like the atheist's notion of death. Non-being was and wasn't a form of existence. Very untidy.

There was no reason why he shouldn't get the soft jobs. He needed all the souls he could get. They might as well go to hell as limbo. Their record could be defined as a major transgression in itself, based on a willful refusal to play the game of salvation-damnation. That would be enough to send them to hell in a deserving way. . . .

On the other hand, shouldn't hell be reserved for the *truly* bad? Maybe it would be better to stuff limbo with legions of Michael Browns, thus denying them to heaven while concentrating essential evil in hell.

He thought about it for a while, and decided against

the idea; when all was said and done, it was better to have a crowd on your side.

He wrote the appropriate memo, replete with subtle argument and elegant logic, and sent it to the other side. It might just work, he thought . . . and it would eliminate the middle-of-the-road desk, which would please the economy-minded front office.

Proud of himself, Satan sighed, wondering if She would go for it.

THE SOLE SURVIVOR

by Rod Serling

Ponderous yet stately; a giant floating city and yet with her vast decks converging into a single point at the bow, there was a suggestion of gracefulness and speed. Her four funnels spewed out trailing black columns of smoke against the cloudless sky. Far off in the distance little patches of fog blurred the horizon, but the visibility was almost unlimited.

The Lookout spotted the object first and called down to the bridge. "Object in the water," his metallic voice rasped through the speaker, "two miles ahead."

On the bridge the Officer of the Watch and the Quartermaster peered through their binoculars. A black dot bobbed in the gentle swell of the ocean, but clearly visible.

"Damned odd," the Officer of the Watch said, lowering his binoculars. "A lifeboat is what it is."

The Quartermaster kept the binoculars to his eyes. "Appears to be . . . appears to be one survivor."

The Captain of the ship entered the bridge and moved to the ship's telephone on the wall, unhooking it and putting the mouthpiece close to his own mouth. "Lookout. Any signs of life?"

"I thought I saw a movement, sir," the Lookout's voice responded, "but I can't swear to it."

The Captain put the ship's telephone back on its hook and turned toward the two men flanking the wheel. "Starboard, five degrees," he said tersely to the Helmsman.

"Starboard, five degrees, sir."

The Captain turned to the Officer of the Watch. "Three long blasts, Mr. Wilson," he ordered.

The Officer of the Watch pulled a cord above him. There were three massive resounding blasts of noise. Then the Captain looked through his binoculars. The black dot grew larger.

"Officer of the Watch," the Captain asked, "who's our best small-boats man?"

"That would be Mr. Richards, sir."

The Captain lowered his binoculars. "Ask him to come to the bridge."

"Mr. Richards to the bridge," the Officer of the Watch said into the ship's phone.

The Captain moved across the bridge to stand next to the Helmsman. Again he lifted the binoculars to his eyes. "I'll be damned," he said softly. "Looks to be a . . . a woman." He chewed on the end of his mustache as the binoculars dropped; then he turned to the Officer of the Watch. "No reports of ships in distress in these waters?" It was a statement with just a shade of questioning inflection.

"No, sir."

"And yet," the Captain said musingly, "that's a ship's boat. There's no mistaking it."

A young Junior First Officer entered the bridge and saluted the Captain.

"Mr. Richards," the Captain said, "I want you to take starboard sea boat. I'm going to drop and recover you underway. Take a Signalman with you."

He turned to peer through the glass in front—the crow's-feet lines contracting with the habit of years. "We'll be making about five knots when we bring the boat abeam," he continued. "The lifeboat is about two miles away." He made rapid silent calculations inside his head. "This will give you seven minutes to waterline. I'll give two short blasts, which will be the executive for un-hooking the forward falls and shearing off. I'll circle ship to port and pick you up in the same position. Understood?"

"Aye, aye, Captain," Mr. Richards said, with a salute.

"Then carry on." The Captain had already turned to the Quartermaster. "Stop engines," he continued.

"Stop engines," the Quartermaster repeated the order, but turned toward the Captain as he did so. Any slowing down, let alone going dead in the water, was a deadly serious business.

"You heard the order," the Captain said.

The Quartermaster nodded, then reached forward to turn an iron handle. "Stop engines," he repeated again.

"Starboard, two degrees," the Captain said to the Helmsman.

"Starboard, two degrees," the Helmsman repeated the order, turning the wheel slightly.

The Captain and the Officer of the Watch moved out to the open deck in front of the bridge. Again binoculars were raised. The black dot now looked about the size of a fist.

"Make out a name yet?" the Captain asked.

The Officer of the Watch shook his head. "Bit of a fog dead ahead, sir. And that lifeboat—or whatever she is—keeps moving in and out of her."

Again the Captain chewed on the corner of his mustache. "Bloody puzzlement," he murmured. "Ship's boat when there's no ship around. One survivor—and a woman at that. A bloody puzzlement." Then his voice took on the crisp tone of command. "Check seaboard," he continued.

The Officer of the Watch peered over the side railing. Halfway down the vast expanse of ship's side, a boat was being lowered. "Lowering away handsomely, sir."

The Captain stepped back inside the bridge. "What's our speed through water?" he asked the Quartermaster.

"Down to seven knots, sir."

The Captain turned to the Officer of the Watch, who'd followed him in. "And the range of the ship's boat?"

"Approximately a mile and a half now, sir," the Officer of the Watch answered.

"All engines slow astern," the Captain ordered.

"All engines slow astern."

"Check your sea boat again."

The Officer of the Watch went back outside and

again looked over the railing. "At waterline, sir—after falls unhooked," he called out through the open door.

"Stand by," the Captain said. "Two short blasts."

The Quartermaster repeated the order.

"Speed?"

"Five knots, sir."

The Captain felt perspiration on his face. "Stop engines," he ordered.

"Stop engines," the Quartermaster repeated.

Again the voice of the Officer of the Watch came in from outside. "Ship's boat almost abeam," he announced.

The Captain wiped his face. "Two short blasts," he ordered.

"Two short blasts," came the Quartermaster's voice, and once again the pulsating crescendo of noise blasted through the stillness of the day.

"Sea boat's sheared off, sir," the Officer of the Watch informed him.

Then Captain nodded. "Slow ahead, Quartermaster." Then he turned to the Helmsman. "Port, ten degrees."

"Aye, aye, sir," the Helmsman said, turning the wheel.

The Captain lifted up his binoculars, and already those gray little ghosts of doubt marched across his mind. The small and insignificant act of compassion, standing alone and embattled against the giant enemy that was war. Stop a ship that size on a clear and waveless day. God—the risk. The miserable risk. But there *were* laws of the sea that transcended the improvised callousness that passed for security in wartime—laws and customs that dated back to sails and oars; codes of human behavior that had to be honored.

The Captain shook his head as if clearing it of the extraneous little ghosts. "Have Signalman report condition of the survivor," he started to say, then broke off abruptly and frowned. "Mr. Wilson," he barked.

The Officer of the Watch reentered the bridge. "Sir?"

"On the bow of that ship's boat—do you make out something?"

The Officer of the Watch squinted through the binoculars. "Very faintly, sir," he said softly. "A name. . . ."

The binoculars fell. He stood there, mouth open. "That's quite impossible," he said to no one in particular. "Quite impossible."

"Impossible," the Captain said grimly, "or the product of someone's perverted sense of humor." He looked through his binoculars. "You'll be entering this in the log after the Dog Watch this evening, Mr. Wilson. I'll initial it." He lowered the binoculars. "Without my official corroboration, they'd have you up in front of a Board of Inquiry for drinking on duty."

He took a deep breath and moved toward the deck entrance. "I'll be on deck," he announced. "I want to be the first person to talk to that survivor—whoever she is."

He walked out on his little, muscle-knotted bandied sea legs, and his braided Captain's hat could be seen disappearing as he moved down the steps to the deck below.

"What did you see, sir?" the Quartermaster asked the Officer of the Watch.

He gestured toward his binoculars. "I can't make out anything now. She's turned in the swell, and her bow's to us."

"Well, I'll tell you, Q.M.," the Officer of the Watch said. "That is, I'll tell you what I think I saw—and what the Captain thinks *he* saw."

The other men on the bridge stared straight ahead, but there was a sudden and absolute silence.

"On the bow of that ship's boat," the Officer of the Watch said, "it appears to read . . . it appears to read . . . 'The Titanic'!"

They gently lifted the blanketed body of the woman over the railing onto A-deck and then placed it on a stretcher.

The small patches of fog had joined, and the sun was now blotted out. The scene looked funereal as passengers and crew surrounded the stretcher and stared down at it.

The Captain approached the group, and the sailors quickly moved aside as if in response to a silent command.

"Unconscious, sir," Richards said to the Captain.

The Captain leaned down, gently pulled aside the blanket to reveal the face of the unconscious body on the stretcher. The face was gray, pale, and bearded.

The Captain looked up towards Richards. "Unconscious . . . and also a man."

"But dressed as a woman, sir—" Richards said.

The Captain straightened, pulled at his mustache, then gestured. "Take him to the Infirmary."

Several sailors lifted the stretcher and started to

trudge down the deck. The Captain moved as if to follow them. Richards touched his arm.

"Captain?" Richards said. "They're pulling the lifeboat in on C-deck. I think you'd best look at it, sir. One blanket, that's all I found. No rescue packets, no life jackets, no flares—"

"Could have been lost at sea," the Captain said musingly. "Swept overboard—"

Richards shook his head. "That's not all that's odd, sir. Her condition—"

The Captain turned to him and frowned. "What about it?"

"She's so barnacled, sir—all crusted up to the waterline. It's as if she'd been afloat for—"

The Captain interrupted him. "For how long? Go ahead, say it: Since the *Titanic* hit an iceberg? And if that were the case, Mr. Richards—what do you suppose the condition of that man would be?"

Richards looked down the length of the deck as the stretcher disappeared inside. "He'd be a skeleton, sir," Richards said softly.

The Captain nodded. "That's a reasonable surmise," he said, his eyes squinting.

Richards couldn't read humor or sarcasm.

"So we come to the obvious conclusion, Mr. Richards," the Captain continued.

"Which is, sir?" Richards' voice was soft and somehow apologetic, as if the conclusions were obvious and were simply eluding him.

"Conclusions as follows, Mr. Richards," the Captain said, and this time there was just a shade of a smile underneath the mustache. "The man's been at sea for a week or two. Possibly three at the outside. But that's all."

"And the name on the ship's boat?" Richards asked.

"I'll tell you what, Mr. Richards," the Captain said. "When the gentleman regains consciousness, we'll ask him!"

The man lay in bed in the ship's Infirmary as night shrouded the ocean outside. There was no sound save for the vast humming turbines of the ship's engines; and then the quiet, hushed footsteps of the ship's doctor, who entered the room, went over to the bed, and stared down at the man. After a moment the Captain appeared at the open doorway. The doctor moved quickly over to him, pantomiming his wish that they converse elsewhere.

They moved into the doctor's office alongside the Infirmary room, and the doctor closed the door.

"Still unconscious?" the Captain asked.

The ship's doctor lit a pipe. "More like a . . . a coma."

"And his physical condition?"

The ship's doctor sucked in on his pipe, looked down at his desk, then up into the Captain's face. "Thin," he answered. "Obviously in shock. And his right foot—"

"What about it?" the Captain asked.

The ship's doctor looked grim and unhappy. "Frostbite," he answered.

The Captain studied the ship's doctor. "Frostbite? *In the month of May?* Let me ask you something, doctor— have you been on deck recently?"

The ship's doctor nodded. "Yes, sir, I have."

"Have you seen any icebergs?" the Captain asked.

The ship's doctor shook his head and smiled. "No, sir. Not a single iceberg."

The Captain leaned over the desk. Not a sarcastic man, he dredged up sarcasm to cover his own bewilderment. "You'd *know* an iceberg if you saw one?" he asked.

The ship's doctor stifled an explosive anger, but even at that his voice came out cold. "I'd also know a case of frostbite, Captain—even if I stumbled across it in equatorial Africa!"

There was the sound of a man's voice from the adjoining room—just the faintest of outcries. Both men tensed instantly; then the Captain followed the ship's doctor toward the connecting door and on into the Infirmary.

The man in the bed was sitting up, his eyes open and staring. Very slowly he turned to look at the two men who'd just entered the room.

"Feeling better?" the ship's doctor asked.

The man just stared at him, not responding.

"I think we'd best have a chat, you and I," the Captain said, with a brief look toward the ship's doctor, who nodded, turned, and left the room.

The Captain pulled up a chair alongside of the bed. He tried to keep his voice neutral. "Now, let's have it from the beginning," he said. "At approximately fourteen:thirty we found you in a ship's boat. On it was written 'The Titanic,' and in it—there was you and there was one blanket. Now, what I'd like to know is—"

THE SOLE SURVIVOR

* * *

The ship's bell rang nine times. Inside his office the ship's doctor checked desultorily the various patients' charts. His mind wasn't on it. At intervals he would lift up his head to listen to the muffled voices from the room alongside.

In that room the Captain had just left his chair. There was nothing neutral in his voice by that time. He felt nothing but frustration and helpless bewilderment. The survivor, after an hour and a half, still made no sense whatsoever.

"Surely you can't have been the sole survivor," the Captain said, obviously persisting along a familiar line. "After your boat was lowered, what about the crew, the other passengers?"

The survivor's eyes looked overly big, set deep in the emaciated face. "I . . . I don't remember," he whispered. "All I remember is just drifting. Waking up in the boat . . . and just drifting."

There was a tap on the door. The ship's doctor entered, looking at his watch.

The Captain made a gesture as if to say he was almost finished.

"And the name of your ship?" the Captain asked for perhaps the dozenth time.

"The *Titanic*," the survivor said.

The Captain pursed his lips, held his breath and then blew it out. "The *Titanic*, you say."

"Yes, sir. The *Titanic*."

The Captain looked toward the ship's doctor with a

shrug, then over his shoulder toward the survivor. "And your name? Tell the ship's doctor your name."

The survivor looked around toward the ship's doctor. He closed his eyes tightly as if deep in thought.

The Captain's voice was much louder now. "The gentleman doesn't remember his name," he half-shouted. "The gentleman doesn't remember very damned much."

The ship's doctor made a little pantomiming gesture as if pleading for restraint.

The Captain shook his head and turned away, pacing restively.

"What do you recall?" the ship's doctor asked as he approached the bed, his voice soft.

The survivor opened his eyes. "We fouled an iceberg. It was a point on the starboard side. Then there was this . . . shuddering noise—scraping—somewhere under the starboard bow." He shook his head. "That's all I remember," he added helplessly.

The ship's doctor turned from the patient toward the Captain, who had halted his pacing.

The Captain looked disgusted. He retraced his steps over to the bed, this time scaling down his voice, though the impatience and distaste showed through. "You were dressed in women's clothing," he said. "Can you explain that?"

Silence.

"Can you?"

Still silence.

"You have no idea?" The Captain's voice was now that of a British officer in a Court of Inquiry. It just happened to take place in the ship's Infirmary. "Perhaps," he said, after a pause, "perhaps you won't mind if I take a stab at an explanation."

The man on the bed kept his eyes averted.

"Perhaps you put that dress on," the Captain said, "to gain access to a lifeboat. Could that be it?"

The survivor whispered. "I don't know."

The Captain moved closer to the bed. "You don't know? Is that what you said? I think you do."

The survivor's face seemed to shrivel, and he cringed, as though half-expecting a physical blow.

The ship's doctor put a restraining hand on the Captain's arm and again warned him with a look.

The Captain nodded, jammed his hands into his pockets, looked up toward the ceiling, then back down to the survivor on the bed. "We'll talk again later," he said. "Perhaps when you've rested, some of the answers that presently prove so elusive will manage to wriggle their way to the surface."

He turned on his heel and walked out of the room.

The ship's doctor looked from one to the other and was about to follow the Captain when the survivor painfully inched his way back to a partial sitting position. "Doctor," he called out hoarsely.

The ship's doctor turned to him.

"What year is it?"

The ship's doctor frowned. "What year do you think it is?"

The survivor lowered his head back down on the pillow. "It's 1912. Isn't it? Isn't it 1912?"

The ship's doctor's voice was very soft. "Try to get

some more sleep," he said. "There'll be someone in attendance at all times."

He moved out into the passageway, closing the door behind him. The Captain was standing there. The ship's doctor tried to smile. "I should very much like to know what this is all about, Captain."

The Captain looked toward the closed door. "And so should I. Obviously it's some kind of hoax. And obviously it's an outrageous one. And there's no doubt in my mind that's he's been carefully coached."

"Coached?" the ship's doctor asked.

The Captain nodded. "And in spite of that—he supplied us a few pieces to the puzzle."

The ship's doctor looked bewildered. "Like what?" he asked.

" 'Fouled the iceberg,' That's what he said." The Captain pointed to the closed door. " 'Iceberg, a point on the starboard bow.' Doctor, that's a sailor talking. *But in whose service?*"

Slowly, his shoulders hunched, the Captain started toward the stairway. The ship's doctor followed him. At the foot of the stairs the Captain stopped and looked straight ahead, deep in thought.

The ship's doctor's voice was tentative. "I don't think I understand," he began.

The Captain turned to him, his voice grim. I'm wondering if it's possible your patient was put adrift for a very specific purpose."

"Purpose? You've lost me, Captain."

The Captain put one foot on the first rung of stairs. "To slow us down, man. To make us alter course. I know that sounds altogether incredible, doctor . . . but you know, there *is* a war on."

He looked down the length of the passageway toward the Infirmary door, then turned and started a slow walk up the stairs, leaving the ship's doctor staring up at him.

On the bulkhead wall a life preserver made a small sideward movement in a sudden swell. On it was stencilled, "The Lusitania."

An infirmary attendant came out of the patient's room into the passageway just as the ship's doctor came down the stairs. The ship's bell rang eleven times. The attendant balanced a tray with two plates of untouched food. The ship's doctor noted it briefly. "Not eating?" he asked.

The attendant shook his head. "Not a morsel, sir which is odd, if you'll forgive me. Poor bloke's thin as a drainpipe. Hasn't got a pound of flesh on his bones. Looks to be proper starving is what he looks." He looked down at the tray. "Still—I couldn't get a cracker into him."

The ship's doctor moved past him to the Infirmary door, opened it, and entered. A small orange night light sent darting shadows around the room. The ship's doctor approached the bed and leaned over.

The survivor was awake, his eyes wide open.

"No appetite, I'm told," the ship's doctor said.

The survivor stared straight up at the ceiling. "What time is it?"

"Shortly after eight."

The survivor's voice sounded hollow, strangely like some kind of sepulchral confession. "Dog Watch just ended," he said.

Again the ship's doctor tried to read something in the skin-tight, unrevealing face. Despite himself, he felt an unbidden thrill. What if the man were a spy? What if he knew something that no one else knew? What if he asked the time because he knew that at a certain hour—

The ship's doctor unconsciously shook his head. Paranoia, he thought. But God, in a ship at sea during wartime, you could conjure up any kind of jeopardy. He forced an evenness to his tone. "Were you a member of the *Titanic*'s crew?" he asked.

"Stoker."

The ship's doctor smiled, or at least tried to smile. "Well," he said in a bedside tone, "if you want to ship out again when we reach London, I'd recommend taking some nourishment."

The man on the bed turned to study him. The over-sized eyes in the undersized face seemed to glow fanatically in the night light. "This ship's the *Lusitania*," he said softly, as if trying to authenticate that which he already knew.

"That's right," the ship's doctor answered.

The survivor lifted a thin, veined hand to his beard-stubbled chin. "It's 1915," he said.

The ship's doctor nodded.

"I've been in that lifeboat for three years."

It was chilling just to hear him say it—chilling. To voice the impossible as if it were a matter of record.

"Well, now," the ship's doctor said, his voice nervous. "Well, now—we both know you couldn't have been in a lifeboat for three years."

The room, the ship's doctor noted, in another portion of his mind, had grown suddenly silent. It was as if the engines had stopped—that constant, rhythmic, pounding noise of dynamos that somehow fused into the subconscious and disappeared—now it was as if they were nonexistent. The room was utterly silent.

The survivor's voice seemed louder in the stillness. "A question to you, doctor," he said. "How do you know what I've told you isn't possible? Listen to me—listen to me and then tell me if you still think it's impossible."

Not a spy, the ship's doctor thought. Spies fitted molds. Cold, callous, always planning kind of chaps. But this man . . . those haunted eyes . . . the anguish that seemed so much a part of him—deranged, of course, but not a spy.

He leaned forward. "Tell me about it," he said.

For a moment the survivor's lips moved with no words forthcoming; then he abruptly tore his gaze from the ship's doctor and stared fixedly toward the wall. His voice sounded choked. "Have you ever been frightened, doctor? I mean, so frightened you'd do anything to survive? Have you?"

Humor him, the ship's doctor thought. Always humor the deranged. Give them at least that much comfort.

"Fortunately," the ship's doctor said, "I've never found myself in that kind of situation."

The skeletal face turned to him again. "I have," the survivor said. He took a deep breath. "She was down by the bow and going fast. When I tried to get into a lifeboat, they stopped me. No crew members. Just women and children."

"That's a traditional rule of the sea," the ship's doctor said, his voice slightly aimless, like a kind of absent-minded teacher.

The survivor stared at him. "Sure. Sure—unless you're standing on a tilted deck heading into icy water that'll kill you in three minutes. Then you don't think about traditional rules of the sea."

A silence. The ship's doctor waited. "So you put on a dress," he said finally.

The survivor nodded. "And a muffler to hide my face. And I knocked a half a dozen people aside and got on. While they were lowering her, one of the cables broke. She capsized. But I hung on. Somehow I hung on. When she hit the water, I was the only one who had."

The silence, the ship's doctor thought—the incredible silence of the room and the ship. No ship's engines. No creaking bulkheads. No metallic tinkle of dishes or glassware. No squeak of a ship's lamp as it undulated slowly in the ocean's swell. There was absolutely no sound.

And then the survivor's voice continued. "The ship's band was playing. Some kind of hymn. And there was this . . . this great wailing cry. I could look up at the deck and see faces along the rail. Hundreds of faces. Then there was this explosion. She was going down by the bow, and everything inside that ship was moving. Pianos, furniture, deck chairs—everything . . . all crashing down into the bow. And then there was this . . . this *cry*. Then one by one the funnels disappeared . . . and then the ship. Then there was nothing but bodies floating. Stars . . . dead calm . . . and bodies."

The ship's doctor felt mesmerized.

The voice of the survivor continued in a dead monotone. The night light swayed back and forth from the ceiling.

"An illusion," the ship's doctor finally managed to say. "Understand? It *had* to be an illusion. You *couldn't* have been on the *Titanic*. You couldn't have survived in an open boat for three years."

He rose from the chair, bewildered and shaken by the spectral voice and the skeletal figure who spoke so calmly and so believingly about something that was beyond belief.

"There is an explanation for this," he said. "A rational, believable, altogether understandable explanation. And it'll come out eventually. In the meantime—"

The survivor interrupted him. "In the meantime, doctor—let me tell you something."

The ship's doctor felt his hand shake, and it was suddenly hard to breathe.

The man on the bed swung his legs over the side and rested them on the floor. Skin and bones. Skeleton. Just a frame covered by a thin parchment of flesh.

"You're going to be hit by a torpedo," the man said, "off the Old Head of Kindale. You're going down in eighteen minutes flat."

The voice was so soft, so matter-of-fact, that for a moment the ship's doctor found it difficult to connect tone with words. What had the man said? Something about a torpedo? Something about going down in eighteen minutes? And what had the Captain said? The man was a spy.

"By God," the ship's doctor said finally. "By God, you *are* a German agent."

For the first time the survivor smiled—thin, slit mouth just slightly turned up. "A German agent? I wish . . . I wish to God I was." He shook his head. "No, doctor, I'm no agent. Not a spy. Not a saboteur. But you know something? I'm beginning to understand just what I *am*."

Again the blanketing silence.

"What . . . are . . . you?" the ship's doctor asked.

The survivor stood up, swaying slightly, holding onto the night table for support. "I'll tell you what I am, doctor," he said. "I'm a Flying Dutchman, built of flesh, blood, and bones. Damned and doomed. An eternity of lifeboats . . . rescues . . . and then—"

"—And then forever being picked up by doomed ships," the ship's doctor said to the Captain as they sat in his cabin. An early-morning light filtered through the porthole as the night gave way to day.

The Captain sat behind his desk and folded his hands behind his head. "Justice, of the poetic sort," he said, smiling.

"He believes it," the ship's doctor said.

The Captain's smile was fixed. "Does he, now? He believes it." He leaned farther back in his chair. "Very fanciful," he said. "Altogether bizarre." Then he put his hands down on top of the desk. "Except for a very notable flaw. If this is *his* damnation, *his* punishment for an act of cowardice—"

"He believes that it is," the ship's doctor interrupted.

The Captain shook his head. "So we take a torpedo and share his punishment?" He smiled. "Not exactly fair, you'll admit, since none of us have done anything to make us damned and doomed, eh?"

"It doesn't work that way," the ship's doctor said, as if pleading a case. "He tells me that when the torpedo hits—only *he'll* be aware of it. We're only here to . . . to people the scene, so to speak."

The Captain rose from behind the desk, the smile gradually fading. "So. And following that logic, it means that you and I are—"

"Phantoms," the ship's doctor said. "Phantoms, Captain. Ghosts of what we were."

The Captain walked over to the porthole and stared out at the brightening sky. "Now, that's interesting," he said. "Especially interesting in light of the fact that I don't feel at all like a phantom. To the contrary, doctor, I feel—"

He turned as he spoke, and whatever words were to follow were choked off and left deep inside his throat.

He was alone in the room. There was no ship's doctor. Inside his mind the machinery of logic roared and pulsated; the mental process that manufactured rationale, that explained away the impossible, that offered up the clues, the excuses, the reasons to explain the totally unexplainable.

The room was empty.

The ship's doctor had disappeared.

And the machinery in the Captain's head stripped gears and went off in screaming tangents, thoughts colliding with thoughts and terror laying claim to the debris. Like some kind of partially destroyed robot, he forced his legs over to the ship's phone on the wall and tried to reach the bridge.

"Bridge, this is the Captain. Come in, bridge. This is the Captain, bridge. Come in—"

Three decks above him the bridge was empty of men. The dials of the instruments moved; the ship's phone undulated gently on its hook; the needle of the giant compass above the Helmsman's wheel moved left and right in sporadic little stops and gos.

And then the Captain's cabin was empty.

The survivor forced himself through empty passageways, down silent decks, into cavernous salons and mausoleumlike dining rooms. When he reached the deck, he went directly to the rail and looked out at the quiet sea. And then he saw it. A tiny black broom handle sticking up above the water.

"Periscope," he screamed. "Periscope off the starboard bow!"

He looked wildly up and down the empty deck. "Periscope," he screamed again, "off the starboard bow!"

He raced up a ladderway to the deck above him. And then he saw the torpedo. It slivered through the water at a breathless speed, leaving a wake of frosty bubbles. Then another torpedo, and still a third. His world exploded into a flash of blinding whiteness. He felt an incredible pain, and then for a time he felt nothing at all.

The ocean liner, gleaming white and graceful as a porpoise, sped swiftly across the quiet sea.

On the bridge came the voice of a Lookout through the ship's speaker. "Object dead ahead," the metallic voice rasped.

The men on the bridge lifted up binoculars and peered through the glass.

"Incredible," said the Officer of the Watch.

"What is it?" asked the Quartermaster.

"A ship's boat," the Officer of the Watch answered. "Appears to be . . . one survivor."

A tall, gray-bearded Captain entered the bridge. "Any sign of life?" he asked.

"One survivor, sir," the Officer of the Watch responded, "but—"

"But what?"

The Officer of the Watch took off his binoculars and handed them to the Captain. "You'd best look for yourself, sir."

The Captain lifted the binoculars and peered through the glass. "That can't be," he said in a quiet little voice. He lowered the binoculars, then turned toward the Officer of the Watch. "Get a small boatman and lower him immediately. We'll stop for a recovery." Again he raised the binoculars. "I think someone must be playing a joke. You read the name on the bow, Carlos?"

The Officer of the Watch gulped. "Yes, sir, I do. It reads . . . 'The Lusitania,' sir."

The Captain took a deep breath. "The *Lusitania*," he said. "Sunk—forty-odd years ago. And this is one of her lifeboats?" He shook his head, rejecting the entire thing. "Stop engines," he ordered.

"Stop engines," the Quartermaster repeated.

"Starboard, two degrees," the Captain said to the Helmsman.

The Helmsman, following his compass, turned the wheel slightly to the right and felt a combination chill and sweat. He had to wipe the perspiration from his brow where little rivulets of water were dripping down from his seaman's cap—a cap which read "S.S. Andrea Doria."

There was a ship's whistle, and then the grinding halt of the engines; and in the little lifeboat the survivor looked toward the approaching rescuers. He wondered how long it would be this time. And how would the death come. Then he felt the jar and scrape of the other boat hitting the gunwales of his own. He fainted as eager arms reached out to pull him to what they thought was safety.